BECAUSE I LOVE YOU

Lucien very carefully placed his sleepy wife on her feet and lit the bedside lamp, turning the wick low. Her eyes remained closed as he began to unbutton her gown, revealing a plain chemise beneath. No corset still, as she feared it would interfere with her ability to conceive. Another notion from yet another pamphlet.

"Why on earth do you put up with me?" he asked as he finished with the buttons and pushed the arms of her dark dress down.

"Because I love you," she answered without hesitation.

"I'm not an easy man to live with, am I?"

Evie smiled gently, allowing him to continue undressing her. Slowly. Gently. She was not quite awake, and yet she was not asleep. "No," she said honestly. "You're not. But that does not make me love you less."

Dress discarded, she sat on the side of the bed and allowed him to remove her shoes and stockings. For tonight, she could sleep in her chemise. He did not think he could bear to strip Evie naked and then put a nightgown on her body. He already wanted her too much.

BOOK YOUR PLACE ON OUR WEBSITE AND MAKE THE READING CONNECTION!

We've created a customized website just for our very special readers, where you can get the inside scoop on everything that's going on with Zebra, Pinnacle and Kensington books.

When you come online, you'll have the exciting opportunity to:

- View covers of upcoming books
- Read sample chapters
- Learn about our future publishing schedule (listed by publication month *and author*)
- Find out when your favorite authors will be visiting a city near you
- Search for and order backlist books from our online catalog
- Check out author bios and background information
- Send e-mail to your favorite authors
- Meet the Kensington staff online
- Join us in weekly chats with authors, readers and other guests
- Get writing guidelines
- AND MUCH MORE!

Visit our website at
http://www.kensingtonbooks.com

SHADES OF SCARLET

Linda Fallon

ZEBRA BOOKS
Kensington Publishing Corp.
http://www.kensingtonbooks.com

With a special thanks to my agent, Richard Curtis.
A rare gentleman. A true shark.
A friend who can make me laugh when I need it most.

One

Eve crept up behind her husband, her footsteps soft on the parlor rug, the rustle of her skirts no more than a whisper. Her approach was quiet enough for Lucien's occupied mind to completely dismiss as he sat on the parlor floor, hovering intently over his latest invention.

With all her heart, Eve wished she could be as nonchalant as her husband. He told her not to worry; he told her everything would be fine. She could tell, by the expression on his face and the serenity in his voice, that he believed every word he said. She did not.

Standing behind Lucien, Eve lowered her hand to his head to stroke his long, dark hair. He looked up, startled to find her there. A moment later, he smiled. "I did say I'd be finished in five minutes, didn't I?"

She nodded. "Half an hour ago. Your supper is getting cold."

Lucien held up one hand. "Five more minutes. I just need to tweak this one connector." He returned his attention to the contraption on the floor. The device was supposed to measure the changes in energy levels when he or anyone else channeled a spirit. He also wanted to test the thing on Lionel Brandon and Hugh Felder, perhaps even O'Hara, to see what kind of energy fluctuations took place in their bodies when they used their psychic powers. To Eve, the thing on the floor looked like some kind of torture device. Wires and the attached metal clips grew like spider legs from a square metal box. On one side of the box were two separate meters with which to take readings. On the end was a sturdy crank.

The concept was a good one, but so far Lucien's newest contraption didn't work. Not at all.

Fifteen minutes later, Lucien finally stood. He stretched his arms over his head, worked out the kinks, and then turned to face her.

She had altered one of the upstairs rooms into a studio for her husband, but he preferred to work here in the parlor, or perhaps in the dining room. He claimed that he enjoyed being close to her while he worked. Even if he did have a tendency to retreat into his own world, he knew she was near.

Lucien wrapped his long arms around her. "Why do you look so glum, love?"

Telling him would only start an argument, but she didn't like to lie. Lucien hated deception of any kind. Besides, she didn't ever want to hide her feelings from the man she loved with all her heart. "We had a letter from Katherine and Garrick today."

He smiled gently. "How are they?"

"Fine. They're still living in that small Texas town, the one Katherine mentioned in her last letter."

"Garrick finally found a place that satisfied him."

"He bought part ownership in a sawmill there."

Lucien's reaction was subtle but telling. His eyebrows arched slightly. "I thought Garrick hated the family business."

"Apparently what he really hated was working for his father. Katherine says he's very happy." Very, very happy.

Lucien bent his head to kiss her on the cheek. "Why does that good news have you looking so somber? Is there something else?"

"Yes," she whispered.

"Tell me."

Eve took a deep breath. "Katherine is going to have a child. According to her physician, she'll have the baby in November."

"That is good news."

Katherine had been with child when she'd written the last letter, early in the summer, but she had said nothing. At that time she hadn't been very far along, and she'd wanted to wait until they knew more certainly when the baby was coming and that the pregnancy would progress smoothly. She had only two months left, and according to the letter she had never been healthier.

Eve pursed her lips. She was happy for her friends; she truly was. But still . . . why wasn't *she* pregnant?

Lucien read the expression on her face too well, and gathered her close. "I thought we had decided not to worry about this for a while longer."

"*You* decided we wouldn't worry," Eve snapped, her face buried against Lucien's chest.

"It's too soon to be concerned," he said sensibly.

Too soon! How could he say that? "We've been

married eight months," she argued. "And we were together for three months before the wedding! Almost a year, Lucien. A year! Some women get pregnant the first time they let a man touch them. Some take a few weeks, or a couple of months. But a year? Buster's been married six months, and his bride is already expecting their first child."

Buster Towry, charter member of the Plummerville Ghost Society and by far the gentlest of their members, was finally married. For two years he'd been afraid to approach the redheaded daughter of a neighboring farmer. After January's adventure at the Honeycutt Hotel, he'd decided a pretty girl was nothing to be afraid of, after all.

Lucien kissed Eve while she pondered the happiness and good fortune of her friends. Oh, she loved the way her husband kissed! His lips soft and strong, his arms all around her, his tongue teasing hers. In a heartbeat, everything changed. Her anxiety faded, and she stopped worrying about what might or might not be. Lucien was warm, tender, and when he kissed her, she was swept away so easily. His kiss touched her everywhere, from the inside out.

Just when she felt herself begin to melt, Eve drew her lips away from his. "You can't make me forget just by kissing me."

"I think I can," he replied softly. His hand cupped her breast, his thumbs raked wickedly across the fabric of her dress and across her nipple. "No corset."

Eve tried to ignore the flash of pleasure that shot through her body; Lucien knew how to touch her to make her want him so much that nothing else mattered. "This afternoon, I read in one of my pamphlets that corsets are not healthy for a woman when she's trying to conceive."

"You and your silly pamphlets," Lucien grumbled as he continued to caress her.

"My pamphlets are not silly," she argued. Her heartbeat changed; her breathing altered subtly. Her knees went weak. She tried to ignore it all. Lucien was going to think the pamphlets more than silly when she told him what else she'd read today.

"Dinner's already cold," Lucien said, laying his mouth on her neck and kissing gently. "What do you say we let it get a little bit colder?"

"Lucien," she argued weakly. "You haven't eaten all day. You really should have supper, and . . . and . . ."

Her arguments died as he began to unbutton the bodice of her warm green dress. . . . Oh, she was going to have to steel her resolve! Lucien wasn't going to make this any easier. He kissed the hollow of her throat while he continued to unfasten buttons without faltering. His fingers were so sure. So talented. Yes, she would have to be very strong.

But not yet, perhaps. Not yet.

No, she had to be strong *now*. Lucien knew how to seduce her; he really did know how to make her forget anything and everything with a kiss, a tender touch. Eve very gently disentangled herself from her husband. Judging by his grin, he expected her to take his hand and lead him up the stairs to their bedroom.

"I also read that if a husband and wife are having relations too often, the husband's sperm can become weak and that can affect their ability to conceive." Eve clasped her hands before her. She lifted her chin in defiance.

"Too often?" Lucien repeated darkly.

"Well . . ." She felt the heat of a blush rise to her cheeks. "Yes."

"Weak?" he said with only a touch of incredulity. Eve nodded.

"I hate to ask," her husband said in a lowered voice. "But what exactly are you thinking at this moment? I can see the wheels turning, Evie."

She licked her lips. "There is a possible solution to our problem that we have not yet considered. Abstinence. A couple of months without sexual relations."

Lucien had to suspect what was coming. After all, she had very gently warned him. Still, he looked shocked at her suggestion. "A couple of *months?*"

"That's not such a long time, really."

"Oh, it's not."

Eve began to button her dress. "Not really."

Lucien crossed his arms over his chest. "This is the most ridiculous thing I've ever heard."

"It is not ridiculous. It's quite scientific, and as a scientist yourself you should understand . . ."

"But *two months?*"

Eve's lower lip trembled. "I want a baby so badly, I'll do anything . . . anything at all."

Her husband leaned closer, and he planted his deep blue eyes directly on her face. "I can assure you, darling, that not having sex is not the way to assure yourself of a child."

"I think we should try everything we can."

"Can't this be our last resort?"

"It is!"

Lucien ran the fingers of one hand through his hair, ruffling the long, dark strands. "Why do you care so much whether or not we have a baby? I'm perfectly happy as we are. If we have babies one day, that will be fine. I will love those children, I know I will. But if we don't ever have a child, I will still be perfectly happy."

"How can you say that!" She wanted a baby so much, she could not imagine how Lucien could be so cavalier about the subject. "I want your child, more than I've ever wanted anything."

"And I am perfectly satisfied with you," Lucien said. "Can't you be content with me? Am I not enough to fill your life?"

Her dress fastened again, Eve stepped forward to tenderly lay her hands on Lucien's face. "I love you," she whispered. "You know how very much I love you. I can't explain why I feel the need to have a child so acutely, but I do. I dream about having a child. I daydream about how it will feel to have your baby growing inside me. Do this for me, Lucien. Two months. It's not such a long time. The weeks will go by quickly."

"I don't think so," he grumbled.

"Please."

For a long moment, Lucien studied her. His eyes went dark; his jaw clenched. "All right, Evie. Two months. Unless you change your mind, that is. If you decide that this idea of yours is as preposterous as I believe it is, all you have to do is say the word and we'll be back in that bed where we belong, naked, shaking the night and making one another moan until the rafters tremble."

"I won't change my mind," Eve said primly, even

as she felt her own unexpected tremble begin in her bones.

Lucien grinned at her. "I think you will."

Lucien made notes on his latest experiments with the newest piece of equipment he was developing, hoping the chore would take his mind off this current untenable situation. His wife's insistence that they abstain from physical affections had lasted, thus far, for four very long days. He had tried to sway her, gently of course, but in typical Evie fashion she had dug in her heels and was having none of his subtle seduction.

And if he went beyond subtle, she would be furious.

"Women," an unfamiliar voice said softly.

Lucien lifted his head sharply to see the ghost that lounged just a few feet away. He had seen this specter before, in his months in Eve's home, but the Confederate soldier had never deigned to speak with Lucien—as he was a Yankee, after all.

"What about them?" Lucien asked as he set his notes aside. He couldn't send this particular spirit on unless he knew why the soldier was earthbound. Until now, he hadn't had a chance.

"Do you think they were created simply to drive us mad?"

Lucien smiled. "Perhaps. But what would our lives be like without them?" His own life without Evie was dull and gray, not *living* at all.

The soldier nodded.

"What's your name?" Lucien asked. It was so important, at times, to call a spirit by the proper name.

"Soldier" simply would not do for a personal conversation.

"Thaddeus," the ghost said. "Thaddeus Miller."

"Thaddeus Miller," Lucien said gently, "do you know that you are dead?"

Miller nodded once. "I didn't for a long time, but since you've been here I have begun to see."

"Why are you still here?" Earthbound. Trapped.

"I'm afraid," Thaddeus whispered.

"Of what?"

"I'm afraid of what awaits me." The soldier faded for a moment, but he did not disappear. "I killed men in war. I laid with a woman who was not my wife. And then I got hurt, really bad, and I couldn't find my way home. I left my Angelina behind, with no one to look out for her, with no one to provide and care for her. There were times I was sorry I married her, other times I loved her so much I couldn't stand it, and still . . . I was a bad husband. I never should've left her behind."

"Did she live in this house?"

Thaddeus shook his head. "No. After I got hurt . . . no, after I *died*, I couldn't find her. I was lost, for a long time, and then I found this place and I've been resting here. Waiting."

"Don't be afraid to move on," Lucien said firmly. "You can do it, you know. You can leave this earth all on your own. Look up, Thaddeus."

The ghost lifted his head slowly, as if he were afraid of what he might see. "Light."

"Peace awaits you there," Lucien said. "Forgiveness, too."

For the first time, Lucien saw the soldier smile. "Angelina?"

And then he was gone. Poof. Sending a spirit home was rarely so easy. Then again, Lucien thought, he'd been living in this house almost a year. It had taken a shared misery to bring Thaddeus to Lucien.

Misery. Yes, this new development was indeed miserable.

Eve kept her hands busy with a new batch of biscuits. The last batch had been much too hard, and since she had nothing else to do . . . She pounded the dough unmercifully.

"Thaddeus is gone," Lucien said as he walked into the kitchen.

Eve's heart lurched at the sound of his voice. "Who's Thaddeus?"

"Your soldier."

Flour on her hands and her apron, Eve turned quickly. "He spoke to you?"

"I might be a damned Yankee, but I am also a fellow miserable male pondering the impossibly complex workings of a woman's mind."

Eve pursed her lips. "That was rather quick," she said, ignoring his blatant insult.

"All he had to do was look up and open his heart, and the pathway was shown to him. Humans and spirits both have an annoying tendency to ignore that which is right in front of them." He reached out and slowly dragged a finger across her cheek. "Flour," he said softly as the finger moved to her neck.

"I really should finish these. . . ."

"Just one question, love. Seeing Thaddeus brought

Viola and Alistair Stamper to mind. They were such interesting spirits."

More than interesting, they had been downright lascivious! In this very house they'd . . . She couldn't think about that, not now. "Yes, they were. Now, I really must . . ."

"Your determination to have a child makes me wonder. Do you want a baby badly enough to take the steps Viola took when she found herself childless?"

"No!" Eve forgot about her biscuits. "I would never, ever resort to . . . nothing is as important as . . . really, Lucien, surely you know me better than that!" Viola had taken another man into her bed, in hopes that she might conceive a child. Nothing could ever make Eve that desperate. "I do love you," she said in a softer voice.

"Then you won't refuse me a single small, innocent kiss."

The kiss Lucien gave her was single, but it was not small or innocent. How was it possible that he knew exactly what to do in order to make her question her resolve? Her knees went weak, her heart fluttered, and her hands itched to touch her husband. A kiss, one kiss, and she felt it everywhere.

And Lucien knew it, too. His eyes were dreamy, filled with passion, when he took his mouth from hers. "I suppose I should get back to work."

"So should I," she whispered.

"Perhaps one more kiss," Lucien said as his mouth came toward hers.

Eve sighed and prepared herself for another kiss. "This is very nice, darling. I could stand here and kiss you all afternoon."

His smile was wicked.

"But I'm not going to change my mind."

The damn thing simply would not work! Lucien had placed the energy-measuring device on the dining room table so he could study it from a new angle. It should be operating properly by now.

Cursed contraption.

He wound the crank on the right end of the device, attached three of the metal clips to his body—one on his left hand, the second on his right hand, and a third on one earlobe—and then pushed the red button on the front. He should be able to collect a normal reading, something to compare with a reading taken while he was channeling a spirit. Instead of sending the needle to a number he could record for future use, the damn thing gave him quite a shock.

Eve waltzed out of the kitchen with a silver tray in her hands. Tea and cookies for a late-morning snack. His wife had been baking a lot in the past week. Cookies, cakes, breads of all kinds. She'd soon be feeding the entire town of Plummerville at this rate.

Lucien yanked off the clips and tossed them onto the table. "This isn't working at all," he said tersely.

His wife smiled at him as she placed the tray on the table. "You'll make it work. You always do."

He narrowed one eye. "I'm not talking about this damned contraption. I'm talking about your new-found love for celibacy."

Her smile died. "I don't like it either," she confessed. "I . . . miss you. But if abstaining for a couple of months is effective and I end up pregnant, it will be well worth the sacrifice."

A couple of months. He had not thought she'd last three days! After all, his wife was a passionate woman. Evie Thorpe dressed primly most of the time. She kept her honey brown hair in a conservative bun, and she was always more concerned than she should be about what other people thought of her and her life. But when they were alone, when they touched, she was passionate and responsive. She did not hold back when she loved him. She laughed and moaned and screamed in their bed. He had expected her to turn to him days ago, agreeing that this newest plan of hers was hogwash.

Here it had been more than a week since she'd presented her ridiculous idea to him. Ten days! He was not sleeping well, and neither was Eve. They were both on edge. Eve baked, and he fiddled with his contraption, trying to make the damned thing function as it should.

He still hadn't come up with a name for this new device. Perhaps he'd just call it The Damned Thing.

Lucien reached for his wife . . . and she danced out of his reach. All he had intended to do was take her hand. Yes, she was every bit as on edge as he was. It wouldn't take much in the way of seduction to get her to agree that for them to stay apart was foolish.

"Evie," he said in a lowered voice.

"Have a cookie," she said brightly.

Lucien took a deep breath. "I don't want a cookie. You know very well what I want."

"Lucien, please . . ."

"I've been doing something wrong." He pinned his eyes on Eve's throat, on the delicate way it worked and on the silky texture and the warmth he knew he would taste if she would allow him near her.

"You haven't done anything *wrong,*" she insisted softly.

"Obviously I have. Otherwise you wouldn't be so damned stubborn."

Someone knocked on the front door, and Eve ran to answer, no doubt glad for the chance to escape. Lucien grabbed a cookie from Eve's silver tray and sullenly took a bite. He was going to have to seduce his own wife. He could; he had no doubt of that. He knew where to touch her, how to kiss her, to make her put aside her newest plan. But when that was done, would she hate him? Would the two months start all over again?

"You have a telegram," Eve said as she returned to the dining room.

Their fingers barely brushed as he took the folded sheet of paper from her. A simple touch of their fingertips, and he felt it to his bones as if a spark of lightning traveled through his veins. Evie shocked him, but in a more pleasant way than the contraption before him.

Lucien unsealed the telegram and read it over quickly. "A plantation house south of Macon. Glover Manor. It has recently changed hands, and the new residents have ghosts. Three of them, apparently."

"Is there any indication that they're dangerous?"

Dangerous ghosts were rare, but since they'd had to deal with a particularly evil spirit a few months past, Eve was cautious about which jobs they took. Lucien had to admit to the occasional bout of caution himself. "No," he said.

"When will you leave?" Eve asked, obviously relieved.

Did she hold her breath? Yes, she did. Her green eyes were expectant. Bright. Was she looking forward to being rid of him for a week or two? Perhaps even a month? Yes, she was more tempted to break her own vow than she let on.

"You will come with me, won't you?" he asked.

Her face fell. "If you . . . need me."

"I do." Since their marriage, Evie had traveled with him to each and every job. She documented each haunting, took notes when he was required to channel a spirit, and handled many of the business details that he always forgot. Like making sure that he got paid when the house they had been called to was free of ghosts.

"Of course, if you really and truly do *need* me . . ." she began.

"I do," he said again.

Eve sighed, and she sounded almost dejected. Lucien smiled at his wife. Yes, she was closer than she knew to capitulating.

At Glover Manor, there would be no opportunity for her to spend the entire day and half the night baking. Perhaps he should leave The Damned Thing here, so he would not have the contraption to fiddle with while she baked. At the end of the day, they would retire together to their room. There would be no sleeping on the parlor sofa, no restlessly pacing the house when they should be in each other's arms.

Evie would have to deal with this desire that shimmered between them, once and for all.

"Will you ask anyone to assist you?" she asked.

A few jobs he handled alone. Most required some assistance. "Lionel and Hugh were halfway across the country last time I heard from them."

"O'Hara, then."

"Probably."

Eve clasped her hands together. "Then I really should ask Daisy to join us. She and O'Hara have been corresponding since January, you know."

"Yes, I know," he said tersely. He heard his wife and her friend Daisy twittering about O'Hara now and then. "But this is not a social outing, Evie."

"She's very anxious to see him," Eve insisted. "When she found out he was at the Jackson haunting, she was very disappointed. He was so close, and still he didn't come to Plummerville for a visit when the job was finished. Since the ghosts at Glover Manor aren't dangerous . . ."

"That we know of," he interrupted.

"We really should invite Daisy to join us."

A chaperon. Daisy Willard was to be his damned chaperon! "Fine," he said sharply. "Whatever you want. I'm sure we can find something for her to do."

Although it did seem to him that if O'Hara wanted to visit with Daisy, he could have made his way to Plummerville at some time in the past eight months. He had not. Poor O'Hara, he might not be pleased to see Miss Willard.

Since Lucien was not totally opposed to giving O'Hara a nasty start, he wouldn't argue with his wife on this matter.

"I'll send O'Hara and Mr. Glover each a telegram this afternoon, and the three of us can catch the morning train," he said.

Eve was accustomed to packing quickly, so she did not complain about the short notice.

She grabbed her cloak from the coat tree in the foyer, so she could walk to Daisy's house and invite the love-struck blonde to join them on the trip. Lucien made a point of following Eve to the door and kissing her good-bye, as a proper husband should. It was a brief kiss, but not too brief. She held her breath at first, and then relaxed and simply enjoyed the touch of their lips.

Pamphlets be damned, he was going to seduce his wife. There would be a few things in the way of his task. Ghosts. O'Hara. Daisy. And Eve's own obsession with getting pregnant.

Somehow he had to make her see that nothing mattered but the two of them and the way they loved each other.

Eve backed away when the kiss ended, bright-eyed and pink-cheeked, the breath she took deep and ragged. "I won't be gone long," she said in a quick, low voice, and then she turned and practically ran from him.

"Two months," he muttered as the door closed on Eve. "Impossible."

Two

Lucien had loaded their luggage on board, and the three of them claimed a seat on the train. Two padded benches with similarly cushioned seat backs faced each other, with room for two on each side. Those benches were awfully small, Eve noted. Not only narrow but short. Did they really expect two people to sit comfortably between the window and the aisle?

"This is so exciting!" Daisy said as she claimed her place by the window. She had dressed in a rose traveling outfit and matching hat that suited her fair complexion and pale gold hair. The hat sported a large bow; the dress was embellished with lace and silk flowers. There were no wrinkles, no piece of the ensemble that was awkward or askew. Everything about Daisy Willard was very well put together, pretty and bright.

Eve felt downright dowdy in comparison, as she always did. Her plain traveling outfit was taupe, and the high neck scratched her throat, causing an occasional shift of her head as she attempted to get more comfortable. She had already removed the hat, which had been driving her batty since she'd left the house, and a strand of the hair she had contained at the nape of her neck this morning had already started to fall.

Since Lucien had come back into her life, Eve had made an attempt to brighten up her wardrobe. She now owned a few dresses that could be called frivolous, and there were a number of colorful calicos in her collection of day wear. But in truth, she was more comfortable in drab colors and simple lines. She would never be at ease in frills the way Daisy was.

Daisy, seated at the window, almost anxiously studied the platform below. Lucien stood behind Eve. Directly behind, so close that she could feel the heat radiating off him. She had a choice, and it had to be made immediately. She could sit beside Daisy, or she could sit beside Lucien, in these small, close, cozy seats.

Her husband placed a large, capable hand against the small of her back, and her heart went pitter-pat. One long finger moved restlessly against her waist, mindlessly caressing. Oh, she could not endure being so close to Lucien for the entire trip!

Eve quickly sat next to Daisy, and Lucien took the seat directly across from her without so much as a small sigh of disappointment.

"I thought you might like the extra room," she explained to her husband. "The seats are smaller than I remember." Though they surely had not shrunk since their last outing, just a few weeks ago. Still . . . "You can have that entire bench to yourself."

Lucien smiled gently. "Very thoughtful of you, dear." He made himself comfortable, stretched out his legs, and slipped his foot up under her skirt. He didn't immediately withdraw that foot, but raked the toe of his shoe against her ankle. Up and down. Up and down.

Eve turned her attention to Daisy, doing her best to dismiss Lucien's wandering foot. "You must be very excited about seeing O'Hara."

Daisy wrinkled her pert nose. "I was, last night and early this morning, but now I'm not so sure. Perhaps I shouldn't be at all excited. He could have come here to visit at any time, but he didn't."

"He's been very busy," Eve said.

Daisy was not convinced. "For a while, I thought he liked me."

"I'm sure he does," Eve said, encouraging her friend.

Daisy sighed, and the bow on her hat quivered. "I do look forward to seeing him again, but I hope he doesn't think I'm chasing after him."

"That would be embarrassing," Lucien said. "It's not too late to change your mind and stay at home. I'd be happy to tell O'Hara that you would not be entirely opposed to a visit, if he were of a mind."

Eve glared at her husband, who managed to appear completely innocent.

"Should I stay at home?" Daisy asked Eve, her voice bright and quick, her blue eyes wide with wonder and a touch of horror. "Will O'Hara think I'm being horribly forward by my very presence?" she raised a hand to her breast. "That would be mortifying."

"Of course he won't think you're being forward!" Eve said reassuringly. "What a silly idea." She glared at Lucien again. "He'll be pleased to see you, I'm sure."

Lucien shook his head and opened his mouth as if to say something, and Eve kicked out her own foot. He closed his mouth abruptly, his comment unspoken.

"Besides," Eve said calmly, "O'Hara doesn't have to know that you're traveling with us in order to see him. We can tell him that you've expressed an interest in writing, and you're to be my assistant on this trip."

Lucien snorted beneath his breath.

"It's a very small lie," she said sharply.

"You know I hate deception," he said. "If O'Hara asks me outright why Daisy is with us, I will feel compelled to tell the truth. She has been smitten and traveled with us in order to get a look at his supposedly handsome face." He ended with a snort.

Eve glared at her husband, trying for her most cutting stare. He glared right back.

Daisy preferred to watch the landscape fly past than to study her friends. They were behaving very strangely today. Lucien was tense, and so was Eve. Several times they'd almost bitten each other's heads off over the silliest disagreements! At the moment, they had settled into an uneasy silence. Best to remain quiet, Daisy supposed. She didn't want to say anything that might be upsetting to anyone.

So she watched the thriving fields the train sped past, and she thought of O'Hara.

Knowing what he could do, that he could touch her and know her deepest secrets, she should be frightened. She had been afraid of him at one time.

Even though he had already touched her and discovered her most mortifying secrets, she *was* afraid still.

But somewhere along the line she had decided to be brave. She had decided to risk her heart and her mind for this extraordinary man. There had been a time when she'd been so sure that he liked her. He had certainly acted as if he did.

So where had he been for the past eight months? He wrote friendly letters. She responded. A few weeks later another letter would arrive. But he never spoke of romance or love in those letters, and he had not returned to Plummerville to call on her.

He had never kissed her. They had come so close, and yet they had never kissed. Did his lips have the same sort of power his hands did? Would he lay his mouth on hers and see into her soul?

Daisy herself had no psychic powers at all, nor did she want them. But her woman's instincts were keen. When she saw O'Hara face to face, she would know if he still cared for her. If he ever had cared for her, that is. Was the O'Hara she remembered just a figment of her imagination? Had she constructed her own hero in her mind, in order to survive the ordeal at the Honeycutt Hotel?

She would soon find out.

The recently renamed Glover Manor was a well-kept plantation house, unlike so many of the once-grand homes that had fallen into disrepair after the war. The plantation home before them was long and two stories high, painted white, with columns encircling the structure and supporting the roof over the gallery that encircled the house. The lawn was manicured, the plants that grew in the garden to the south well-tended and mannerly. The trees that grew near the house were ancient, gnarled, and magnificent in their own way, and they offered lots of shade and atmosphere. The view from the front drive, late on this autumn afternoon, was impressive.

Lucien assisted Daisy from the carriage, and then he helped his wife. He did not release Eve's hand as soon as her feet touched the ground, as he had Daisy's. He wanted to hold onto that fine, soft hand as long as possible.

The driver, a shy young man who had introduced himself as Jim when he'd met them at the train station, began to unload their luggage. His eyes flitted to Daisy now and then. Jim didn't do a good job of hiding his admiration for Daisy's beauty, but she seemed not to notice. While Jim worked furiously and Daisy continued to stare at the splendid house before them, Lucien grasped Eve's hand.

When would she admit that her celibacy scheme was ridiculous? He had certainly gone for more than two months without a woman in his bed during his lifetime, but not while the woman he loved and wanted was right beside him, sleeping in his bed, teasing him with what he wanted but could not have.

He lifted her hand to his mouth and kissed her knuckles. "I'm sorry I snapped at you earlier."

Eve looked not at him but at the house before her, much as Daisy did. "That's quite all right. It's been a trying time."

He wanted to understand, but in truth he did not. Not entirely. Eve wanted a child, as most women did.

And yes, many women conceived rather quickly. But not all. Some women took months and even years to conceive. Why couldn't Eve just relax and enjoy this time they had together?

She was enough for him. Was he not enough for her?

Eve very gently withdrew her hand from his grasp. "I must say, this is by far the most beautiful haunted house I've ever seen."

"It is magnificent," Daisy said, awe in her voice.

Lucien's eyes remained on his wife. "Magnificent, indeed."

The front door opened, and a servant stepped onto the gallery. The old woman's skin was black as night and well wrinkled, her hair had gone completely white, and her posture was regal. The austere gown she wore was midnight black and without a single feminine embellishment. The woman had to be in her sixties at least, but she had the bearing of a much younger woman. Her spine was rigid, and her movements did not speak of old age but of vigor and youth.

"You must be Mr. Thorpe," she said solemnly.

"Yes," Lucien said, stepping forward. "I'm here to see Mr. Edwin Glover."

Was it his imagination, or did the old woman's eyes sparkle? "Mr. and Mrs. Glover vacated the premises early this morning." Her manner and her voice were oddly formal, even for a servant. Distant, almost as if his presence was distasteful to her.

"Really?" He had expected to find the new residents at home. It would save him a lot of time if he could ask them about the history of the house and the ghosts who lived here.

"I was told to make you at home here, to give you whatever assistance you need and to offer the Glovers' most heartfelt apologies for their absence. They had a fright last evening," the woman added ominously.

Daisy raised a hand to her chest. "A fright?" She glanced back to Eve. "You said they weren't dangerous! I don't want to go through an ordeal like . . . like . . ." She blushed. "Like last time."

None of them wanted to face a Scrydan again.

"What happened?" Lucien asked as he took Eve's arm and together they walked toward the front door.

"One of the spirits decided to join the Glovers in their bed, shortly after midnight."

"Dear me," Daisy muttered.

"Which one?" Lucien asked.

"I'm not sure," the old woman replied, a decided chill in her voice.

Through the open door, Lucien saw that the home was finely furnished and very clean.

"I'm Eve Thorpe." Eve smiled at the servant. His wife had a way about her; everyone liked Eve. Of course they did. She was warm, honest, and caring. Judging by the old woman's expression, the servant immediately discovered an unexpected liking for the visitor before her. "And this is my good friend Daisy Willard."

The woman nodded. "My name is Ruth. If you need anything, come to me. There are not many servants in residence these days. Jim and I are the only ones who live on the premises."

"Isn't that unusual for such a large place?" Lucien asked. The upkeep of such a plantation house would surely require the services of more than one old woman and a stable boy!

"Yes," Ruth said. "I'm afraid when the Glovers moved in this past summer and started talking about making the place a working plantation again, as well as a house of hospitality for their many friends, the ghosts became more active. Most of the help left, scared off by the hauntings, though I did manage to keep a few day girls and a boy to help Jim with the animals. There's no need for you to deal with any of them. I am in charge of the running of the household," she said proudly. "I supervise them all, and if you need anything you need only come to me." She looked the new arrivals over carefully. "I was told to prepare three rooms. One for each of you?"

"Yes," Eve said brightly.

"No," Lucien replied. "My wife and I will share a room. The third is for a colleague who will be joining us in a few days."

Ruth nodded at Lucien. Yes, the old woman liked Eve. But Lucien was in charge, and she knew that quite well. "I'll have Jim bring your luggage in."

She opened the door wider and invited them into the house. As Lucien stepped inside, he felt the presence of the ghosts. He could not see them, not yet, but they were strong and he would see them before long. Of that he had no doubt.

They were mischievous. Lively. Beneath it all, there was a hint of malevolence that could not be denied. No wonder the servants had been scared away.

And there were more than three ghosts residing in this house.

* * *

Eve busied herself unpacking while Lucien was downstairs setting up his specter-o-meter and the ectoplasm harvester in the main parlor, in hopes of a busy and productive night.

She should have known that he would never allow them to spend the night in separate rooms, not even until O'Hara arrived. But it had been a nice thought, for a few naive seconds.

She'd lived all her days without a man's touch, until Lucien came back into her life last year. So why was it now so difficult to get along without him in her arms and in her bed? She readily admitted that she missed him; what she would not confess was that she craved his touch until it made her a little crazy.

One month and nineteen days, and their self-enforced abstinence would be over. It wasn't such a long time, not really. Especially not if it meant conceiving the child she wanted so badly.

When she'd married Lucien, she hadn't known she'd crave a child to distraction, that the need and the want would fill her every waking hour until it became an obsession. When she closed her eyes and imagined the life she wanted, there were children. Boys and girls, babies and older children. They would fill her house and her heart, these children she and Lucien would make together. To see everyone around her gifted with what she wanted so badly only made matters worse.

Eve told herself, as she unpacked her brush and combs, that she was an adult, a woman in charge of her own life and her own body. A month and nineteen days was nothing to her. Nothing at all. After all, she was a reasonable woman, a practical person. Passion was very nice, but it wasn't necessary. She could do without her husband's touch for a short period of time.

Tomorrow morning her sentence would be reduced to one month and eighteen days.

"My room is gorgeous!"

Eve almost jumped out of her skin as she spun to face Daisy. Her heart thudded against her chest. "You scared me half to death!" she said as her heart rate gradually returned to normal.

"Sorry," Daisy said as she walked to the French doors that opened onto the gallery. She threw back the doors, and a soft autumn breeze made the gauzy white curtains dance. That same breeze ruffled Daisy's pink skirt. "This room is beautiful, too," she said. "I imagine there's not a corner in this house that's not exquisite! It's rather like a castle, don't you think? The furnishings in every room I've seen are perfectly matched and extravagant. The paintings on the walls are framed in gold. You should see the pillows on my bed!"

"Yes," Eve said, glancing around her own room. "It is lovely." She had not paid the close attention Daisy had to her surroundings, but her friend was right. The gleaming mahogany four-poster bed was draped in pale green silk; the chaise against one wall matched that silk precisely. The entire room was decorated in shades of pale green and white. There were fresh autumn flowers on the polished mahogany dresser, clean towels laid out by the wash basin, a plush carpet on the floor.

"So," Daisy said brightly as she spun away from

the open doors. "When do you think O'Hara will arrive? Lucien said it might be a few days." She sounded disappointed. Patience was not one of Daisy's attributes.

"A day or two. Perhaps three."

Daisy wrinkled her nose. "Lucien won't really give away our little tiny lie, will he? I will be mortified if O'Hara discovers that I came here for the express purpose of seeing him again."

Eve wished she could be sure. Lucien was a wonderful husband and she loved him madly, but he was rarely obedient. "I'll do what I can; I promise."

That promise was enough for Daisy. Her smile widened, and she walked briskly for the door. "I must finish unpacking. I don't want my gowns to wrinkle!"

Dismayed, Eve looked down at her own gowns. Most of them were plain and drab. A few were always wrinkled! She didn't have much patience for ironing and mending, and she had even less tolerance for bows and frills that always seemed to get in the way. Daisy wore bows and frills as easily as she wore her own skin.

Daisy left the room much as she had arrived, a pink whirlwind who closed the door behind her.

Alone again, Eve resumed her sullen pouting. She rarely succumbed to such a childish display, but as she saw no practical way out of the corner she had painted herself into, she allowed herself to pout.

Lucien's voice drifted through the large house. He was too far away for her to hear his words, but she caught the timbre of his voice, the occasional word as he instructed the men Ruth had assigned to assist him. Jim and his helper, Eve imagined, since the voices below were all obviously male.

She felt her husband's voice most of all. Was it possible to *feel* a voice? To have it work beneath the skin and touch the bones? A sudden sharp shout, and she was certain. Yes, she could feel Lucien's voice.

In spite of the trials she knew she had before her, Eve smiled. In another half hour or so—no, much less time than that—those assistants who were trying to help Lucien would be dismissed. Lucien was never satisfied unless things were done exactly as he wished. *Exactly.* When it came to his contraptions, no one else handled them properly, as far as he was concerned. He always ended up working alone.

Or with her. He trusted her with those blasted instruments as he trusted no one else. He allowed her to adjust the machines, to check the readings, to fiddle with them on occasion.

He loved her. Angry, happy, petty, passionate, annoyed—it didn't matter what mood she found him in. He always loved her, and she loved him. They had been to hell and back, and nothing could ever tear them apart. Nothing and no one.

Daisy had left the French doors opened, so when a new breeze kicked up, Eve felt the wind wash over her. It would soon be dark, and there was a decided crispness in that wind. A touch of ice, a precursor of winter. The gauzy curtains danced, a new chill filled the room, and the wind whispered.

Eve turned to face the portal, to watch the curtains that whipped furiously. She had once dismissed anything out of the ordinary as her own imagination. No more. She'd seen and heard too many things to dismiss even the smallest inconsistency.

As the curtains danced, she heard something not of this world. A faraway voice. A trill of laughter. Movement, a soft footstep, as if someone ran toward her. Goose bumps ticked her arms, but Eve was not afraid.

"Hello?" she said softly.

The wind died; the curtains dropped. The soft and disembodied voice of a child whispered,

"Mama?"

Three

Lucien turned his head just in time to see Eve rush down the stairs, a blur as she raced downward. He had moments earlier told the incompetent workmen Ruth had assigned to assist him to take their hands off his property and busy themselves elsewhere, and they had gratefully made their escape shortly before Eve's arrival.

She came upon him quickly and stopped well short of running him over. "There's a child," she said breathlessly.

He knew she wasn't with child herself, so she had to be talking about the ghost he had already seen briefly, a boy who didn't appear to be more than four or five years old. "Yes, I know."

"I heard him, Lucien." Her pink face paled a little. "He called out for his mother. The wind blew into my face and I . . . I smelled something sweet, like . . . like . . ."

"Caramel."

Startled, Lucien and Eve both turned to face Ruth, who had entered the room so quietly neither of them had heard her approach. She stood not five feet away.

"Tommy always loved my caramel candy. I made

it for him often. I never make it anymore," she said,
her wistful voice at odds with her austere bearing.
"There's no one here who will enjoy my caramel
candy the way Tommy did, so I don't make it anymore. But I sometimes catch a whiff of it myself."

"Tommy," Eve repeated softly.

Ruth nodded.

"You've been here a long time," Lucien said, his
eyes on the older woman.

She looked directly at him, regal and fearless. "I
was born on this land, I was a slave in this house,
and now I am a paid servant."

"Why did you stay?" Eve asked. "After the war,
you could have gone anywhere."

"This is my home, and besides . . ." At last, Lucien
saw a touch of emotion in the old woman's eyes. "I
couldn't leave them."

"Couldn't leave who?" Lucien took a single step
forward, watching the woman's face closely.

"Tommy and Margaret and Isabel, of course,"
she said, all but snapping at him. "Why else would
I stay? They need me here. What remained of their
family after the war died long ago, and others come
and go. What am I to do? Leave them to the whims
of strangers?" Again, Ruth laid strong eyes on Lucien. "You're going to try to send them away."

"Yes."

She lifted her chin, and in spite of her almost
combative stance, her chin trembled. "They won't
leave, and you can't force them to go. They are a
part of this house and they always will be."

"You don't want them to go," Lucien said kindly.

Ruth did not respond.

"They are not at peace," he explained, hoping to

win the servant over to his side. He suspected he would need her assistance before this was done. "Spirits who are at peace do not linger on this earth. It's time for those you care about to move on."

"How can I know that you won't try to send them to a place they don't know—a place where they will be afraid and lost and without . . . without friends?"

"You have my word."

She did not say as much, since such a response from a servant would be unacceptably hostile, but he saw the truth in Ruth's dark eyes. She did not have faith in his word.

"Since I was a child, I have seen spirits all around us. Contented spirits do not haunt. They have no reason to disturb the world of the living, as they are happy in their own world. They might look in on us now and then, but they do not haunt. Ghosts remain behind because there is some business that remains unfinished, some crime unpunished, some thing undone. Tell me what holds them here, Ruth. Help me send them to a happier place."

For a moment she did not respond, and her stoic face did not reveal her thoughts. Finally, she said, "I will not be here to tend to them forever. I'm seventy-four years old. What will they do when I am gone? Who will care for them then?"

"Indeed," Lucien said in a serene voice. "You can give the spirits who haunt this house this final gift of peace and serenity, which they do not now have. Help me set them free, Ruth. Help me send them on to a place where they will no longer be filled with pain."

"They are not in pain," she insisted.

"They are," Lucien insisted, just as assuredly. "I

can feel it. If they will talk to me and share that pain, perhaps I will not need your help at all. But if they won't talk to me . . . I'm not sure what I can do to help them."

"Tomorrow," Eve said as Lucien tossed restlessly. "Ruth said she'd tell you everything tomorrow, after she's had a chance to collect her thoughts."

He turned to her in the dark and rested his face close to hers. "She could have said everything that needs to be said tonight. This delay is unnecessary and annoying."

"You're so impatient," she said softly.

"Do not speak to me about patience, Evie. I believe I have proven to you that I have an abundance."

She smiled. "I suppose you have."

Lucien had tried several times to tempt her to break her vow, with a kiss, a hand, a wandering foot. But he had never insisted that she give up on what he openly called a ridiculous idea. In all the time she had known him, he had never treated her as if her desires and wishes had any less importance than his own.

"You're very good to me," she whispered.

"I could be better," he answered, his voice just as low as hers. A wandering hand rested on her hip.

Their bed was large enough, but the mattress sagged and they both rolled to the middle, where they lay too close. After this afternoon's encounter, Eve wanted nothing more than to hold her husband, to let him hold her, to forget everything but the way she loved him.

But if she did, she'd never be able to keep her hands to herself.

"I don't think I'll be able to sleep," Lucien said with a sigh.

"Of course you can sleep. I'm exhausted, myself." Eve rested her head on Lucien's chest and closed her eyes. Sleep—she needed to drift off to sleep so she'd dismiss the annoying notion that he'd been right all around and this business of staying apart was ludicrous.

She closed her eyes, but she didn't sleep. The hand at her hip drifted around to rest comfortably on her bottom. Lucien would not be still! He shifted; he squirmed; he managed to hold her so that she fit against him in such a way . . .

Eve rolled over and away from Lucien, keeping her eyes closed. Maybe he'd think she was asleep. She had to grab the edge of the mattress to keep from rolling back into Lucien. Maybe once he was asleep she'd let go. Until then, she was going to hold on for dear life.

They sat in the south parlor, Lucien and Eve on the love seat, Ruth perched on the edge of a chair that faced them. Eve had to admit, her husband could be a persuasive person, especially when he was so passionate. And he was passionate about his work; it was one of the things that had first drawn her to him.

After last night, she knew doubly well that she needed to maintain a little distance from her husband in order to keep her pledge, but yesterday's ghostly encounter above stairs and the expression on Lucien's face as he waited for Ruth to begin her tale made it impossible for her not to reach out and take his hand.

"Margaret and Isabel were born in this house in 1845. I assisted in the delivery myself. They were beautiful girls." Her eyes became misty, but she shook off the emotional response quickly. "And horribly spoiled by their father. They were the McBrides' only children, and both Mr. and Mrs. McBride doted on them. They were identical twins, you know," she said.

Lucien nodded. Of course he knew. Eve had not.

"When they were very small, only a few people could tell them apart."

"You among them?" Lucien asked.

"Yes," Ruth answered. "They could never fool me, though they did try."

Eve's eyes scanned the parlor. She saw nothing out of the ordinary, heard no more ghostly cries. But were the twins present? Did they listen as Ruth told the tale of their lives?

Ruth squirmed slightly, as if she were still not sure about this sharing of information. "As they grew older, their personalities differentiated them. Margaret was shy, sometimes painfully so. Isabel was more demonstrative. She wasn't a bad child by any means, but she was certainly more likely to get herself into a bind than Margaret. Isabel would climb trees while Margaret watched from the safety of solid ground. Isabel would swim in the pond on a cool day while Margaret worried that her sister would catch a cold. As they grew older, the differences became more pronounced. They were sixteen when the war began. Isabel already had a bevy of suitors. Margaret had only one, a boy as shy and withdrawn as she."

No one in the South had been untouched by the War Between the States. What must it have been like for two spoiled sixteen-year-old girls? Their world had been turned upside down.

"The men left us," Ruth said in a lowered voice. "For a while we were safe here. We got along very well, in fact, until three years into the war, even though things were very different for us all. Eighteen sixty-four." She shuddered very slightly. Only her trembling fingers gave her away. "The Yankees came, and the war found us at last. We should have hidden from them; I know that now, but we didn't know until too late that they were upon us. The girls . . ." Ruth wrung her hands. "Margaret was upstairs mending some clothing, and Isabel was in the garden. By the time we gathered them together, it was too late to run.

"Mrs. McBride tried to stand in front of the door and keep the soldiers out, but they pushed her aside. Poor woman, she wasn't well. Mrs. McBride wasn't meant for hard times. She'd picked up a persistent cough over the winter, and it never quite went away. Seeing those Yankees run over her house, breaking things and stealing and making themselves at home . . ." Ruth shuddered as if she remembered too well. "The Yankees' invasion sent her to her bed, and she never left it. She died a few days later in that bed, and she never knew . . ." Ruth laid hard eyes on Lucien. "You're a Yankee, aren't you?"

"I suppose I am, though I was much too young to serve in the war in any way."

"I'm not sure that matters," Ruth said softly. "The

girls won't like you, because you have that accent they learned to hate."

"What happened after the soldiers came?" he asked.

Ruth no longer looked at Lucien but instead stared directly at Eve. "I didn't know until later that the men who invaded us were not with the army. They were deserters, renegades. Worthless thieves, each and every one of them." Anger, a pure rage, shone in her dark eyes. "They kicked me out, sent me to the old slave quarters to live while they took over this house as if they had a right . . ." She took a calming deep breath.

"They wouldn't allow Margaret and Isabel to come with me. Mrs. McBride was ill—dying, though we didn't know it at the time. The soldier in charge, an awful man with a nasty beard and a sword he brandished as if he were anxious to have someone's head, he said that if the girls tried to leave, he'd toss the mother out, too. And he would have. He would have tossed a sick woman out on the porch to die."

"So the twins stayed here," Eve said when Ruth hesitated.

"Yes. I thought they would allow the girls to care for their mother, perhaps make them cook and clean and do their laundry, but I never . . ." Ruth took a moment to gather her wits. "Mrs. McBride was not the only woman here who was not prepared for war."

Eve could tell by the fire in the old woman's eyes that she blamed herself for everything that had happened. "Were they . . . harmed?"

"They were beaten, tortured. Raped."

"And one of the soldiers is Tommy's father."

"Yes."

"Which twin is the mother?" Lucien asked.

Again, Ruth turned her attention to Lucien. "I don't know. No one does. No one but Margaret and Isabel."

"How is that possible? You said they were very different, that by this time in their lives everyone could tell them apart."

"I moved back into the house after the Yankees left," Ruth said angrily. "It was very thoughtful of them not to burn the place down, since Mrs. McBride was dead and they had defiled two beautiful, innocent young girls until no one, not even I, could see the girls they had once been. After that, they were the same. Not Margaret, so shy and kind. Not Isabel, full of life. They were identical women, sad and quiet and broken."

"And one of them was with child," Eve said.

Ruth nodded. "They refused to say who the mother was. One of the girls told me that it didn't matter, that it could have been either of them who gave birth to a bastard child of rape. I believe they decided to suffer together, to bear the shame together."

"And after the war was over?" Lucien prompted.

"Some of the men they knew returned, but the immediate family was gone. Mr. and Mrs. McBride were both dead, and of course the girls had no way of keeping the plantation. They could have married, of course, but they refused all suitors. When the house was purchased by a distant cousin, the new owners were kind enough to let the girls and the baby live in the guest house. They made a nice home there for the three of them, and I saw them often."

"And made them caramel candy," Eve said.

Ruth gave in to a small smile. "Yes, I did."

"Did they ever show any sign of their individual personalities as the years passed?" Lucien asked.

"No. Oh, they did not remain broken forever. They healed. They loved Tommy. Some days they smiled." Her earlier smile was long gone when she said. "In the last year of their lives there was talk about men, men who visited one of the girls in the guest house late at night."

"Which sister?" Eve asked.

"I don't know."

And if she did know, Eve suspected she would not tell. Ruth protected the girls still.

"How did they die?" Lucien asked.

Ruth took a deep breath, as if she needed strength to finish telling her story. "Someone set the guest house on fire late one night. They burned. Tommy was five years old. Isabel and Margaret were twenty-five. Another body, the remains of a man, was found with them, but no one ever knew who he was. I don't suppose it matters.

"I saw the flames," she continued. "The light from the fire woke me. But by that time it was too late. They were gone."

"Are you sure someone deliberately set the fire?"

Ruth laid ancient, depthless eyes on Lucien at his question. "Yes. Someone deliberately started that fire; I'm sure of it. The girls and the child died in their beds. They had no chance to escape."

"Was there a thorough investigation?"

Ruth shook her head. "No. In truth, no one

cared, but for me, and even though I was no longer
a slave, I was just as powerless as I had been before
my emancipation."

Eve grasped Lucien's hand tightly. It was a truly
horrible story, one she would not soon forget.

Margaret and Isabel might be bound to the earth
until the identity of their killer was revealed.
Tommy apparently wanted to know which of the
twins was his mother.

As she sat on the couch, holding Lucien's hand,
Eve was almost certain she caught a whiff of
caramel in the air.

Along with a whiff of perfume.

Glover Manor was, as she had said often since ar-
riving here, a beautiful house. She'd slept well last
night, surprisingly so. As she'd gone about her
morning rituals and dressed for the day in a peach-
colored gown, Daisy had felt very much at home
in her room. A few minor adjustments to her hair,
and she'd be ready to face the day with a smile.

So why did she feel as if a cold wind were creep-
ing down her back, beneath her gown?

She'd learned to deal with the concept of ghosts,
but she was not anxious for another face-to-face encounter. With any luck, she wouldn't see or hear
any ghostly activity this time. Lucien was the one
with the gift for speaking to the dead. Daisy preferred ignorance where the presence of ghosts was
concerned.

She didn't want to think about ghosts. Her mind
was busy enough with thoughts of O'Hara. What if
he arrived early? She couldn't very well allow him

to find her skittish about the situation and distracted and, well, less than perfect.

A shuffling in the hallway outside her room caught her attention. The footsteps in the hallway didn't sound ghostly, but she wanted to be sure.

Daisy opened the door an inch or two, just in time to see Lucien and Eve pass by. They were obviously on their way somewhere, their matched stride was so sure. So determined.

"Where are you going?" Daisy asked as she stepped into the hallway.

"The attic," Eve said. She smiled back but did not slow her step. "Ruth says she believes there's a portrait of the twins stored up there."

"Ghostly twins?" Daisy asked.

Eve nodded.

For a moment Daisy hesitated, then she followed her friends. "Why do you need a portrait? Can't Lucien tell you what they look like? Can't he see them?"

"I see them as they are," he said softly. "I need to see them as they were."

That made no sense to Daisy, but she didn't question Lucien further. She adored Eve, and Eve loved her husband. But Lucien was an odd man, and Daisy still hadn't quite forgotten what Lucien had been like when Scrydan had possessed his body.

"Why do you need to see them?" Daisy asked Eve as they reached the doorway that opened into a narrow attic stairwell.

Eve looked up. Another door at the top of the stairs was closed, making the stairway itself quite dark. They didn't carry a candle or lamp, since it was fully light outside.

It was morning, a time of peace and beauty and normalcy, not a time for ghosts. Goodness, she hadn't even had breakfast yet!

The hairs on the back of Daisy's neck stood up in warning. She had the distinct feeling she was, once again, about to come face to face with a haunting spirit.

An anxious Lucien climbed to the top of the stairs, and Eve followed. Daisy waited a moment, but finally she climbed the stairs as well. At a near run. This was no place to be left behind.

Lucien walked slowly to the center of the small attic room. Cobwebs hung from the ceiling, catching the morning light that shone through a very small window set in one wall. Dusty trunks had been placed here and there, along with a cracked mirror, a broken rocking chair, and a stack of framed pictures leaning against one wall.

It was all rather distasteful. And dirty.

Eve glanced around the room, searching for the portrait they had come here for. Daisy helped. The attic was interesting, as some attics were, home to a multitude of discarded things. Daisy looked beyond the dirt and spotted a couple of pieces of furniture that, with a little work, would be perfectly suitable.

She realized, after a moment, that Lucien had hardly moved at all since stopping in the center of the room. When he turned his head toward her, she saw that his face was white, his eyes hooded.

"It happened here," he said in a lowered voice. "Dear God, right here. Both of them. They screamed. They cried. They . . . they . . . ." He placed one hand over his stomach and doubled over.

"Out," Eve ordered, taking her husband's arm and leading him toward the stairway.

"No, I want that portrait."

"I'll get it," Eve assured him.

"I won't leave you here alone." Lucien stopped at the doorway, glanced down the long, dark stairway as if he could not wait to escape. "There's so much pain. Can't you feel it? Can't you . . . hear?" He placed both hands over his ears and pressed them tightly to his head, as if he could smother the sounds.

Daisy glanced around the perfectly quiet, ordinary attic. She didn't see anything, she didn't hear anything. But Lucien's word was good enough for her. "Maybe we should go, Eve. We can send someone else up for the portrait."

Eve made her way toward the framed pictures covered in cobwebs and dust. "Take Lucien down the stairs," she insisted. "I'll be right behind you."

Lucien wasn't exactly with them at the moment. He mumbled and glanced about the room as if he saw things she did not. Of course, he did just that. Whatever he saw, it was horrible.

"Come along, Lucien," Daisy said as if she were talking to a child. She reached out to take his arm.

He allowed her to take his arm, but he glared at her. "Not without Evie."

Daisy leaned slightly forward. "You shouldn't worry so. She doesn't see what you see."

"That doesn't mean it isn't here."

True enough. "Eve!" Daisy called, only a little bit frantic. "Haven't you found what you're looking for yet?"

"Got it," Eve said. Her declaration was followed

by the sound of heavy objects being moved aside. When she reappeared, she held a good-sized portrait before her.

"Why are you still here?" she asked Lucien, her voice sharp and her eyes concerned.

"Not without you, love," Lucien said. "Never without you."

Lucien took the framed portrait and insisted that Eve descend the stairs first. When Daisy, who was directly behind Eve, had made it halfway down the stairs, she heard the attic door above her close solidly.

It occurred to Daisy, as she gratefully made her way into the main hallway, that handsome and charming as he was, O'Hara was likely not worth all this trouble.

Four

In the portrait that stood before him, propped against the dresser in the room he shared with Eve, it was easy to tell which twin was Margaret and which was Isabel, thanks to Ruth's description.

Isabel's smile was wider than her sister's, and the artist who had painted this portrait had captured the sparkle in her eyes. Margaret's smile was more subdued, but she had a serenity about her that made her somehow more beautiful than Isabel, even though they had identical dark brown hair in ringlets, dark brown eyes, and wore girlish pale blue dresses with frills and bows.

According to Ruth, the twins had been fifteen when this portrait had been painted. Not women, not children, but caught in between. They should have had their entire lives ahead of them, and instead . . .

What Lucien had seen and heard in the attic stayed with him still. It was as if the spirits had yanked him back in time. Disturbing images had flashed through his mind in rapid succession. The rope that bound the sisters, the knife that had been used to threaten and cut them, a fist. Blood. Mingled with the images were the emotions the girls and the attackers had felt. Unable to move, unable to fight, they had been completely and totally over-powered. Helpless. Frightened.

The girls had not known at first what was going to happen to them. Not until one of the soldiers started ripping and cutting off their clothes. And even then . . . All their lives the McBride twins had been so protected, so sheltered, that the violence inflicted upon them had turned their neat world, where things like this did not happen, inside out.

Lucien had almost vomited onto the attic floor, the pain had been so great. He could still feel it, the fear and the horror. The anger and the confusion.

And the love. Through it all, he'd felt Margaret and Isabel's love for each other.

Eve laid a hand on his arm. He'd almost forgotten that she stood beside him.

"You're not to go up there again," he commanded in a soft voice.

"Yes, dear."

"I should send you home in the morning. Daisy, too."

Eve shook her head. "No. That's not the way it works, Lucien." She wrapped her arm through his. "I won't leave you, either."

A part of him wanted to lay her on the bed behind them and make love to her until he forgot what he'd seen and heard. Pamphlets and vows aside, he knew she would not refuse him. She probably needed that closeness as much as he did.

But that wasn't going to happen.

Lucien wished, not for the first time, that his life could be simple. He wished he could be like Buster, a farmer whose only challenge, before joining the

Plummerville Ghost Society, had been working up the nerve to talk to a redheaded girl. Or Garrick, who could turn his back on what he disliked about his life and start again in another place. But he couldn't do either of those things. He would never be a farmer. He could never turn his back on who—*what*—he was.

"Evie," he said, his eyes on Margaret and Isabel, "I hope we never have children."

"What?"

Lucien didn't turn his head to look at his wife, and he didn't need to. He heard the disbelief, felt it in the arm that remained entwined with his.

"Not one," he said, "not a dozen. Not a number somewhere in between."

"You're upset," she said. "You'll come to your senses in a—"

"I have come to my senses!" He dropped her arm, unable to touch her any longer. "Look at them!" He pointed to the twins in the dusty portrait before them. "They were beautiful, and innocent, and loved. Their parents doted on them, spoiled them, did their best to give them a good life. And look at what happened to them!"

"I know. . . ."

"You don't know. I do. In a matter of seconds, I smelled it, felt it, tasted it." Blood and tears, sweat and panic. "Seconds, and it tore me apart. It wasn't over in seconds for them, Evie. They suffered for what seemed like an eternity. They're suffering still. Do we really want to create a child so it can live in a world where men do such things?"

"There's more good in the world than—"

"Where?!" he shouted. "Show me where!"

Eve reached out and took his hand in her own. He loved the feel of her touching him, even in such a simple way. What had he done without her for so long? How had he lived? She lifted his hand and placed it over his own heart, his palm down so that he felt the thud of his heartbeat, her palm against the back of his hand. "Here."

"It's not enough," he whispered.

"It has to be." She dropped his hand slowly. Reluctantly. "We'll talk about this after you calm down. You'll forget what you saw today. The images will fade, as they always do."

Lucien turned his back on his wife and left the room abruptly, without telling her that the images didn't always fade. He pushed them to the back of his mind, tried not to dwell on old pain, but he carried a piece of that pain with him always. She thought he would change his mind, that when he was far enough away from the experience to dismiss what he'd felt and heard that he would want children as much as she did.

Unlikely. He was glad their first year together had not produced a baby. If he was very lucky, he would prove unable to father a child and would never have to worry about the impossibility of protecting an innocent from the horrors of the world.

On more than one occasion, he had promised Evie that he would gladly give her everything she wanted, and he'd tried. He'd tried with all his heart.

He wanted his wife; he loved her . . . but they no longer wanted the same kind of life.

* * *

As the evening wore on, Daisy found that every noise, no matter how insignificant or ordinary, made her jump. Her eyes continually drifted to the parlor doorway. O'Hara might arrive early, she supposed. Maybe even tonight.

Dinner had been simple, and Daisy had helped Ruth place everything on the table and clear it away again. Apparently, the day girls had seen a ghost in the afternoon, and they'd quit their jobs and run for home together, leaving Ruth to handle the chores alone. Ruth had grumbled that it was *that one* who agitated the spirits. She meant Lucien, of course. And she was probably right.

Glover Manor was very much like a castle, and Daisy had spent a good part of the afternoon exploring. She stayed well away from the attic, of course, and the Glovers' personal rooms upstairs. But downstairs she could allow herself to snoop and admire as she wished. Lucien had claimed this parlor near the front of the house as his own, but there was another parlor that overlooked the garden, a music room, a library, and what looked to be Mr. Glover's office. She hadn't spent much time in that room, as there were what appeared to be personal papers on the desk. Besides, it was the least beautiful of all the rooms.

Daisy liked the room she called the garden parlor best. It was bright and airy, delicate and inviting. She could definitely see herself spending a quiet afternoon in that room, stitching or reading poetry.

But since Eve and Lucien were spending the evening in the parlor, so was she. She did not want to be alone in this big house any more than she had to!

Lucien was busy making adjustments of some sort to one of his thingamajigs. He had a habit of sitting on the floor as he worked. Daisy could not imagine why. She would find such a position uncomfortable. Then again, Lucien didn't have a corset to take into consideration.

Eve watched her husband solemnly. This morning's misadventure had affected them both in some deep way Daisy did not understand. Poor Eve—she wanted a baby so badly, and there was nothing Daisy could do for her friend. Nothing at all.

All of a sudden, Eve's head popped up, and she looked toward the fireplace. "Did you hear that?"

A chill danced down Daisy's arms. "No. I didn't hear anything."

Lucien lifted his head. "It's nothing, Evie. They're restless, that's all."

Restless. He was talking about the ghosts. Daisy clasped her hands together tightly. Thank goodness she hadn't heard or seen anything! It was bad enough to know they were about.

But she was curious. "Why does Eve hear them when I don't?"

"There's one who's showing himself to me," Eve said, obviously distracted.

"They can do that?" Daisy asked with a shiver. "They can . . . choose?"

"Sometimes," Lucien said as he returned his attention to his work. "If there is a connection of some sort, if the spirit believes the person in question has a sort of sympathy for the injustices that keep them earthbound, then they might be able to . . . break down a wall, as it were." He ended the explanation with a wave of his hand.

"That's interesting," Daisy said softly. And terrifying, though she didn't say so aloud.

The minutes ticked past, and Daisy thought about what Lucien had said. Why did Eve have a connection with one of the spirits in this house?

Luckily for Daisy, there was nothing to connect her in any way to any of the ghosts in this house. All she wanted was to see O'Hara, get her heart settled one way or another, and then go home.

Eve's eyes remained closed as Lucien crawled gently beneath the covers. He had not lit a candle or a lamp but had found his way beside her by moonlight alone. Was he afraid of what she might say or do if he woke her?

She wanted to dismiss his earlier vow that he wanted no children. True, he'd never shown any real enthusiasm for building a family, but she had never imagined that the idea of having babies was distasteful to him.

He saw things others did not; she was well aware of that. But did he truly believe the world was such a terrible place that it was not fit for a child?

Tonight was the first night Lucien had not tried, in a subtle or not-so-subtle way, to convince her to forget her two-month bout of abstinence. Maybe she wouldn't have to worry about getting through the next month and seventeen days with his doing his best to seduce her. She should be relieved. Why was she so sad instead?

Lucien slept, but the house did not. He awakened it with his very presence. Walls popped and moaned. Floors crackled. And while Eve lay beside her husband and wondered what would become of their marriage, a mist formed near the window. At first she thought it was her imagination, but she had encountered a ghost or two herself. Not as Lucien did, with strength and clarity, but when a strong spirit wanted to make itself known, it managed.

It was not Tommy, the child she had seen tonight so very briefly, but a woman, Eve realized as the mist took shape. One of the twins. She wore her dark hair in a plain bun, and her dark eyes were older than those of either girl in the portrait. She was alone, without her sister or the boy, Tommy. The ghost was dressed in a plain, drab dress that had seen better days. This was the woman she had become after the soldiers had done with her.

"Hello," Eve whispered.

The ghost smiled, but not brightly.

"I wish you could speak to me."

The woman of mist shook her head.

"We want to help you—you and your sister and the boy."

The ghost's smile faded. She shook her head slowly, sadly, as if to say, *No one can help us.*

The story Ruth had told was heartbreakingly sad. No wonder the twins were trapped here after all this time. Would saving them, seeing them at peace at last, change Lucien's mind about having children?

Lucien had said on more than one occasion that he should be enough for her. He was, in many ways. Her life had never been so happy as it had been since he'd come back into it. Someone to love, to laugh with, to lie beside. Someone to argue with, even. She took care of him; he took care of her. Did they really need children to complete their lives? When she thought of the moment she'd hold a baby in her arms, the answer was *yes*.

But if she never had a child, she wouldn't love Lucien any less. They did belong together, whether their family was comprised of the two of them or a house-full.

The ghost made no attempt to communicate, but she did not disappear. Perhaps she was content to show herself to a living being who was not afraid. Eve wondered, should she wake Lucien? He was so tired, drained by his experience in the attic. She hated to disturb his rest. And yet, this was the reason he had been called here.

Eve was considering waking her husband when the door to their room burst open and Daisy came flying in, nightgown dancing around her body, loosened blond hair doing the same. The ghost disappeared. Lucien sat up like a shot.

Daisy ran to Eve's side of the bed. "Scoot over!" she commanded.

"What?" Eve had no choice but to comply as Daisy proceeded to join her and Lucien in the bed.

"There's a ghost in my room," Daisy said as she pulled the covers to her chin.

Eve was snugly sandwiched between her husband and her friend, on this mattress that had a tendency to sag. The other sister had visited Daisy's bedroom, she assumed, since one had been here until Daisy burst into the room.

Lucien lifted his head. Long dark hair was slightly mussed; his face was dusted with a dark, rough beard. He looked not at all civilized at the moment. "You did understand when we started off on this trip that we were coming to a *haunted* house?" he asked dryly.

"Well, yes, but . . ."

"There are usually ghosts in haunted houses."

"I know that, but . . ."

"You can't stay here!" Lucien said sharply.

"Why not?" Daisy asked innocently. "It's not as if I might interrupt anything, since, well, you know . . ."

A long moment of uncomfortable silence passed. Eve held her breath.

"You told her," Lucien said in a lowered voice. "For God's sake, Evie!"

"Eve didn't exactly tell me," Daisy said. "I gave her a pamphlet, and after she'd had a chance to read it over I asked what she thought of the suggested methods, and so I perhaps know more than I should about personal matters that are best left between a wife and a husband, but . . ."

"*You* gave Evie that damned pamphlet?"

"Yes."

"And you think that gives you the right to share our bed."

"Just for tonight," Daisy said. "Until I get accustomed to the . . . the ghosts."

"You've seen ghosts before," Lucien reminded her.

"Yes, but I didn't have to face them alone."

Eve closed her eyes, caught in the middle, literally, of this conversation.

"Fine," Lucien said, returning his head to the pillow and turning his back on Eve. "Darling, does your friend know that I sleep naked?"

"Eww, you do not," Daisy insisted. "You're just trying to shock and disturb me so I'll go back to my room and be forced to face the ghosts all by myself. Well, it's not going to work. That doesn't make any sense, anyway. Why on earth would anyone sleep . . . that way?"

"Naked," Lucien said sharply.

Eve wondered if she should tell Daisy that Lucien did indeed sleep nude. Since her marriage, she'd slept that way herself on many nights.

But not lately.

"Go to sleep, Daisy," Eve said as she settled in, closer to Lucien than she should be, given the circumstances. She still thought a brief bout of celibacy might be the answer to her problem, and he . . . If he didn't want children, did that mean he would never touch her again? She could not imagine such a turn of events.

Daisy and Lucien both fell asleep rather quickly, but Eve remained awake. The ghost did not return, but Eve's thoughts would not be still. In her mind she heard the ghost of Tommy moaning, *"Mama."* She saw Lucien double over in the attic. She listened again to Ruth's story, saw the pain in Lucien's eyes. How could she possibly sleep tonight? How could they?

Some time in the middle of the night, Lucien rolled over and took Eve into his embrace. His long arms wrapped around her, and she found herself being cuddled against his chest, in that very spot that was hers and hers alone. She fit here. She was safe here. A few minutes later, she was fast asleep.

Lucien kept himself busy during the morning hours fiddling with the specter-o-meter. Until he shook the remaining horror of what he'd seen in the attic yesterday, it would be foolish to open himself up in order to channel one of the sisters. Or both of them. He would prefer not to channel the child if he had a choice. The spirits of children were unpredictable, and they did not always communicate as fully as the ghost of a departed adult.

He didn't want to visit the site of the fire until O'Hara arrived. It would be best if the grounds of the cottage where the sisters had lived and died remained undisturbed until then. In these circumstances, it would take a combination of their powers to see everything that needed to be seen.

He didn't have a shortage of ghosts to study to pass the time—not in this house. They were everywhere. The specter-o-meter was constantly reading one spirit or another, and the ectoplasm harvester stayed full. The ghosts were past residents of the plantation, mostly, drifting in and out. He hadn't seen either of the twins today, or the child, but there were other ghosts present. Curious, harmless, restless ghosts.

The spirit of a soldier peered over his shoulder. Since this was a Confederate soldier, Lucien didn't need to wonder if the spirit of one of the men who'd committed atrocities in the attic had returned to pay penance.

Another man, one less curious about Lucien's work than the soldier, stood a few feet away. The intensity with which he stared finally made Lucien lift his head in acknowledgment. "What do you want?" he asked, testier than he should have been with a spirit who had apparently come to him for help.

The ghost was not perturbed, but continued to

stand as if he were lounging against the end of the table. "I want you to save them."

The spirit of a man long past this world made a sound no one else could hear—no one but Lucien. His gift. His curse.

"Why?"

"I love her."

Lucien shoved the specter-o-meter aside. It was impossible to work on the contraption when this spirit—who was not the one he had been called to clear away but was very present all the same—was making the needle jump so. "You loved one of the twins."

"Love, not loved. Emotion survives death. You know that. Love survives most of all."

"Which one?" Lucien asked. "Which sister?"

The ghostly smile faded. "I don't know."

"How can you not . . ." Lucien stopped in mid-sentence. He had assumed he was speaking to the spirit of a man who had courted one of the young girls before the war. Apparently, that was not so. "You met her . . . after."

The ghost nodded.

"How could you not know her name? What did you call her?"

"She said I was to call her 'darling,' that no other name was necessary."

"What am I to call you?" Lucien studied the clothing the ghost wore, trying to piece together the clues. The plain trousers, Union shirt, and tall black boots the spirit displayed now would be something he'd worn at some time during his life.

"Thomas," the spirit said as it faded away. "My name is Thomas."

Lucien stood. "Is the child named for you? How is that possible, if you didn't meet them until after . . . ?" After. Their entire short lives had been divided into before and after.

Thomas faded away, leaving too many questions unanswered.

His job would be so much easier if the spirits would cooperate! Instead they came and went as they pleased, told him half-truths, and teased him with secrets they would not, or could not, share.

Thomas was no different.

Eve came into the room, not knowing how close she had come to seeing yet another ghost. Would she have seen Thomas? Perhaps, perhaps not.

He didn't always tell his wife what he saw. If he did, they'd spend half their life living—no, *re*living—someone else's years.

At the moment, they had enough problems with their own.

"Did you sleep well?" he asked.

"Yes. You?"

"Fair enough." The nightmares had not been nearly as violent as he had expected they would be. "And Daisy?"

Eve grinned. "She was still sleeping when I left the room."

"I hope this new arrangement isn't a permanent one," Lucien said.

"No, no," Eve assured him. "I'll make sure she understands that last night was a one-time event. If she's going to be a member of the Plummerville Ghost Society, she's going to have to face a ghost on her own now and then."

He loved his wife, and he always would. The only

thing that stood between them and a perfectly happy marriage was her insistence that they needed a child to achieve happiness . . . and now his decision that he didn't want children at all. He had to make her see that they didn't need a child to complete their lives. Their love was enough.

He could not bear to have a child and watch it suffer as Margaret and Isabel had suffered, as Tommy had suffered, as children suffered every day. Somehow he would make her understand that he was right in this.

And until he unearthed a method of birth control—French letters or herbs, he imagined—he would not touch her. It was a chance he could not take.

"Daisy is a delicate young woman. Perhaps you and she could share a room for a few days, and I could sleep in the other room. Alone." The plan should delight Eve, since she had been trying to keep him at a distance for more than a week now. Almost two.

She did not look particularly delighted as she said, in her coolest voice, "Whatever you think is best."

Lucien turned his back on her. God help him, he had no idea what was best, not anymore.

Five

Since Lucien didn't seem to want any assistance this morning, Eve busied herself in her room. She made a few notes on what she'd seen thus far, and then gently cleaned the portrait that remained in the bedchamber she shared with her husband. Or would she now share it with Daisy?

No. She had a feeling that if she gave in on this one, if she allowed Lucien to draw away from her, they would never get back what they'd once had. A few days ago she would've welcomed such an arrangement. She had even hoped, at one point, that he'd travel to this job without her! But that was before . . . before everything had changed.

No one had ever told her marriage would be so difficult. The love was easy, but the rest could be damned hard.

The doors to the gallery were opened, and had been for a while. The breeze that wafted through the portal was cool and fresh. With the French doors closed, earlier, Eve had felt absolutely trapped in this room. Closed in and suffocating.

A new breeze made the curtains dance, and the unmistakable aroma of caramel teased Eve's nose. She dropped the rag she'd been cleaning the portrait with and stared at the open doorway. She held her breath and waited. Finally, a whisper on the wind reached her. *"Mama?"*

It was unusual that she heard the ghostly cry, as she had upon her arrival. She did not have Lucien's gift, and in many hauntings she saw and heard nothing while her husband went about his work. But one thing she had learned in her years of working with Lucien and the others. Just when you thought you knew what the rules of this game were, they changed. There were no rules. No precise order. No book of facts and figures.

"Tommy?" she said softly. The scent of caramel became stronger. The curtains danced more than they should, given the light afternoon breeze.

"Mama."

It broke her heart to think of this child who had never had a chance to grow to adulthood. Who had never known his father, perhaps had never even been sure himself which of the twins was his mother. She wanted to wrap her arms around him and hold him close. But of course, that was impossible.

"No," she said softly. "I am not your mother."

The wind died; the scent of caramel vanished very suddenly. "But I would like to be your friend," Eve said quickly. Too late. Tommy was gone.

Why did it seem that she was surrounded by children these days, when she was so desperate for her own? Garrick and Katherine, Buster and his bride. And it seemed that when she walked the Plummerville streets there were more babies than usual, more women swollen with child. It seemed as if everyone but she was blessed with children.

She and Lucien had not yet conceived. Perhaps they never would. Perhaps nothing she learned from any pamphlet would help them have children of their own. And now Lucien had doubts about bringing babies into the world! She could change his mind on that point. At least, she thought she could. Perhaps.

Maybe it wasn't meant to be. Perhaps she was barren or Lucien was unable to father children, and they would have to be happy with each other.

At the moment, she was anything but happy.

A soft knock sounded at the door, and a moment later it swung open and Daisy walked in. Daisy had spent the afternoon in the kitchen with Ruth, learning to cook. Since the day girls had quit and the chore of feeding three visitors became too much for the old woman—not that Ruth would ever admit to as much—she needed assistance. Daisy had never much cared that she wasn't the best of cooks, but lately she had become obsessed with becoming the perfect housekeeper and cook.

All thanks to O'Hara, Eve suspected.

"What are you doing?" Daisy asked brightly.

Today Daisy had chosen a pale blue gown that showed off her figure and accentuated the fairness of her skin and the rosy tint in her cheeks. She looked like a doll, porcelain and delicate, complete with bows and frills and a ribbon in her blond hair.

"Nothing important," Eve said, deciding not to share her most recent ghostly encounter with Daisy. The news would rob Daisy of her smile and likely make what Eve was about to say impossible. "I made a few preliminary notes and have been cleaning the portrait of Margaret and Isabel."

Daisy stood beside Eve and studied the painting. "They were very beautiful," she said softly, her smile fading. "And young. I hope Lucien can help them."

"He will," Eve said confidently. "Speaking of Lucien, he had an idea regarding the sleeping arrangements."

Daisy's smile returned. "I know. He mentioned it downstairs. I am so relieved. I can't tell you . . ."

"I don't think it's a good idea," Eve interrupted her friend.

"Why not?"

Eve found a spot of dust on the picture frame and very gently wiped it away. "Lucien needs me. He won't admit to such a thing, and I'm sure he thinks what he's suggesting is best. But I don't. I'm afraid if we start to draw apart now we'll never repair the damage done."

"Just a night or two . . ." Daisy began.

"No."

Daisy nodded and offered no more argument. "All right. Lucien did assure me that these ghosts are unable to physically harm me, so I suppose if I see one again I should just close my eyes and wait until it goes away."

"Thank you," Eve said softly. "Now," she said more energetically, dismissing her marital problems from her mind. "Help me hang this portrait. I think it would look best over there." She pointed to an atrocious landscape painting, too drab and dull for this lovely room.

The family who now lived in this house had no connection to the McBrides, not by blood or marriage. There was no reason for the portrait of the twins to hang in this house. But Eve could not relegate them to the attic, and they deserved to hang on the wall and be admired, not be propped in a corner somewhere in a dismissive manner.

Eve and Daisy lifted the framed painting carefully and carried it across the room. "So," Daisy said casually. "When do you think O'Hara will arrive?"

"Lucien said perhaps as early as tomorrow."

"I'm beginning to think that maybe I shouldn't have come." Daisy didn't look at Eve as she helped to take down the landscape and hang the portrait. "After all, O'Hara hasn't expressed any interest in me in a romantic way, not since we were snowed in at the Honeycutt Hotel. For all I know, he makes romantic overtures to a different girl in every haunted house he studies."

"I don't think so," Eve said, grateful to turn her mind from her own troubles to someone else's. "And you did say he'd been writing."

"Yes." Daisy sighed. "Friendly, cordial, completely unromantic letters. Did I do something wrong? I was so certain, when he left Plummerville last January, that he would be back by spring."

"O'Hara is . . . odd," Eve said.

Odd in the same way Lucien was, but in his own way. O'Hara did not speak to the dead, but if he laid his hand on an object he could see visions of the past, and sometimes visions of the future. Most of the time he was an overly friendly, outgoing, frequently smiling man. What set him apart was the power in his hands.

"He probably met someone he likes better than me," Daisy said softly. "And I will feel like a complete fool when he shows up here with a wife in tow."

"I doubt very much . . ." Eve began, but Daisy was paying her no mind.

"Men. They will tell you that some things don't matter, that everything is fine, and then . . ." She pursed her lips. "Oh, I am such an idiot."

"O'Hara is not going to show up with a wife!" Eve insisted. "He is sweet on you, I know it. He just has a hard time sharing his feelings, that's all. Beneath his outgoing exterior, he's very . . . shy."

Daisy stared at her friend and snorted. "O'Hara? Shy? No." She steeled her spine and lifted her chin. "It's a good thing I came. I have to know, once and for all, if I'm a fool for wondering . . . every time someone knocks on my door, or I hear the whistle of the train . . ." She laid clear blue eyes on Eve's face. "I have to know."

Nothing could take Lucien's mind off his personal problems like those of a ghost or two. Margaret and Isabel were present but not cooperative. At least, not yet. They did not fear him, as he had thought they might, but they were wary of him and the way he could call to them.

Thomas made brief appearances but divulged no pertinent information. There was also the weaker spirit of an older woman, the twins' mother; the Confederate soldier; a young girl, a slave who had died by falling down the stairs; and a male spirit who never stayed long enough for Lucien to get a reading on him.

Then there was Tommy. The child had a strong spirit, stronger than a child's should be. He'd been gone from this earth almost seventeen years, and while the image he presented had not changed, his spirit had grown and matured in some ways.

But in other ways he remained a child.

He wasn't sure why the twins haunted this place. Was it because they had been murdered? Or because they had been violated and tortured in the attic of this very house? Lucien shuddered; his stomach did a sick flip. He would never forget what he'd felt in that attic room.

"I do not blame you," a soft voice whispered.

Lucien turned his head and found himself face to face with one of the twins.

"Do not suffer for me," she said.

"How can I not?" Lucien asked softly.

The specter before him smiled, but still he could not tell which twin he spoke to. The smile did not have Isabel's vivaciousness or Margaret's serenity. The deserters who'd hurt the sisters had taken their true smiles from them. "Your wife is right: you are a good man. I don't blame all men, the way Sister does."

"Your twin, she . . . never recovered?"

The ghost shook her head, and her smile faded. "Did you?"

Again she shook her head, this time softer and easier. "But I did not find solace in anger, as Sister did. I did not try to smother my pain by taking men into my bed and then . . ." The shade took a step back. Today she was dressed all in black, as if she were in mourning. "It took a long while, but I finally discovered that there are good men in the world. Men like you."

He could feel her fading, feel her drawing away

from him already. "Wait. Who are you? What's your name?"

The ghost gave him another sad smile. "You can call me 'darling.'"

Lucien had remained withdrawn over dinner. Eve had practically dragged him from the parlor, where he'd been tinkering with the goo he'd collected in his ectoplasm harvester, to the dining room table for the magnificent feast, prepared by Ruth with Daisy's help. He'd barely eaten a thing.

He'd been surprised when she'd told him that she'd heard Tommy again, but not shocked. When she'd asked him why the boy revealed himself to her, he'd told her that perhaps her own desire for a child had drawn the spirit. One sentence, and things between them grew awkward again. Eve decided to eat and forget more conversation with her distracted husband.

Daisy retired shortly after dinner, already twittering about what she might wear tomorrow in case O'Hara arrived. She was not anxious to retire, worried that perhaps a ghost might show itself again tonight. Apparently, it was more important that Daisy be prepared for O'Hara's impending arrival. That meant a good night's sleep and a fancy dress laid out for tomorrow, so worries about spirits were dismissed cleanly if not easily.

Once she'd said good-night to Daisy, Eve joined Lucien in the parlor and sat on the settee, spreading the skirts of her dark blue gown around her. She felt as if she were about to do battle.

For a while, they both remained silent while

Lucien played with his equipment. Eve was restless, though—not content simply to be with her husband as she often was. He seemed to sense her discomfort, or else he was uncomfortable for his own reasons. He kept glancing up, trying to catch a glimpse of her when she wasn't watching him.

Finally, he set his contraption aside and sat up to look at her. He didn't bother to stand but made himself comfortable there on the floor.

"Perhaps you should go to bed," he said. "You know Daisy doesn't like to be alone in this house."

Eve took a deep breath and prepared herself to do battle. "I'm not sleeping with Daisy tonight. I'm sleeping with you."

"Evie . . ."

"You don't want children. I do. That's a pretty big problem, Lucien."

"Yes, I know."

"But it isn't big enough to make me turn my back on you. I won't allow this to divide us. I love you. I know you love me. Somehow we'll make this work."

"How, exactly? I'm not going to change my mind about what I want. You *never* change yours. There are many things on which a man and woman can compromise, but a child is not one of them."

"Just a few days ago, you were not so adamant about the subject," she said softly. "In fact, you seemed agreeable where the idea of a child was concerned. Your experience in the attic was traumatic—I can see that—but . . ."

"You can't blame this entirely on yesterday's episode," Lucien interrupted. "I have never been as keen on the idea of reproducing as you have. I agreed for your sake, because it's what you wanted."

"It's not as though we have a choice, Lucien," Eve said. "Not if we want to continue to be intimate." She could not believe that he would end their marital relations, not for this matter or anything else.

"There are ways to prevent conception," Lucien said logically. "If we're very careful . . ."

"I don't want to be careful!" She wanted their marriage to continue as it had been. Wild. Impulsive. Passionate.

"I can't talk about this tonight," Lucien said. "You go on to bed. I'll join you . . . later."

He wouldn't. She knew that too well. If she went to bed without him, he'd end up sleeping right here on the floor. She might as well sleep with Daisy.

"I believe I'll wait for you," she said softly.

Lucien glanced over his shoulder. She would be angry with him if he didn't look so miserable. "I will probably work for quite some time yet, and you need your sleep."

Eve leaned back and made herself comfortable. "I'll wait."

The twin he had spoken to that afternoon must have been the sister Thomas had fallen in love with. Had she been telling him as much when she told him to call her "darling"?

Apparently one twin had survived the assault mentally intact, and the other had not. That news didn't do Lucien a lot of good, as he still did not know which twin was which, which was Tommy's mother, and who had murdered them all.

Lucien glanced over his shoulder. Eve was sound asleep on the sofa and had been for more than an hour. He should wake her and insist that she go to bed, but insisting never did any good where Eve was concerned.

He never should have married her. It had been selfish of him to think of his own happiness when he knew, deep in his heart, that he would never make any woman a good husband. His life was not his own. He was called to speak to spirits, to lead them home, to speak for those who could no longer speak for themselves. No, he never should have married Evie.

But he loved her so much, sometimes he hurt with it.

"Take her," a soft voice whispered.

As he had this afternoon, Lucien turned his head to see a twin standing near. Very near. Instead of a prim black dress, this twin wore a very low-cut gown of scarlet. Again, her smile did not reveal her true identity.

"You want her," the ghost said. "I can feel the heat radiating off of you, you want her so badly. So take her, there where she lies."

"I can't do that."

Her grin grew wide. "Afraid of making a baby. That's so sad. Would you truly deny your wife and yourself on the grounds that life is not fair? How pathetic."

There were no true secrets in this world; he knew that. Spirits were everywhere, even when no one could see them. "Let's talk about you."

"Oh, let's not." She reached out and touched him with cold, misty fingers. It was as if a breeze drifted across his face. "Too bad I have no body to share. I could satisfy you, Lucien Thorpe. Perhaps

I will visit you in your dreams and show you what I can do."

"I'd rather you didn't." Ghosts didn't visit him in his dreams. They often appeared to others that way, but since he saw spirits so clearly in his waking hours, they left him alone while he slept. Still, he never knew what another day, another spirit, might bring.

"You're one of those tiresome men who loves his wife."

"Yes, I am."

"Then *take* her."

"I can't."

The ghost waved a pale hand. "Of course you can. If she finds herself with child, that can be remedied easily enough. A particular herb in her tea, a push down the stairs, a quick and painful surgery . . ."

"Stop it," Lucien commanded. "I would never do such a thing."

"It does hurt," she said softly. "More than you expect. Much more. No one warns you that it will hurt for days and weeks and years. No one warns you that the emptiness does not go away, that nothing can fill that emptiness, that watching someone else's child grow to be healthy and happy makes you regret . . . but regrets are for fools, and I'm not a fool."

"No, you're not," Lucien agreed.

The ghost reached out again, took a silent step forward, and hovered so close to Lucien he felt the chill of her presence along the length of his body. "I'm so cold. Make me warm again."

"I want to help you," Lucien said sincerely. "But you have to help me. What's your name?"

She smiled wickedly. "You can call me 'darling.'"

The ghost faded quickly, vanishing on the tail end of Lucien's whispered curse.

Both twins had been with child after the attack. One had carried her child, Tommy, and raised him. The other twin had aborted her baby somehow and had regretted the decision.

But he still didn't know which twin had learned to forgive and which had become a scarlet woman who searched for love where there was none.

Lucien turned his back on the ghost, the specter-o-meter, and the ectoplasm harvester, and walked directly to Eve. When he woke her, she opened her eyes slowly. And then she smiled at him. Perhaps marrying her had been a mistake, but he did not regret it. He did love her, more than life itself.

"Come along," he said, taking her hand. "Time for bed."

She narrowed her sleepy eyes suspiciously. "Are you coming with me? Or do you plan to tuck me in and disappear?"

He helped Eve to her feet, and while she yawned, he lifted her into her arms. She was so surprised, she squealed as he swung her up. "I will crawl under the covers with you, hold you close, and sleep."

At least, he hoped he slept. This house drained him, exhausted him in unexpected ways.

"Good." Eve rested her head on his shoulder as he carried her toward the stairs. "I don't sleep well without you. When you work late, I am always rest-less until you join me in bed."

"I believe you were the one who suggested that I stay in O'Hara's room until he arrived."

Eve sighed. "What a foolish idea. I only suggested

such a silly plan because it is so very hard to be close to you and not touch you."

"Nothing about you is foolish or silly, Eve Thorpe," Lucien said.

"Some days I would agree with you; on others . . . perhaps not." She yawned as he carried her down the second-floor hallway, snuggled against him as he opened the door to their bedchamber.

Lucien very carefully placed his sleepy wife on her feet and lit the bedside lamp, turning the wick low. Her eyes remained closed as he began to unbutton her gown, revealing a plain chemise beneath. No corset still, as she feared it would interfere with her ability to conceive. Another notion from yet another pamphlet.

"Why on earth do you put up with me?" he asked as he finished with the buttons and pushed the arms of her dark dress down.

"Because I love you," she answered without hesitation.

"I'm not an easy man to live with, am I?"

Evie smiled gently, allowing him to continue undressing her. Slowly. Gently. She was not quite awake, and yet she was not asleep. "No," she said honestly. "You're not. But that does not make me love you less."

Dress discarded, she sat on the side of the bed and allowed him to remove her shoes and stockings. For tonight, she could sleep in her chemise. He did not think he could bear to strip Evie naked and then put a nightgown on her body. He already wanted her too much.

"I love you, too," he confessed.

"I know you do." Eve fell back and twisted so that

she could snake her legs beneath the covers, and Lucien began to undress himself. "What are we going to do?"

Lucien tossed his clothes over a nearby chair. "I don't know."

Eve sighed and drifted toward sleep as Lucien finished undressing and put out the lamp. He crawled beneath the covers with his wife, and against his better judgment he took her in his arms and held her close. Already more asleep than awake, Eve squirmed until she was where she wanted to be. Her head rested on his shoulder, one arm draped over his waist, one leg entwined through his.

He wanted his wife so much he hurt. His body throbbed, his erection pressed against her soft flesh. A shift of her underthings, and he could be a part of her, the way a husband should be a part of his wife. Inside Evie there would be no more pain, no more doubts.

He wondered for a moment if prayer was an effective form of birth control.

Now that the room was in darkness, he saw the drifting lights of spirits. Misty bits of colored light danced above his bed and around the portrait Eve had hung earlier in the day. Scents teased him. Caramel. Perfume. Blood.

Lucien was never truly alone, but he could, when necessary, close himself off to the spirits that haunted him. It was a talent he had learned in order to save his sanity, and he called upon it now.

"Go away," he whispered while he closed the doors in his mind that allowed the spirits to communicate with him. "I wish to be alone with my wife."

One by one the lights faded. The scents that had filled the room disappeared.

Lucien drew a sleeping Eve tighter into his embrace. They had to come to an agreement, and soon. He could not continue to live with her, to see her every day and hold her and touch her, and yet not truly *have* her. Judging by her reaction earlier tonight, unless he was able to change her mind about having children, she would not embrace the notion of birth control.

And he still could not imagine creating a child only to watch it suffer and die.

There had been a time when he'd been sure he was meant to live his life alone. That there could be nothing for him but his calling, his blasted gift that was so often a curse. For years he had dedicated himself to his work. Nothing else mattered. There had been women now and then, but none he ever thought to make a part of his life. Not since the foolish age of seventeen, anyway.

And then he'd met Eve, and she'd made him see and want more.

He should have listened to the moments of doubt that had plagued him. He should have had the strength to walk away from Eve months ago. Maybe, in the back of his mind, he hadn't forgotten their first planned wedding after all but had listened to a deep and insistent voice of warning.

By taking Eve into his life, he had ruined hers.

Six

Eve dreamed of Lucien loving her and woke with her arms and legs wrapped around him, as if they truly had made love in the night.

They hadn't. She knew that by the fact that her underthings were intact and, more important, by the unsatisfied throb between her legs.

Lucien slept restlessly, and Eve tried to soothe him by stroking his back and kissing his throat, by holding him close and whispering sweet words into his ear. She knew how to soothe him, how to pull him gently from the other world into this one, where he belonged.

He did very quickly grow still, and his breathing eased.

She had asked for two months of abstinence, and after two weeks she felt as if she were starving for her husband. By the gray light of dawn, still lost in the memory of her wonderful dream, her plan seemed ludicrous.

But she was awake enough to know that if they made love now, half-asleep and thinking only of this moment, Lucien might not be happy with her. This matter of a baby was not settled between them.

Then again, the matter might have been settled

all along. A year together, and there was no child. Perhaps they had no choice at all; perhaps God or nature had taken that choice from them.

O'Hara would know, perhaps. Like Lucien, he didn't see everything. But he was uncannily accurate in his readings, and if she asked him to take her hand and tell her whether she and her husband were able to have children, he would tell her.

And if it turned out that she could not have a child, or that Lucien was unable to give a child to her . . . she would mourn for the children she would never have, but she would not love her husband any less than she did at this moment. He had asked her if she was willing to go to the lengths Viola Stamper had years ago, taking another man into her bed in order to make a baby. Her answer had been a resounding no, and that had not changed.

Eve closed her eyes. Why had she become so obsessed with the idea of a child? Of course she wanted babies, but if it was not to be . . . then it was not to be. When they were finished with this house and the tragedies of the past, perhaps Lucien would leave behind his insistence that he didn't want a child.

And if he didn't?

"You've always been very tempting in the morning," hc whispered.

Eve smiled. "Have I?"

"You know it well, love," Lucien said softly. He cupped her breast through the linen of her chemise and teased the nipple that hardened at his touch. He rolled her onto her back and laid his mouth upon her neck. Wicked lips kissed and teased, and the throb deep in her body increased.

In moments, her mind was cleared of everything but Lucien, his hands, his mouth, the way she loved him. The way she needed him. Nothing else mattered to her. And what about him? Did he think of his own anxieties at this moment? No. There was nothing in the world but the two of them. That's the way it was meant to be.

As if he knew she craved his touch, Lucien parted her thighs and stroked her through the thin layer of cotton that kept her from being as bare as he was. A spark shot through her body at that touch; her legs parted wider.

Perhaps he wasn't completely awake. Should she remind him of his newly found aversion for babies, before they went too far?

"Lucien . . ."

"Don't talk," he rasped. "Don't think. Just feel."

She did. And what she felt was so much better than any dream.

Eve reached out to touch Lucien, to take his erection in her hand and stroke gently. She ceased to care about babies and ghosts and lost herself in the way Lucien caressed her.

He shoved her chemise high and began to untie the tapes at her waist. Her body burned for his, so she helped him. Together their hands fumbled as they hadn't since the beginning. Lucien didn't fumble anymore, he knew her too well. He could undress her in the dark, with his eyes closed, anywhere, anytime . . .

Suddenly he stilled, one hand on her hip and the other propped beside her to keep his weight from her. Eve opened her eyes to find that he looked not at her but at the empty pillow beside her head.

"Go away," he said gruffly.

Apparently, that pillow was not empty after all.

"You do not belong here," Lucien said after a short pause during which, apparently, the ghost who shared their bed responded.

Lucien's face paled visibly; he withdrew from Eve in a way that was more emotional than physical. A moment later he rolled away.

Eve lifted herself up onto her elbows. They had been so close; her drawers had been pushed to her hips, but no farther. "What's wrong?"

"You know what's wrong. I shouldn't have . . ." He rolled up and sat on the edge of the bed, his back to Eve. "What happened to your blasted two months of celibacy?"

"I suppose I forgot all about them. You told me I would," she added softly, sitting up tall and reaching out to touch his back. "Come back to me," she whispered as she ran her fingers down his bare back. He had such nice muscles, such a wonderful, familiar shape. "If we make a baby, fine. If we don't, that will be fine, too. We're both worrying too much, you know. Worrying about things over which we have no control."

He didn't leave the bed, but he didn't return to her, either.

"Who was here with us?" she asked.

"One of the twins," he said. "The one in the red dress. She said . . . I won't tell you what she said, Evie. Don't ask it of me."

"All right." If the exchange had upset Lucien this much, Eve didn't want to know what had been said. "Is she gone?"

Lucien glanced over his shoulder, not to Eve but to the pillow at her side. "No."

"Make her leave and come back to bed."

Lucien stood abruptly and reached for his clothes. "I can't."

Since there was a possibility that O'Hara might arrive today, Daisy took special care in her morning rituals. Her hair was perfectly styled; her gown was a very special one, made of pale green Liberty silk and decorated with the finest lace. The last time she'd been trapped in a haunted house with O'Hara, she'd been forced to wear the same outfit day after day. This time she would impress him with her finely put together ensembles.

A small spark of unease twittered in her stomach. He might not be impressed at all. She had been so certain that there was something special between them, but his letters had been cordial, not romantic.

Perhaps he was distressed by her past. No one else knew about the man who had promised to marry her, taken her virginity, and then walked away. O'Hara knew about that time in her life; he knew because he'd touched her hand and seen her greatest regret. She'd given herself to a man who was not her husband, and a couple of months later she'd lost his child. There had been a time when she'd been certain that baby she'd lost was the only one she would ever carry. Men were not to be trusted, much less loved.

She'd felt that way for a long time, and then she'd met O'Hara. Why was he so very different?

He was not terribly tall, and while he wasn't ugly, he wasn't particularly pretty, either. His tastes in clothing tended to be less than tasteful. He was given to wearing checks and stripes and seemed to have an affinity for brown suits and loud vests.

But his eyes . . . his blue-green eyes were beautiful, and warm, and kind.

She had to know whether he cared for her at all, as she had once believed he did. And the only way to know was to look into those eyes and see for herself.

Lucien and Eve were both in a foul mood over breakfast. Daisy had to wonder if perhaps she should have kept the newest pamphlets to herself. Her friends were usually so happy, so perfectly content with each other. Since coming here, they had not been at all content.

The three of them sat at the long dining room table. Ruth had cooked breakfast on her own, but Daisy and Eve both helped set the table for three and carry the food from the kitchen to the dining room. Ruth had prepared an abundance of food: eggs, biscuits, grits, stewed apples, ham, and coffee. Daisy was the only one of the three who ate well. Eve picked at her plate of food, and Lucien hadn't even bothered to eat at all. He just sipped coffee and stared at the center of the table.

When he rose to his feet, so did Eve. "You didn't eat anything," she said.

"I'm not hungry."

"Eat," Eve commanded. Lucien reached out and grabbed a biscuit, and carried it with him as he left the dining room. Daisy expected Eve to follow, but she did not. Instead, she sat slowly and sighed.

"I thought marriage would be easy," Eve said. She pushed at her eggs with a silver fork. "I thought the wedding would be the end of all our troubles, and for a while it was. It truly was." She sighed again.

"Maybe it's the house," Daisy suggested. "Once you two get out of here, everything will be lovely again."

Eve shook her head. Poor thing, she looked as if she had quickly dressed in the first thing she'd laid her hands upon: a simple dark gray gown. Her hair had been twisted up quickly and almost neatly. "It's not the house," she said. "Not this time." Eve lifted her head and laid wide green eyes on Daisy. "What if we never have children?"

"It's much too soon to . . ."

"But what if it never happens?" Eve interrupted. She lowered her voice. "Not only have I not conceived after a year, now Lucien has decided he doesn't want children at all. What if I can't change his mind?"

"Would you rather have Lucien and no children, or another man and a house-full?" Daisy asked.

"Lucien, of course," Eve said.

"You love him so much."

"I do." Eve relaxed visibly.

"And he loves you."

Eve nodded.

"Then where is the problem?"

After a moment Eve smiled. "Leave it to you to cut right to the heart of the matter."

"Everything's going to be fine," Daisy said with a smile.

Eve nodded, but in truth she didn't look as if she believed those words. It was distressing to realize, even for even a moment, that sometimes love was not enough to make everything right.

Daisy lifted her head at the sound of horses' hooves approaching the house. The soft sound grew ever closer, and she smiled. O'Hara would likely not arrive by carriage, as they had, since he would have much less in the way of luggage. Men could travel much lighter than women, a point Lucien had pointed out several times on their short journey. O'Hara would come by horse, she imagined.

She started to rise, then sat again. No, she would not rush out to meet him. First of all, she didn't know that he would be pleased to see her. Second, she did not want to appear too eager. And third . . . the approaching horseman might not be O'Hara. Wouldn't she feel foolish to rush out onto the porch with a welcoming smile on her face for a stranger!

Daisy sat very still. The hoofbeats came near, then ceased. A few moments later she heard a sharp rap on the front door. Ruth swept through the dining room on her way to answer the knock. Eve leaped from her seat and was soon right behind the servant. Daisy sat still for about ten seconds; then she jumped up and followed her friend.

Standing behind Eve, Daisy saw Ruth open the door. She heard O'Hara's familiar voice as he introduced himself. Something in her eased and coiled at the same time. He was here. Soon she would know if he felt as she did. If he dreamed of the kiss they had never shared, if he thought of her and missed her on lonely nights.

Ruth stepped back and opened the door wide, and O'Hara, dressed in an atrocious checkered suit, stepped into the house. He had been riding a long time, or so it seemed by the disheveled state of his clothing and his brown hair. So why did he look suddenly beautiful to her eyes?

He smiled that lovely smile and turned to someone behind him. "Come along," he said in a kind voice. "It's all right."

Daisy's smile faded. Oh, no. Her worst fears were coming true. O'Hara had brought a woman with him. A wife. No wonder his letters became shorter and more distant as the months went on. He had found someone else. She held her breath and waited for the brazen hussy to make an appearance.

She released her breath slowly when a young man—a boy, really—stepped into the house. His eyes scanned the large entryway as if he had never seen such a magnificent house before. Perhaps he had not. Though his dark hair was neatly trimmed and the bag he carried was without patches, the gray suit he wore was a little bit too short for him in the sleeves and the trousers.

"O'Hara!" Eve said, stepping forward to greet her friend with a smile. "We didn't expect you quite so early."

"I didn't expect to arrive so early myself, but my young friend here insisted that we not dilly-dally."

Daisy took a step back, so that she had to peer around the corner to see O'Hara. Anxious as she had been, she now wondered if surprising O'Hara was such a good idea after all.

"And who is your young friend?" Eve turned her eyes to the boy.

O'Hara glanced nervously past Eve. "Is Lucien here? I really need to speak to him."

"He's tinkering," Eve explained. "You know how he is when he starts fiddling with his specter-o-meter."

"Yes," O'Hara said absently. "I know."

When O'Hara did not introduce the boy, Eve offered her hand. "My name is Mrs. Eve Thorpe."

The boy placed his bag on the floor and offered his own slender hand. "I'm Nathaniel Th—"

"And a fine young man Nathaniel is," O'Hara interrupted.

"A pleasure to meet you," Eve said.

Nathaniel did not look particularly pleased. His face remained solemn. His handshake was brief and unenthusiastic.

Lucien was drawn to the entryway by all the commotion, Daisy supposed. He entered from the parlor, where he liked to work, and made a beeline for O'Hara. "You're early," he said without a smile.

"Yes, well . . ." O'Hara began.

Lucien's gaze cut sharply to the left of O'Hara and the boy. He came to an abrupt halt, his spine straightened to a new height, and his eyes went wide with . . . not horror, exactly, but close. Very close. "Good Lord, what are you doing here?"

No one said a word, and still Lucien responded. "That's preposterous."

A ghost stood there—apparently, one Lucien knew.

Everyone began to speak at once. Ruth offered to move everyone into the dining room for coffee,

O'Hara tried to explain how the boy Nathaniel had found him, and Eve wanted to know exactly who Lucien had spoken to.

Lucien held up a hand, commanding silence. When all was silent, he turned on his heel. "The parlor."

Everyone started to follow, and upon hearing the parade Lucien barked. "Not everyone! Just Zella."

"Who's Zella?" Eve asked as she came to a halt.

"My mother," Nathaniel said in a soft voice.

There was an awkward moment of silence, and Daisy decided now was the time. She stepped forward, head high, smile on her face, so that she was no longer concealed behind the corner. Time to be brave, to see what O'Hara's response would be.

That response came quickly. His eyes cut to her, his face went pale, and he said, "Damnation, what are you doing here?"

Lucien slammed the parlor door behind him. Ruth excused herself to return to the kitchen. Daisy turned and ran, and O'Hara took off after her.

Leaving Eve alone in the entryway with the young man who had arrived with O'Hara.

Nathaniel was a handsome young man, a couple of inches shorter than Eve and perhaps a bit thinner than he should be. His dark hair was nicely cut, and he had inquisitive blue eyes that cut this way and that, only occasionally landing on her.

"Well, Nathaniel, are you hungry?" she asked.

"Yes, ma'am," he said solemnly.

Eve headed for the dining room, and Nathaniel

followed silently. A tickle of warning she didn't like danced up her spine.

Since Lucien had not put anything on his plate, she instructed Nathaniel to sit in the chair Lucien had vacated earlier. He stared at the food on the table.

"Go ahead," Eve said as she sat at her own place beside Nathaniel. "I'm afraid we haven't done the meal justice this morning. Take whatever you'd like."

The boy cut a suspicious glance her way, and then he began to fill his plate.

"So," Eve said curiously. "How do you know O'Hara?"

After he'd finished a bite of eggs, Nathaniel answered, "My mother directed me to him."

"Is your mother a friend of O'Hara's?"

"No, ma'am. I don't believe they ever met."

As the child dug into his breakfast, obviously hungry, Eve let the questions lie. There would be plenty of time to query the child after he'd eaten.

Her mind was divided between the child and wondering about the spirit that had upset Lucien so. Zella, he'd said. Not one of the McBride twins but Nathaniel's mother, if she'd understood correctly. So much had been going on at the time, she couldn't be certain she'd heard the child correctly. Was Zella yet another ghost who haunted this house? And what had she done to upset Lucien?

After a few minutes of eating almost furiously, Nathaniel's movements slowed. He finally set his fork aside and lifted the linen napkin beside the plate to wipe his face and hands.

"Thank you, ma'am," he said politely. "I was very hungry."

Linda Fallon

"Hasn't O'Hara been feeding you?" She smiled, and the boy turned his head to look at her.

"Oh, yes, ma'am," Nathaniel said seriously. "It's just that lately I've been hungry a lot."

"You're a growing boy," Eve observed. "How old are you?"

"Thirteen, ma'am."

Eve could not for the life of her imagine why O'Hara would bring a child into a haunted house.

Nathaniel stared up at her, and for a moment, just a moment, there was something eerily familiar about his eyes. That shade of blue, the shape of the lids . . .

"Your name is Mrs. Thorpe," Nathaniel said.

"Yes, that's right."

He blinked once. "Are you my father's wife?"

Zella hadn't changed in fourteen years. She was still shapely, and her face had the same exotic beauty Lucien remembered. Her dress was somehow conservative and alluring at the same time; her black hair worn loose these days. But then, ghosts didn't have to worry about convention.

"I do not have a son," he said.

"Yes, you do," she insisted.

He had loved Zella once, a very long time ago. She'd taken him into her bed, taught him what love was about, physically and emotionally, and after a few short months she'd taught him about heartbreak as well.

"When you ended the affair, did you know you were going to have a child?"

"Yes," she admitted.

"And yet you didn't bother to tell me." He seethed with anger and with fear.

"You were seventeen years old," she said gently. "You were a boy, Lucien, not a man. And I was, well, older."

"Ten years older," he reminded her.

Zella was not a woman who would have taken aging well. She loved her beauty and her appeal to men too much to be graceful about wrinkles and gray hair.

"None of that matters now," she insisted. "Nathaniel is your son and your responsibility."

Lucien shook his head. His worst fears, thrown in his face. "No. This is a trick. You . . . you witch."

The ghost of Zella sighed. "You did not seem to mind my vocation when we were lovers."

"I didn't believe you at first," he admitted. "I thought it was just . . . talk. Fantasy."

Zella gave him a wide grin, then looked upward, and the grin faded. "I have very little time, Lucien. I stayed earthbound in order to deliver Nathaniel into your hands, but I can't remain forever and argue over the past."

"He could be someone else's child. I suspect I was not the only man in your life. . . ."

She laid steely gray eyes on his face. "For those months we were together, you were the only man in my bed. What came before or after is none of your concern. Nathaniel is your son. Accept it."

"Why should I believe you?"

Zella gave him a softer, gentler smile. "I had such great plans," she said, and then she laughed lightly. "You did not realize how great your gift was. You still don't, not entirely. I knew if I had your son, he would have the same gifts. I saw riches. My child would be a phenomenon. I didn't plan for him to end up as you have, clearing out haunted houses for a paltry fee. I saw lecture halls, rich clients, newspaper articles and books, and . . . fame and fortune. A child who speaks to the dead."

"Since I've never heard of him, I assume your plans failed. What happened? Was the child born without the ability to see the other side?" He held his breath and waited for an answer.

Soft and misty, Zella looked gentler than she had in life. "I did not expect to love him so much. I did not expect to be filled with the need to protect my child from the pain you suffered. He has been sheltered, Lucien. I schooled him myself, and brought in tutors when his intelligence proved too challenging for me alone. I passed up the opportunity to marry, many times, because I knew I could not fully protect Nathaniel if I brought strangers into our life." Her expression softened. "You never said much about your own mother, but there were times . . ."

"I do not want to talk about my mother." Lucien covered his eyes for a moment, but he knew nothing so simple would make Zella go away.

He had not been able to make the twin in red depart this morning, and he couldn't force Zella to go, either. That only proved to him that women could be difficult beyond death. Why was he surprised?

"I named him Nathaniel Thorpe Mead," Zella said gently. "I hope you don't mind. I wanted him to have your name, in at least that small way."

"Why didn't you tell me?" Lucien asked as he dropped his hands.

"You didn't want to know," she whispered.

Lucien closed his eyes. This could not be happening. Not here, not now. "And yet here you are."

"Of all the things I did not expect, dying before Nathaniel reached manhood was the most startling. A house full of herbal and magical cures, and what happens? I get run over by a carriage and break my neck." She rubbed her neck, which looked fine at this point, and grimaced.

"Does he have it?" Lucien asked. The gift, the curse, the power.

"Yes," Zella whispered, dropping her hand slowly. She continued with a smile. "I wanted to be a better mother to your son than your mother was to you. I had an advantage over her. I understood Nathaniel's gift. It never frightened me. Never."

"I told you, I do not want to talk about . . ."

"Forgive me, Lucien."

"For what?" he snapped.

"For robbing you of the opportunity to see your son grow."

He sank down, sitting on the settee where Eve had fallen asleep last night. A son. A son who shared his abilities. A son who was a complete stranger.

Zella placed her hands on her hips in a provocative pose and smiled. "I'm going now. Take good care of our son. He's special, as you are. And he needs you. He needs you, Lucien, so much. And I think he needs that wife of yours, too. She's solid and reasonable. Very warm. Nathaniel is going to need that in the coming years. I like her," she said, as if that realization surprised her. "Your wife and your son are getting acquainted as we speak."

Lucien jumped to his feet, and his heart almost pounded through his chest. *Evie.*

Seven

O'Hara followed Daisy as she ran from him. She weaved her way through the opulent rooms and down a thickly carpeted hallway, never glancing back. Her skirt danced around her as she rushed, her step dainty but quick, through open doorways. She finally made her way to a pair of French doors in what looked to be a library. She opened those doors as he called, "Wait!" then burst through them and into the cool morning.

He was an idiot for reacting as he had. Daisy had taken him by surprise, that's all, stepping into the room without warning.

"Daisy! Stop!" he called as he chased her. She held the shirt of her green gown high as she ran.

She couldn't outrun him, and he wasn't going to give up. As they passed the trunk of an ancient oak tree, he managed to grab her arm and make her stop.

"Let go of me!" she commanded.

O'Hara wanted to release her. Touching Daisy, he felt her hurt and confusion. He felt the tears she held back, as if they burned his own eyes.

"I'll let go if you stop running," he suggested.

After a moment's hesitation, Daisy nodded and he dropped his hand.

He had forgotten how beautiful she was. How flawless and feminine. Why did Daisy care for him? She could have any man, any man she wanted. With a face like hers, a perfect figure, and a personality so sweet . . . she could have any man in the world.

"I'm sorry I didn't greet you properly," he said. "You surprised me."

"Obviously," she said coldly.

"It is wonderful to see you again."

"As evidenced by the curse that exploded from your mouth when you laid your eyes on me." Her cheeks flushed pink; her eyes shone too bright.

"I was . . . surprised."

"So you said," Daisy responded coolly.

There had been a time when he'd considered pursuing Daisy Willard. He'd ridden away from Plummerville so certain he'd be going back soon.

But then he'd received her first letter, and things had changed. Somehow he had to convince her that they could be friends, nothing more.

"How have you been?" he asked, stuffing his hands in his pockets.

"Fine," she said sharply. "Just fine. Very fine, in fact."

"I'm glad to hear it."

"You?" she asked simply, with an arch of her finely shaped eyebrows.

"I've been well. Very, very well."

They were both such bad liars.

Daisy's eyes cut toward the house. "Who's the child?" she asked. "Nathaniel. Is he . . ." She paled. "Yours?"

"No," O'Hara answered sharply.

She sighed, apparently relieved. "Is he an orphan? How did he end up in your care? He really must have a new suit. He's quite outgrowing the one he's wearing."

Like everyone else, Daisy would know the truth soon enough. "Nathaniel is Lucien's son."

Daisy's blue eyes grew wide. "Oh, no. Oh, this is terrible." She began to run again, toward the house this time. Again O'Hara gave chase.

"Stop," he commanded. This time she obeyed, though the expression on her face as she turned to him was less than kind. He suspected she stopped on her own so he would not touch her again.

"Eve will be crushed. I'm her friend; I should be with her."

"Give them a little time," he suggested in a lowered voice.

A *little* time would likely not be nearly enough, but he suspected the newly expanded family needed at least a few moments alone.

"Fine, Quigley," Daisy said, chin high and eyes hard in a way they had not been a few moments ago. "What do you suggest we talk about while we wait?"

He flinched. "No one calls me Quigley," he reminded her. She didn't need to be reminded; she knew very well that he never used his given name. It was a low blow. "Tell me," he said, quickly changing the subject. "What has become of the Plummerville Ghost Society?"

Daisy sighed. "Our little group fell apart after that horrible experience at the Honeycutt Hotel.

You know Garrick and Katherine were married and went out west."

"I heard."

"And Buster was married, as well. Buster's wife and Katherine are both in the family way."

O'Hara felt himself blush, the heat rising in his cheeks. "How very nice for them all."

"Yes, it is." Again her eyes flitted to the house.

Looking at her, he could almost make himself dismiss his reservations and try to give her what she wanted. But he couldn't. No matter how badly he wanted to do just that. What she wanted of him was impossible.

Eve stared down at the boy beside her. "Am I . . . what?"

Before the child could answer, Lucien burst into the room. "There you are," he said breathlessly.

Eve rotated her head slowly to glare at her husband. As usual, his long hair was mussed and his jacket was askew. His face was not usually so pink.

It was too much to take all at once. If Nathaniel was Lucien's son, then her husband was certainly capable of producing a child. Which meant she was the one who might not be able to conceive. It was her fault that they had no baby, and she might never be able to have a child of her own.

Then again, here beside her was the living, breathing evidence that Lucien had once had another woman in his life. She knew, of course, that her husband had not been a virgin when she'd met him. From the beginning, he had been much too talented in the ways of making love to be a novice.

She understood that, accepted it, pushed it to the back of her mind. But if Nathaniel was indeed Lucien's son, she would have that unwelcome knowledge pushed to the front of her mind on a daily basis.

Perhaps it was a ploy. Someone had the mistaken notion that Lucien was rich, and they had sent this blue-eyed child—who did look a little like Lucien, Eve conceded—to see what he could get. If that was the case, they were out of luck. Lucien was an extraordinarily talented man, but he was terrible with money. He had little.

"I see you two have met," Lucien said as he walked cautiously to the table. He moved as if walking toward a poisonous viper and awaited the first strike. So, who was the snake: Eve herself or the child?

"Yes," Eve said in a calm voice. "We have."

Lucien's eyes flickered past Eve to the boy at her side, a child who stared up at the tall man. All of a sudden, Nathaniel pushed back his chair and stood, offering his fragile-looking hand in a very formal way.

"How do you do, sir," he said, his eyes planted squarely on the middle button of Lucien's jacket.

After a moment of silence, Lucien took the child's hand and shook it. "Nathaniel," he said warily. "Uh, pleased to meet you."

The two men—one short, one tall—studied each other with caution and wonder. Eve's heart sank. If this was a trick, the child had been well chosen and well schooled. There was an eerie similarity in the way the two stood, in the tilt of their heads and the slight curl in their hair, even though Nathaniel's hair was much shorter than Lucien's.

"I'm sorry to disturb you," the child said seriously. "After she died, Mother insisted that I find you right away."

Eve's heart sank. *After she died.* It could be a part of the scam. . . .

"May I ask a question, sir?" Nathaniel asked primly.

"Of course you may," Lucien replied.

Nathaniel laid his serious eyes on Eve. "Who is the child who clings to Mrs. Thorpe?"

Eve's heart jumped into her throat. "Child?"

"Tommy. His name is Tommy." Nathaniel tilted his head. "He . . . holds fast to you. He says that sometimes you see him, but at other times you do not." The boy lifted his eyes to Lucien again. "Do you not see him, sir? Mother said you could see and hear the dead, as I do. Do you not see Tommy clinging to your wife's skirt?"

Lucien looked down at her, wrinkling his brow and leaning closer. "I see a small light, a hint of a spirit, but he is not showing himself to me."

"He has dark hair and brown eyes," Nathaniel said. "And he's wearing a yellow shirt and brown knickers. No shoes, but not because he has no shoes but because he likes to feel the grass and the carpet beneath his feet."

"You see all that," Lucien said.

Nathaniel nodded. "Yes, sir."

"What else do you see?"

Nathaniel looked around, as he had often since entering the house. "A soldier who is curious about all this, a man who watches and waits. A woman . . .

no, three women. Two strong, one weak. There's another, but she's more a girl than a woman. She fell. She . . ."

"That's enough," Lucien said.

Eve listened, stunned. She did not feel or see Tommy at the moment, but Nathaniel insisted he was here and clinging to her. Why?

"Sir?" Nathaniel asked shyly. "My mother said that you could perhaps teach me to . . . to make them go away." His face paled slightly, and in spite of his formal manner he suddenly looked to be the child he was. "For a while, at least. Can you? Can you teach me to make them go away?"

Eve ran from the room and toward the stairway. Lucien followed.

"No." She spun on him at the foot of the stairs. "Stay with . . . Nathaniel." She couldn't say it yet. *Your son.*

"I can explain," Lucien said.

Eve stared at her husband, wide-eyed. "No explanation is necessary." He had a child. It was not hers. What else did she need in the way of explanation?

Lucien glanced back toward the dining room, where Nathaniel waited. "Are you going to our room?"

"Yes."

"I'll be up in a few minutes, as soon as I get the boy settled. I don't think I should leave him alone for very long. He's . . ."

"Like you," Eve finished when he could not. She turned away and ran up the stairs, wanting only to be alone to absorb everything she'd learned in the past few minutes.

She closed the door behind her and leaned against it. Only then did she let the tears fall. There were not many, and they were silent tears. Eve didn't think of herself as a demonstrative woman, but life with Lucien had taken her emotions and shaken them up to the point where she could no longer contain them.

A child. A son. And she wanted so very badly for that child to be hers.

The smell came first, almost overwhelming her. Caramel. A breeze stirred, in a room where all the windows and doors were closed.

"Don't cry, Mama," a child's voice whispered.

Eve searched the room for a visual sign of the ghost, but she saw nothing. "I can't see you."

"Hold me, Mama," the ghost whispered.

She would never hold a baby, Eve realized as she stood there. Lucien was obviously capable of having children. She was not. If she were, she'd be carrying a baby by now. Even if Lucien did change his mind about having children—*more* children—it didn't matter. She could crave a child all night and all day, and it would not make a difference.

"I can't hold you if I can't see you," she said as a pair of tears slipped down her cheeks.

Without warning, the French doors were flung open by an unseen hand. The drapes there fluttered, and a mist formed. The mist swirled, it took on color, and finally, it took on form.

Tommy was as Nathaniel had described him: small for five, dark-haired and dark-eyed, barefoot and smiling. As she watched, the child lifted his hand. "Hold me, Mama."

Eve approached the specter, knowing in her heart that she would never hold a child of her own, that no one would ever call her Mama, that this child who pleaded with her for love needed her in a way no other child ever would.

As she walked toward Tommy, he stepped back onto the gallery that circled the house. He looked so real, almost solid. Those soft cheeks were so pure and white, the eyes so innocent.

"Hold me, Mama," Tommy said again, his voice fading. His form began to fade, too.

Eve ran to reach him before he faded completely. "Don't go!"

"It's too hard to stay here," Tommy said in a voice that was now faint, as if it reached over a great distance. He reached the railing that surrounded the gallery, and passed through it, but he did not drop.

Eve stopped when she reached the railing. "Come back," she said. "You'll fall."

Tommy laughed. "I won't fall. You won't fall, either." He lifted a hand in invitation. "If you want to hold me, you have to come to me."

"I can't."

Tommy looked down, and fear grew on his face. "Oh, you were right. I'm going to fall! Save me, Mama!"

Eve reached over the railing, leaned forward as far as she could. "Take my hand." Panic grew in her heart. Tommy was frightened. He wanted her to save him. Only her.

He lifted one arm but was too far away. His hand floated in the air several inches from hers. Eve rose up on her tiptoes and reached out as far as she could. Still her fingers did not reach Tommy's. "Come on, sweetheart. Don't be afraid."

"I am afraid," he whispered.

So was she. She felt Tommy's fear as if it were her own. No, what she felt was stronger than fear. She could save him. No one else. Not Lucien, not O'Hara, not Tommy's real mother, whoever she might be.

"Help me, Mama," he said, and then he began to cry. "Help me!"

Eve crawled onto the railing. It creaked beneath her weight. She leaned forward and reached out again. She could almost touch him. "Come on, sweetie. Take my hand."

He backed away from her, very slightly, as if the breeze carried him.

In a panic, Eve lunged. Too late, she realized that she had nowhere to go. Her weight pitched her forward, and Tommy disappeared as her control vanished. For the first time she saw the ground below her and realized how far up she was, what a long way she had to fall. The railing splintered, and she began her descent.

Eve closed her eyes, but the ground did not come up to meet her. She jerked back, then dangled in the air. Someone had grabbed on to the back of her dress; she knew by the way she hung and by the ominous pop of stitches.

"Give me your hand, Evie," Lucien commanded.

She hung there without control, the ground below suddenly looking so far away. If she fell . . . Another stitch in her dress popped, and she twisted slightly as if caught by a strong breeze.

"Evie, your hand!"

Reaching back and around, she did as he asked. At least, she tried. She couldn't see Lucien. She could only see the ground. The way she hung in the air, so perilously, made her dizzy. She continued to reach back, and when Lucien's hand closed over her wrist, she heard his sigh of relief.

For a moment, a second or two, he just held her. Then, with a heave he pulled her up and deposited her on the gallery. *Dumped* was a more fitting word.

Sitting on the floor in a very unladylike position, Eve looked up at her very angry husband.

"What the hell were you doing?"

He didn't understand. He would *never* understand. Lucien had a child. He was the one who didn't want children, and yet a son who was so much like him that she could not deny his existence had simply been deposited in his lap, like a gift. Lucien did not know yet that child was a gift, but he would. He would.

A child's voice whispered in her ear. *"Don't tell him about me, Mama. He'll be jealous of us."*

"I was admiring the view," she said breathlessly.

"The view."

"Yes. Its breathtaking. The . . . the railing must've broken beneath my weight. Perhaps the wood was rotten."

Lucien detested lies of any kind, but what was she to say? He was the one man in this house who could send Tommy away, and he would if he realized what had happened.

And she wasn't ready to let the child go.

* * *

Daisy knocked very softly on the door to Eve's room. A moment later, she heard a very soft "Come in."

She was disappointed that O'Hara was obviously not excited to see her, had in fact been dismayed. But her pain was nothing next to Eve's. Finding out that her husband had a child from an old relationship was painful enough, but considering the way Eve had been obsessed with having a baby lately, the news must have been like having salt poured on a nasty wound.

Eve sat on the edge of the bed, pale and disheveled.

"Hi," Daisy said with a weak smile. "Are you all right? Lucien said you almost fell off the gallery."

"I wouldn't have fallen," Eve said defensively. "Lucien overreacted, as he sometimes does."

"I see." Daisy sat in the upholstered chair in the corner. From here, she and Eve were face to face.

"How are things with O'Hara?" Eve asked.

Daisy took a long, calming breath. "'Damnation, what are you doing here?' That's what he said when he saw me. How on earth do you think things are?"

"He was surprised."

Daisy snorted. "So he says."

"I do think he likes you."

Leaning slightly forward, Daisy said, "No, he hates me. He despises me. He sees me and what does he say? *Damnation!*"

Eve did not try to defend O'Hara. "I'm sorry."

Daisy relaxed and leaned back. "Me, too. Why was I foolish enough to think that maybe, just maybe . . . ?"

No, there were no maybes. She should know that

by now. It would be safest, for her heart and her sanity, if she continued to live as she had for the past several years. She had good friends, a nice home, a place she belonged, in Plummerville.

"You know what our problem is?" Eve asked.

"There are two of them," Daisy said sharply. "Lucien and O'Hara. They are our two great, big, annoying . . . problems."

Eve actually smiled. "Yes, but the real problem is that we had the poor sense to fall in love with them! We should have fallen in love with ordinary men, like Buster and Garrick, or any other man in Plummerville."

Daisy thought of a few of the men who had called on her in the past. "Well, not *any* man."

"Almost any man."

"Why them?" Daisy asked. She actually pouted for a moment. "Oh, if you had married the mayor and I married the judge, we could rule all of Plummerville."

Eve laughed. "The mayor is fifty-seven and bald and married, and the judge has got to be more than sixty-five years old!"

"Yes, but he's a widower and therefore available, and he has some of his hair left. You must sacrifice to have real power." She found herself laughing, too, in spite of everything.

The laughter didn't last. "I shouldn't have come," Daisy said softly. "Lucien was right. I have no business here."

"We'll just be here a few more days. Now that O'Hara's arrived, Lucien wants to channel the twins. Tonight, he said. After dinner."

Daisy had no love of such things. How on earth

had she ended up in this predicament? Here she was trapped once again, in an entirely different way than before, in a haunted house. "Do I have to watch?" She wrinkled her nose as she imagined participating in an actual séance.

"No," Eve said gently. "You can go on to bed after dinner, if you'd like."

Daisy's heart leaped. "Alone? Maybe that's not a good idea, either." Lucien would stir every spirit in the house up with his séance!

"Perhaps you should join us."

Daisy stood. What choice did she have but to participate in Lucien's silly séance? "I suppose I will."

So far, Eve had said nothing about Nathaniel Thorpe. Lucien's son. "Are you . . . all right?" Daisy asked in a lowered voice as she walked toward the bed.

"Of course I am," Eve said, chin high and spine straight.

As Daisy watched, Eve's chin quivered. She sat on the edge of the bed beside her friend and draped an arm around Eve's shoulder. Without warning, Eve began to cry. Not gently, not quietly, but sobs accompanied by large tears that poured down her face.

"Now, now," Daisy said gently. "It's all right. Cry. Sometimes nothing else works." She wrapped both arms around Eve and held on snugly. Eve's arms wrapped around her, as well. She continued to cry, not holding back in any way. Her heart was broken, and she released a flood of emotion that had been held back too long.

"You'll get through this," Daisy assured her friend. "Lucien loves you and you love him."

"I know that; I do. I don't know why I'm crying like a little girl." She sniffled once. "I never cry. Well, almost never."

"I try not to cry," Daisy said gently. "It makes my eyes all red and puffy."

But she did cry, sometimes, when no one was around.

Eve's bout of sobbing ended almost as quickly as it had begun, and she dropped her arms and drew away. "I apologize. Here I am, feeling sorry for myself, when you have problems of your own."

"Only the one," Daisy said with a sigh.

Eve's head suddenly jerked to the side; her eyes grew wide as she stared into the corner of the room. "Did you hear that?" she whispered.

Daisy shook her head. "I didn't hear anything. What is it? A ghost? A mouse?" She wasn't sure which would be worse.

Calmer than she had been a few minutes earlier, Eve took a deep breath and let it out slowly. "Nothing. It was nothing."

Eight

Lucien stared down at his son. *His son.* Why had he never suspected, never even imagined . . . ?

Nathaniel looked a little like Zella, in the shape of his mouth and the tilt of his nose. But Lucien could not deny that his son also looked like him. It was the eyes, he knew, that were the most startlingly like his, not only in color and shape but in what they saw.

"How was your trip?" he asked.

"Fine, sir," Nathaniel responded.

All these *sir*s. If nothing else, his son was polite.

They stood in the parlor, facing each other, both of them nervous and awkward and unsettled. Why had Zella left so soon? She could have stayed around a few days to smooth things over, to introduce father and son. But no, in typical Zella fashion she had stirred up a hornets' nest and then disappeared.

"As soon as we're done here, we'll go . . . home. You'll like it in Plummerville. There are lots of boys about your age around and about."

"I've never spent much time with other children," Nathaniel said. "Mother thought they would not understand. There were times when contact could not be helped. It usually did not go well." The boy's face paled.

Lucien didn't need further clarification. He himself had grown up isolated, different, an oddity not to be tolerated. His mother had been afraid of him and had done her best to *fix* him, to drive the devil out, to pray and wail until his curse disappeared once and for all. As for other children, saying those encounters had not gone well would be an understatement. The child Lucien had been had always been too quick to tell those around him what he heard, too determined to make others see what he saw. He hadn't had much tolerance for deception even then.

His life had been difficult until Eve had come into it. He wanted better for his son.

"Sir, what should I call you?" Nathaniel asked.

Lucien's heart took an unexpected leap. "Whatever you'd like. Lucien. Fa—" The word stuck in his throat, and he had to clear it before continuing. "Father, if you'd like. Papa. Daddy. Good Lord, I have no idea."

"I'll think on it, sir," Nathaniel said, as if it were a momentous decision. Maybe it was.

Lucien nodded, and was relieved when his son turned away. He didn't remember his own father, which didn't help matters any. Horatio Thorpe had passed away when Lucien had been a small child. Lucien had been two years old, so he had no memories of the man. Like his mother, his father had never popped in to say hello or guide him, as Zella had done for Nathaniel.

"What is this device?" Nathaniel asked, walking toward the table where the specter-o-meter sat idle.

Finally! Something he could discuss without stammering. "This is the Thorpe Specter-o-Meter. It's been in production for several years now, and I've almost got it working correctly."

Nathaniel leaned down to place his face close to the contraption, but did not touch anything. "What does it do?"

Lucien explained how the device he'd invented and built trapped and measured ghostly energy in the air, and Nathaniel listened carefully.

Most people tended to stare into space with a pained expression on their faces after a few minutes of explanation, but not Nathaniel. He not only paid close attention; when Lucien was finished, Nathaniel asked a few questions about how the device worked.

When they were done with the specter-o-meter, they moved on to the simpler ectoplasm harvester and the samples Lucien had collected in this house.

After a short discussion about how the harvester functioned, and an examination of the ectoplasm itself, Lucien explained the new device, the one he'd left at home, to Nathaniel. He couldn't very well call it "The Damned Thing," not in front of the child, so it remained nameless.

While Lucien was telling Nathaniel about The Damned Thing, the child's attention began to wander. Lucien was disappointed, but not surprised. Most people didn't last nearly this long when he started talking about his inventions. But he soon realized that it wasn't boredom that drew Nathaniel's attention from their discussion, but a spirit of some kind.

"What do you see?" Lucien asked in a lowered voice.

"A woman. She won't go away."

He led the boy to the settee, a steady hand at the child's elbow. At thirteen, no one had been around to help Lucien deal with his gift. No one had explained anything; he'd had to learn it all the hard way, until Hugh Felder came into his life. He was sure Zella had done her best with Nathaniel, but only someone who endured the same visions could truly understand what it was like.

"She's following me," Nathaniel whispered.

Lucien lowered himself to the settee, and he instructed Nathaniel to sit beside him. The always obedient child did as he was told.

"Close your eyes."

Nathaniel did just that, and a moment later he said, "She's still here, whispering in my ear. Can't you hear her?"

No, he could not, which was rather disturbing. Which ghost spoke to the boy?

"There are doors in your mind, Nathaniel," Lucien said calmly. "A corridor lined with many doors. These are the portals the spirits use to reach you. Find the door this spirit uses, and close it."

"I don't understand."

"You will. It takes practice. Now is as good a time as any to start." Lucien draped an arm around Nathaniel's shoulder, only slightly nervous about the gesture. "Find the door. See it. Touch it. Close it."

Nathaniel's concentration showed on his young face. Eyes were closed too tight, mouth pinched, neck rigid. Spots of color bloomed on his pale cheeks.

"Close it," Lucien said again.

A moment later, Nathaniel's eyes popped open. A wide smile grew quickly on his usually solemn face. "It worked! She's gone!"

Lucien found himself smiling, as well. His son was a quick study. Quite intelligent.

But did Nathaniel realize that the spirit was not actually gone? The ghost was still present, but Nathaniel's eyes and ears to the apparition were now closed.

"Thank you, sir," Nathaniel said.

"Glad to be of help."

It had taken Lucien years to gain control of his abilities, and still . . . there were days when the spirits did not cooperate and he felt helpless all over again. Nathaniel would have to learn, as well, and it would take many years. A lifetime.

"While we're in this house," Lucien said almost casually, "I want you to stay away from the attic."

He expected Nathaniel to ask why, but he didn't. Instead, he responded with a soft "Yes, sir."

How could he protect this child from bad places, bad spirits, bad people? Was it even possible? All his fears about parenthood came rushing back, for all the good they did him. Nathaniel existed; he was *here*.

Lucien almost told Nathaniel about the séance they had planned for the evening, but changed his mind quickly. The child should be in bed and asleep before they roused and channeled the spirits that haunted this house.

O'Hara paced restlessly in the parlor while Lucien arranged mismatched chairs around a small round table and Eve and Daisy whispered to each other, heads together in that way only a woman might understand. Ruth, the only servant who remained in the house, kept to herself, standing near the parlor door as if she might make her escape at any moment.

Everyone currently residing at Glover Manor was present but for Jim, who didn't live in the main house but had his own residence on the property, and Nathaniel. Lucien had insisted that his son retire for the evening, and the boy had obeyed—reluctantly.

Nathaniel would be sharing O'Hara's room for the duration of this investigation. A pallet had been constructed on the floor of the huge bedchamber, and since they had traveled together for a couple of days, Nathaniel was comfortable with O'Hara. More comfortable than he was with his father, apparently.

A fire blazed high in the brick fireplace, and a number of lamps had been lit and placed about the room. Lucien had never been one to believe darkness was necessary for calling upon a spirit.

When Lucien was ready, the others moved toward the table and chairs. O'Hara hung back, hoping for an opportunity to grab a seat that was *not* next to Daisy.

He had learned over the years to shut his abilities down at will. It took a great deal of concentration at times, but it could be done. At least for a while.

Try as he might, he could not block Daisy. He had attempted to numb his talents when she was near, on more than one occasion. He had even tried to block the sensations that overwhelmed him when he touched her letters, but it was a futile exercise. Laying his fingers on the paper she had touched, he knew Daisy Willard to her core. He not only knew her emotions, he felt them. He not only saw her secrets, he tasted them. No one had ever affected him so acutely.

Worse, he knew what Daisy wanted of him, deep in her heart. She wanted forever happiness. A wedding, a home, a marriage bed, children. Laughter and companionship. Day after day and night after night. She deserved that, but he could not give such ordinary pleasures to her, or to anyone else.

There had been a time, a brief time, when he had believed he might be the man to offer that life to her. Over the past eight months he had reasoned that it was the extreme severity of that haunting at the Honeycutt Hotel that clouded his judgment.

Even if an ordinary life could be his . . . how could he live the rest of his days with a woman he could not block? Every time he touched her, he'd know her thoughts, her feelings, her fears. It was draining to be so in touch with another human being, even for a short time. But *forever?*

She was angry with him for reacting negatively upon seeing her this morning. Just as well. It would be best if she did not forgive him. Once she cleared her impossible hopes for them out of her heart, she could get on with her life and find a proper husband.

By placing himself between Eve and Daisy and turning them about, then wedging himself between Ruth and Eve, O'Hara managed to grab a safe chair. Unfortunately, his attempts to take a place that would keep him from holding hands with Daisy were more obvious than he'd intended. Both Eve and Daisy glared at him.

Just as well. He should go out of his way to distance himself from Daisy, to drive her from him. To kill all her ordinary dreams.

"I am hoping one of the twins will speak through me tonight," Lucien said gruffly. "As you know, I usually prefer to channel unassisted, but as the twins are resistant, our combined energy might be necessary. We will join hands. No matter what, do not break the chain until I give that instruction."

He offered his right hand to Daisy, who sat at his side since O'Hara had maneuvered those present to his advantage, in a not-so-deft manner. Daisy offered her right hand to Eve, Eve to O'Hara, O'Hara to Ruth, and Ruth to Lucien.

O'Hara did his best to block the servant and his friend. Ruth was easy, and while he saw no specifics where Eve was concerned, he did get a sense of turmoil before he shut those emotions out completely.

There was power in this little group. He and Lucien were the only ones present who had evident unnatural abilities, but each of the five possessed something that added to the energy that thrummed in and among them.

His hands tingled, and a chill danced up his spine. Yes, there was most certainly a potent energy here.

"Margaret and Isabel," Lucien said in a soft voice. "Come talk to us, please. Use my mouth. Use my body. I can give you substance and a voice, but you must trust me. You must let me help you."

Daisy wrinkled her nose. She didn't much care for this ghost business; O'Hara knew that well. But

she cared even less for the only other option—
waiting above stairs, alone.

Nothing happened. The clock on the mantel
ticked loudly. The flame in the fireplace remained
steady and strong. No spirits appeared, not in any
way or form. Lucien was obviously annoyed. Daisy
seemed almost relieved. Eve was distracted, her
mind elsewhere.

Ruth stared straight ahead, chin high and the
fingers that touched O'Hara's hand rigid. Suddenly, those fingers tightened.

"I won't speak through him," Ruth said. "He
scares me."

The voice that came out of Ruth's mouth was not
that of an old woman, but of a girl.

Daisy exclaimed, startled and perhaps scared, but
Lucien and Eve held on to her hands tight and
would not let her go.

"You have no reason to be afraid of me," Lucien
said gently.

"I do. You would tear me away from my sister;
you would wrench her from my grasp and separate
us forever."

"No," Lucien said. "I only want to send you both
home. Tell me, what is your name?"

"I don't have a name," Ruth—not Ruth—whispered.

"Of course you—"

"No one can separate us; no one can come between us." The voice drifted and changed, and by
the time Ruth finished the sentence, it sounded as
if two identical voices came from her lips. *Almost*
identical. One girlish voice was slightly higher than
the other, giving the words a harsh and discordant

harmony. "I give her my strength and she gives me hers. Our unity is all that keeps me from screaming until the end of time."

"You will still be together. Both of you and Tommy and Thomas . . ."

Ruth turned her eyes to Lucien. "You don't know," the voices whispered. "No one can ever know." With that, Ruth went limp—her fingers, her face, her body. The old woman slumped in her chair, and O'Hara caught her before she fell to the floor.

With the circle broken, the energy O'Hara had felt earlier died. Hands were unclasped. Lucien stood.

"Let's move her to the settee," he ordered.

Ruth was very light, not much more than skin and bones, so no assistance was necessary. O'Hara swung her up and carried her to the short sofa, then gently deposited her there.

"Is she all right?" Daisy whispered.

"I think so," O'Hara answered. Once she was positioned on the settee, he took her wrist in his hand. The pulse was steady but slow. "She'll be fine. She's just exhausted by the experience."

"Why her?" Lucien asked absently. "I am much easier for the spirits to enter. I'm open, where Ruth is not. Why did they choose her?" He mulled over the question for a moment, then laid his eyes on O'Hara. "Take Ruth's hand."

Kneeling beside the settee, O'Hara did just that. He grasped the woman's small, wrinkled, black hand in his own, and he let the curtain down. As if a dam had been broken, he was assaulted with sensations, memories, and emotions and fears. They were not all her own.

He knew of the injustices the girls had suffered. Lucien had warned him to stay away from the attic, and he had. But he didn't have to enter the room to feel the pain, to hear the screams.

But there was more. A knife. Blood. Anger that went beyond anger. Fire, the flames so hot and bright they burned his skin.

When O'Hara had seen all he cared to see, he dropped Ruth's hand and scooted away from the sofa. He had no desire to accidentally touch her, not now, not yet. He was too shaken to put up the shields he needed in order to survive with his sanity intact.

"What's wrong?" Lucien asked.

"Is he all right?" Daisy whispered.

"O'Hara?" Eve leaned down to get a look at his face. The three of them surrounded him in a protective circle.

He did not attempt to stand, not yet. He didn't have the strength in his legs to rise on his own. When Lucien offered his hand, O'Hara took it and stood.

"Which of the twins was a murderer?" he asked.

"What?" Daisy screeched.

O'Hara laid his eyes on her. She shouldn't be here. She should not be exposed to the life he led, the hell he lived in. "Murderer," he said again. "It wasn't clear, like a memory, but was mixed with the memories of the other sister and Ruth herself. But I saw the knife, and I smelled the blood, and I heard screams that were not theirs."

"I told you," Lucien said, "the twins were—"

"No," O'Hara interrupted. "This was later. Much later." He had never been subjected to such a jumble of emotions. "Men," he said. "She . . . seduced these men, and then she killed them. There were at least five that I could see. Maybe more."

"Are you sure?" Eve asked. "The girls didn't seem at all like . . ."

"Of course I'm sure!" O'Hara ran a hand through his hair. That hand trembled. He could still see and feel too much. "I don't doubt what I saw." He turned his eyes to the unconscious old woman on the couch. "And she knew," he added softly. "She knew."

Ruth sat on the settee, sipping at the tea Daisy had fetched from the kitchen. The old woman shook visibly, but she did not remember what had happened.

Lucien had pulled his chair around so that he faced Ruth directly. "You have been less than forthcoming with us," he said in a low voice.

The others—Eve, Daisy, and O'Hara—stood behind him.

"I told you everything I know," Ruth insisted.

"You forgot to mention that one of the girls murdered at least five men, possibly more."

Ruth's hands twitched; the cup of tea danced and then fell, landing on the carpet at her feet. Cool tea splashed along the hem of her dark gown, but the teacup did not break. "I don't know where you got that preposterous idea." She sounded very convincing, but her eyes refused to be still. She was lying.

"We got that idea from you, Ruth."

"How . . . that's not possible."

"O'Hara." At the mention of his name, the man who had seen this new revelation stepped forward.

"Yes?"

"Take Ruth's hand."

O'Hara leaned in and stretched his hand out, and Ruth recoiled. "What is he doing?"

"O'Hara's abilities are not the same as mine, as you might have assumed. He can touch a person and see inside their mind. He can touch an object and tell you what the person who last held it was doing at the time, no matter how long ago that might have been."

Ruth stared in horror at the man who continued to offer his hand. "You're of the devil."

"Really?" O'Hara said, apparently not offended. "I've never killed anyone, nor have I ever covered up the murder of an innocent man. Innocent *men*, I should say."

"In her mind they were not innocent," Ruth countered hotly.

O'Hara let his hand drop.

"Margaret or Isabel?" Lucien asked.

Ruth pursed her lips, refusing to answer. She had already said more than she'd intended to say.

"I cannot help them if you insist on standing between us!" Lucien said. "That's why they went to you and not to me. They're using you as a shield."

"I have to protect them." Ruth squirmed on the sofa. "It's my fault. . . ."

"What's your fault?"

She shook her head. "I never should have left them here." Tears welled up in her ancient black eyes. "When the soldiers came, I should have insisted that the girls stay with me. If the soldiers wouldn't let us go, then I should have killed them all myself."

"That wasn't possible; I'm sure you know that."

"But I should have tried," Ruth said. "I should have known that the men were evil, that they intended the girls harm. I left them here, and . . . and you know what happened."

"It's not your fault," Daisy said kindly. "Even if you had known, you could not have taken on all those soldiers by yourself."

"I should have tried."

Eve jumped in. "If you had, there would have been no one here to care for them afterward."

Ruth stared down into her lap. "I did a poor job of caring for them," she whispered. "I didn't tell you everything, Mr. Thorpe."

"I'm well aware of that, Ruth."

She lifted her head and stared at him. "After the soldiers left, the girls cried day and night. They clung to each other and would let no one else in. They buried their mother and they nursed their physical wounds, but they did not heal on the inside.

"A few weeks later, the girls discovered they were both with child, and they cried more. One twin refused to accept the news. She said she was not going to have a monster's baby."

He could not see those who stood behind him, but he could feel Eve there. As if she knew he was thinking of her, she laid a hand on his shoulder.

"She took herbal potions that made her ill," Ruth continued, "but the baby remained strong. She tried to starve herself, but her sister would not allow her to die." The old woman took a deep breath that seemed to hurt her. "When she was seven months along, she rose from her bed one morning and threw herself down the stairs. The baby was lost, and she was almost lost herself."

"And you didn't know if this sister was Isabel or Margaret?"

Ruth shook her head. "I told you, I could no longer tell one twin from the other . . . and that was the truth. They changed. They called each other 'Sister,' and when I asked . . . they said Isabel and Margaret were dead. They were right, in a way."

"So, one of the twins lost her child," Eve said. The hand at Lucien's shoulder tightened slightly.

Again Ruth nodded. "Yes. Shortly after that, distant relatives, cousins on their mother's side, moved in and took over what was left of this place. They could afford to pay the taxes on the property, and the sisters could not." She shook her head at this injustice. "The girls moved into the guest house on the south end of the property. The cousins were not cruel. They kept me on and paid me a decent wage. And even though they barely knew their younger cousins, they couldn't imagine throwing the poor girls out into the cold, not with one pregnant and the other . . ." She swallowed hard.

"Crazy?" O'Hara finished.

"I thought with time she would get better, and she did. At least, I believed she was healing."

"One twin had her child—Tommy," Eve said.

"Yes," Ruth whispered. "But . . . the other twin, she came to believe that Tommy was her child. The girls both called him their baby. Growing up, Tommy called them both mother."

"No wonder he's so confused," Eve said softly. "Poor child."

"Who is Thomas?" Lucien asked.

Ruth shook her head. "I can't talk about this anymore, not tonight. My head hurts; my heart is beating too fast." She pressed a hand to her chest. "Let me think about what happened then, what I remember and what I have forgotten. Give me tonight to try to bring it all back. Tomorrow morning I will tell you everything I know. I give you my word, I won't leave anything out this time."

Lucien nodded. Channeling a spirit always exhausted him. Ruth, who was healthy for her age but had no powers to call upon and no experience in these matters, had channeled two at once. He did not want her heart to give out where she sat.

"Tomorrow morning, then." Lucien stood. "I really must have all the facts before continuing."

Ruth nodded, and O'Hara offered a hand of assistance. She recoiled from that hand, and he stepped back.

"Let me help you," Daisy said, stepping forward with a swish of her skirts. "You don't have to worry about me seeing anything I shouldn't when I touch you. I have no abilities at all, except for the cooking you have taught me and a bit of a green thumb."

"Then why are you here?" Ruth asked as she took Daisy's hand and stood, the simple moves shaky and uncertain.

Daisy glanced at O'Hara. "I'm not quite sure," she said as she led the woman toward the exit.

When Daisy and Ruth had gone from the room, O'Hara turned to Lucien. "We should send Daisy and Nathaniel back to Plummerville. Tomorrow morning. Eve, too."

"I'm not going anywhere!" Eve said hotly.

"Perhaps . . ."

"No *perhaps* about it, Lucien," O'Hara said hotly. "Something is very wrong here, and while you said the ghosts are not dangerous . . . I don't believe it. I felt so much anger when I touched Ruth, and it wasn't *her* anger. It was a rage that lingered from one of the twins."

"You had a sense of both girls," Lucien said.

O'Hara nodded.

"Could you differentiate Margaret from Isabel?"

"No." O'Hara walked away, stuffing his hands into his pockets as he turned his back on Lucien. "And neither can they," he said in a lowered voice. "The sisters have clung to each other so tightly and for so long that they no longer know where Isabel ends and Margaret begins."

Nine

Eve knew she dreamed, but it was such a vivid dream! Warm and real, with bright colors and sensations of all kinds.

The sun shone warm in the bedchamber, breaking through the filmy curtains that hung from the French doors and flooding the room with bright, pure light. Flowers filled vases throughout the room, their fragrance reminiscent more of spring than fall. Eve sat comfortably in the green silk chair, with Tommy snugly and solidly situated on her lap.

Here, in this vivid dream, he was warm and real, as solid as she. Eve ruffled her fingers through Tommy's dark hair. The strands were silky and fine. He tipped his head back and smiled at her. His cheeks were pink, his eyes dark and innocent.

"I love you s-o-o-o-o-o much," he said, reaching his little face up for a kiss Eve gladly gave him. His cheek was warm and soft beneath her lips.

This was what she craved with all her heart: a child to hold and love. She wrapped her arms around Tommy and held him close. He rested his head on her chest.

"I wish we could be together all the time," Tommy said softly.

"Me, too," Eve whispered.

"I wish you could be my mama."

"So do I." She ruffled her fingers through his hair again. "But you have a mama, don't you?"

Tommy shrugged. "I guess. But they don't love me the way you would. Sometimes they hate me." Suddenly his eyes were old, not at all innocent but touched with pain too deep for one so young. "Sometimes they look at me and wonder which one was my father. The fat one, one of my mamas said. No, the one that cut her so much, my other mama said. She said I have his eyes."

Tommy looked up, silently pleading with Eve for something only she could give him. "There's a wall between us, Mama. You can knock that wall down, and when you do, we'll be together."

Nothing about Tommy's short life had been fair—not his creation, not his death. This connection they had found wasn't fair, either. "We can't be together," Eve said sensibly, even though the truth hurt. "We truly do live in different worlds."

"You can come into my world, Mama," Tommy whispered. A single tear fell down a fat, pink cheek. "And when you do, you can hold me all you want. You can hold me every day, from now until the end of time. We would be together forever. Wouldn't that be nice?"

"I would have to die," Eve whispered.

"It's not so bad."

Eve cradled Tommy and rocked back and forth gently. He was so warm, and he filled that empty place inside her. "I can't," she said. "Lucien needs me."

"I don't like him," Tommy said sullenly.

"You would if you got to know him." Eve tried for a brighter tone of voice, even though inside she hurt in a way she could not explain. "Lucien can be distant and difficult to understand until you get to know him, but once you do know and love him, you'll see what a remarkable person he is."

"Do you love him more than you love me?" Tommy asked.

"It's a different kind of love," Eve said.

"You do!" Tommy left her lap abruptly and ran for the French doors that blew open for him. "You love *him* more than me! I hate him! I hate him!"

Eve jumped up and followed Tommy onto the gallery. "Come back!" she shouted, but it was too late. Tommy was gone.

Daisy took a long time to fall asleep, and when she did sleep, her dreams were restless. Restless and senseless and disturbing.

Until one of the sisters arrived, real and bright and smiling, to push the rest of the senseless dream away.

The twin was dressed all in white. What she wore was not a wedding gown—at least Daisy didn't think so—but it was very fancy and snow white.

"Why do you love that one?" the twin asked.

"O'Hara? I don't love him. He's . . ." She wrinkled her nose. "Not at all my type."

The girl smiled widely, but the grin was cold, without humor. "You do not lie well, not to me and not to him. He knows you love him, and that is a very bad thing."

"Why is that bad?" Daisy asked.

The twin walked toward her. "If he snaps his fingers, you will come running, and he knows that to be so. In order to regain control over the situation, you're going to have to seduce him."

"What?"

"Don't look so shocked. Sex is all about power, not love. It's naive to romanticize what happens between a woman and a man. The coming together is raw, and fraught with many emotions. Sometimes that emotion is hate, sometimes it's nothing but a need so great it's like a gnawing wound. But love?"

"There can be love," Daisy insisted.

The spirit shook her head as if she were dismayed. "You have more power within you than you've ever imagined, Sister," the ghost said. "If you walked into O'Hara's room at this very moment, took off your nightclothes, and joined him in his bed, he would not be able to refuse you."

"I couldn't possibly . . ."

The ghost wouldn't let Daisy finish her objections. "Worried about the child who shares his room? Then take your O'Hara's hand and lead him to your bed. The result will be the same. He will adore you. He will love you, at least for a while. He will think you the only woman on the face of the earth."

That *was* the desired result. . . .

"I couldn't possibly be so bold."

The twin rolled her eyes and lifted her hands in supplication. "Fine. Be subtle in your seduction, if you must." She looked Daisy up and down. "First, you must stop dressing like a child."

"I do not dress like a child!"

"Bows and ribbons and lace and fluffy sleeves

and petticoats and colors a child would choose."
The ghost shook her head in disgust.

"I like pastel colors!"

The ghost, which did not look at all like a ghost at the moment, placed her face close to Daisy's. "You should wear scarlet, and you should show this O'Hara the womanly gifts with which you have been blessed."

"My . . . what?"

The ghost reached out with a very pale hand and touched Daisy's breasts.

"Stop that!" Daisy said, jumping back.

"Look your O'Hara in the eye and imagine what he would be like in your bed," the ghost said, ignoring Daisy's protests. "Let him see how the imagining affects you. Lick your lips; let your breasts heave and your fingers tremble. Let him look into your eyes and see the endless possibilities."

"He's not *my* O'Hara."

"He could be," the twin said softly. "With a word, a gesture, a whispered invitation. Don't you want him? I thought you did."

"I don't want to just . . . seduce him." Daisy hissed those last two words, afraid to say them aloud. "I want O'Hara to love me."

"If he is capable of love, he will."

"I want him to marry me," she whispered.

"Why?"

Daisy knew what she wanted, so much, so strongly. And it wasn't going to happen. "I want O'Hara to love me so we can be together forever."

The ghost waved a dismissive hand. "That's easy enough. But first you have to make him yours in the way no man can resist."

"I don't know." She really shouldn't be listening to this interfering spirit. But this was, after all, just a dream. "How can I become irresistible?" She tried so hard to be beautiful, for O'Hara, and now this spirit had her wondering about her own wardrobe. Did she dress like a child?

The twin smiled. "I have an old red dress stored in one of the trunks in the attic. You're welcome to borrow it, if you'd like."

The attic. "I'm not going up there again," Daisy said anxiously. No, not even for the opportunity to make herself attractive to O'Hara would she return to that terrible place. "I'm . . . I'm so sorry for what happened to you there. It wasn't right. It never should've happened."

The ghost's expression did not change. "I died there; I was born there. Pain brings change and rebirth and . . ." Something in her eyes flickered. "Some days I don't even remember what happened there. Some days I can push those memories to the back of my mind, so that I no longer feel the agony and the terror. Sister did not forget, though—not ever. She remembered too well."

"There are good men in the world," Daisy said softly.

The ghost smiled. "Men like O'Hara?"

"Yes," Daisy whispered.

The expression on the spirit's face hardened, and suddenly she looked older. Ancient. "Do you know how many women your O'Hara has bedded?" the vision in white asked. "I can't even count them all, there are so many. And you know what? This *good man* of yours has never bedded the same woman twice."

Daisy could feel the blush on her cheeks. "And yet you claim I should seduce him and bring him into *my* bed?"

"You're different from the rest. You will be the last woman he takes, Daisy," the ghost assured her. "The very last."

"How do you . . . ?"

The ghost disappeared, leaving Daisy alone . . . in the attic.

"Go away," Lucien said halfheartedly.

"No."

The twin in scarlet sat on the edge of the bed. It was a dream, not a flesh-and-blood visitation, so Lucien did not feel guilty for trying to send the ghost on her way.

He was never visited by spirits in his dreams, so he found her presence annoying. Maybe it wasn't a ghost he spoke to. Maybe this really was just a dream.

"Another night goes by," she said, "and still you do not take your wife."

"That's none of your business," Lucien said. He sat up and looked at the portrait on the wall. The ghosts he'd seen bore little resemblance to the girls in the painting. "Did you kill them?"

"Does it matter?" The apparition sat beside him on the bed, and he scooted over to accommodate her. Eve was not here at the moment, sharing his bed as she did every night, but then, this was only a dream.

"It does. I must know what happened in order to help you."

"I don't need your help."

"I believe you do."

She stretched out beside him, her red silk dress touching his bare leg. "If your wife truly loved you, she would not make you wait to take her."

"You don't understand."

"Neither do you." She smiled at him, wicked and comfortable in his bed and in her body.

"Go away."

She did not obey. "Are you afraid of what I see that you do not?" the ghost whispered. "Poor Lucien, you must be terrified of the truths I can tell you. Your wife doesn't love you anymore, because you can't give her what she wants most in this world. She loves another."

"She does not." And yet, his heart skipped a beat.

Warm fingers danced over his face, and the ghost in red moved toward him. Close, too close. It was as if she were trying to creep beneath his skin. "Perhaps you should forget about her and lie with me."

"You're dead," Lucien said practically.

"But I am also *here*," she said. She laid a hand on his chest. He felt the weight of it, the movement of her fingers. "In your dreams I am as real as she is. As warm. As tangible. Touch me and you will see." She leaned in as if to kiss him.

Lucien caught one ghostly wrist in his hand and quickly moved his head away from the spirit's kiss. She did not pursue him but smiled and backed away. "If you won't go away, then you should at least give me your name," he said. "I need a name. Something besides 'darling.'"

"Why do you need a name? It doesn't matter; it means nothing." Her smile vanished and she licked her red lips. "I will open myself to you, make you weep with pleasure. And when I am done, I will take my knife and stab you where your heart should be to see if you bleed. Will you bleed Lucien? Will you bleed, for me?"

He came away with a start, sitting up to find himself in his bed with Eve sleeping restlessly beside him.

"Great," he said as he fell back and covered his eyes with both hands. "Just great."

Eve searched everywhere for Tommy, but she couldn't find him. She was in a panic. What if she didn't find him before morning? What if she didn't get the chance to hold him one more time before dawn?

"Tommy? Sweetheart?" she called as she walked through the house. The place was bigger than she had imagined, with more twists and turns, higher ceilings, and rooms Ruth had kept hidden from them. She searched them all, trying to find Tommy, but he continued to hide himself from her.

As she searched, the empty place inside her grew deeper and darker. What if she never saw Tommy again?

Finally there was only one room left to explore: the attic.

Eve stood at the bottom of the stairs and looked at the closed door at the top of the steep, dark stairway. Was he hiding there? Would he dare?

Moving cautiously, she took the first step of her long ascent. Someone was up there; she knew it. The child she needed to hold had hidden in the one place in the house he thought she wouldn't look. "Tommy?" she called softly as she approached the door. Beyond the closed door, someone screamed. Someone else cried. The screams and the sobbing seemed very far away, and yet she knew they came from the attic. She did not stop. Tommy shouldn't be up there all alone!

She ran. The door got farther and farther away, but finally she was able to reach out and grab the door handle. She swung the door open.

It wasn't Tommy she'd heard moving about, but Daisy. Daisy, dressed in red silk and dancing alone in the attic, her golden hair down in endless waves.

"What are you doing here?" Eve asked.

"Dancing," Daisy responded with a grin.

"Why?"

"I am going to make him love me, no matter what."

"O'Hara?"

"Of course, O'Hara," Daisy said as she continued to dance. The red silk hugged her body and swayed around her legs. Waving blond tresses twisted around her body. "I've been going about this all wrong. O'Hara is not a subtle man. It was wrong of me to be so indirect with him."

"Indirect?" Eve's eyes scanned the room. Daisy's love life was not her problem! "Have you seen Tommy? He's just a child. He shouldn't be here alone."

"No," Daisy said, not at all concerned about the lost child. "It won't take long for me to make O'Hara mine, now that I've decided on a more direct approach. I'll be surprised if it takes an entire day." Her grin grew wider. And much too wicked for the Daisy Eve knew.

"Be careful," Eve said absently as she continued to look for the child. "Men are not to be trusted." Where had that come from? She could trust Lucien . . . couldn't she? "Are you sure you want O'Hara? After all, he is a scoundrel. He might break your heart, and then where would you be?" Eve's mind would not remain on Daisy's problems. "Are you sure you haven't seen Tommy?"

Daisy danced in a widening circle, the red silk whirling around her legs, her pale tresses lifting up, floating around her head. She didn't wear any shoes, Eve noticed.

"No man will break my heart, not ever again," Daisy said happily. "Not if I don't allow it."

"But . . ." Eve began.

"Don't worry about me, Sister," Daisy said as she tossed her head back and spun until she was no more than a blur of red and gold. "I'm going to be the last woman O'Hara ever loves."

O'Hara sat on the side of his bed, wide awake even though it was nearing dawn. How could he sleep? Everything he'd seen when he'd touched Ruth still lingered inside him, and the child who slept on a pallet on the opposite side of the room did not sleep quietly. Nathaniel, Lucien's son, tossed and turned and occasionally talked nonsense in his sleep.

And then there was Daisy.

He could not fall in love with her. No matter how sweet, beautiful, and kind she might be . . . he could not love her. And he could not allow her to love him.

O'Hara lay back on the bed and closed his eyes. He needed sleep in order to get through tomorrow, even if only a couple of hours. Exhausted, he finally drifted off.

And found Daisy.

"Where have you been?" she asked, her smile positively wicked. She was dressed all in red and her hair was down, and her cleavage . . . Daisy had cleavage. Lots of it.

She joined him on the bed. "I've been waiting for you," she whispered as she leaned down. Her face was close to his, so close, amazingly close. When he'd left her running on the platform of the Plummerville train depot eight months ago, she'd complained that he'd never kissed her. Perhaps this was the time. A kiss in a dream was likely all he'd ever get.

But Daisy did not kiss him. She slipped one sleeve off her arm and let it fall, exposing one breast. A flick of her fingers, and the other sleeve fell, as well. A moment later, she was naked and so was he.

"See what you've been missing?" she teased. "Silly man."

"This isn't real," he said, as if to remind himself that he was dreaming.

"It could be." Daisy leaned closer; she brushed her cheek against his, raked her breasts against his chest. Golden hair fell across her face and drifted down to touch him, soft and silky. It all felt so real.

A small birthmark on Daisy's side very slightly marred her perfect skin. Unable to help himself, he traced the birthmark with his fingertip. He felt nothing. It was a miracle. He touched Daisy, and all he felt was her skin, her gentle response.

Just a dream, he reminded himself. That's why he could touch her and feel nothing. Because this wasn't real. She wasn't real.

The Daisy of his dreams reached down and grabbed the length that had hardened the moment he'd seen her. Gentle fingers raked up and down, teasing him, testing his limits.

"Haven't you wanted this?" she whispered.

"From the moment I first saw you," he confessed.

She teased him with her mouth, those rosy lips coming near his but never touching. He had never known Daisy to smile this way, so sensual. So full of secrets.

After she'd driven him beyond the point where he cared whether this was a dream, she straddled him and guided his erection to her wet, hot center. Her eyes closed and her lips parted slightly as she lowered herself to take him into her body; she smiled when he was buried deep, then she licked her lips.

"When you come near me, I shudder," she whispered as she began to move. "You walk by and I feel your touch, deep inside, where I am a woman. Your woman." She moved slowly, rising and falling. She was creamy skin and golden hair and red lips. She was heat and pleasure. "Tell me that you need me, darling."

"I need you," O'Hara rasped.

"Tell me that you would do anything for me."

She was wrapped around him, hot and tight, and the way she moved . . . "I would do anything for you." He reached up and caressed a nipple, tweaked it, stroked the tender skin of her breast. Again he felt nothing in his hands but Daisy's flesh. Yes, this was indeed a dream.

Daisy began to shudder. He felt her response all around him. Her eyes were closed once again, but she no longer smiled. She tossed her head back so that a waterfall of golden hair fell down her back. She found completion in a cry of his name and a thrust that took him deep. His own release was coming, just one more . . .

"Mr. O'Hara!"

The hand shaking his shoulder was not Daisy's.

O'Hara opened his eyes to find Nathaniel, still dressed in his nightshirt, standing beside the bed with a concerned expression on his face. Still breathless and caught in his dream, O'Hara was rendered speechless.

"Are you all right, sir?"

"No, I am not all right," O'Hara said abruptly.

Nathaniel backed away from the bed. "The man, Thomas, he told me to wake you."

"Oh, he did. Quite a trickster, that Thomas."

Nathaniel shook his head. "No, it wasn't a trick. He said if I didn't wake you, you would die."

The kid's eyes were so wide, O'Hara couldn't tell him that some ghost had played a trick on them both.

The dream was gone, and unfortunately there would be no reclaiming it. O'Hara sat up and took a deep breath. "Nathaniel, has your father taught you how to block a ghost?"

Nathaniel nodded. "We began working on that

right away. It will take some time, he said, to perfect the procedure."

"I suggest you practice on blocking this Thomas, whoever he is," O'Hara said sourly.

"I will try, sir, but he didn't seem . . ."

"Trust me," O'Hara said. It was fully morning, and after they spoke to Ruth, he and Lucien would visit the site of the fire that had taken the life of the twins, a child, and a man. He didn't look forward to that outing, not at all, but it was a necessary step if they were to complete this job.

The images from his dream stayed with him, refusing to fade as dreams usually did. How on earth was he going to look Daisy in the eye?

The kitchen was cold, and there was no sign of Ruth. Lucien was not surprised. Last night's episode had drained the old woman. She needed her sleep. He never cared much for breakfast, anyway, particularly when he was on a job. And after last night's strange dreams . . . he had no appetite at all.

But the others apparently did have an appetite. It wasn't long before everyone was bumping into each other in the kitchen, trying to scrounge together breakfast for five. They were all silent this morning. Jumpy, too.

Lucien found what he'd been searching for in the pantry. Coffee. He wanted no more of that bitter tea Ruth had given them last night after dinner.

Eve was slicing a loaf of bread, Daisy cut slices of

ham, and O'Hara and Nathaniel were gathering the plates and cups necessary for the meal.

"I had the strangest dreams last night," Lucien said as he turned about with the can of coffee grounds in his hand.

Eve dropped her knife. Daisy squealed as she cut a too-thick slice of ham. O'Hara dropped a plate, which crashed to the floor. With a bit of juggling, he managed to save the other dishes. Only Nathaniel seemed unaffected by the simple statement.

"What about the rest of you? Did the séance give anyone strange dreams?"

"No," O'Hara said abruptly. "I must clean up this mess I've made. Clumsy of me." He headed for the pantry, searching for a broom.

"Neither did I," Daisy said without looking at him. "I slept so well, I'm quite sure I had no dreams at all." Her face blushed beet red. "I think I'll go check on Ruth. She really shouldn't sleep so late." Daisy skittered out of the room, down the hallway that would lead to Ruth's room.

Lucien turned his attention to Eve, who had said nothing. "What about you, love? Bad dreams? Intense dreams? Anything of note?"

She turned and looked him squarely in the eye. "No. I slept quite well."

Lucien said nothing. What could he say? His lovely wife had just lied to him, as had they all. It didn't surprise him that O'Hara would lie. Daisy had obviously been embarrassed by her dream.

But Eve . . . she had promised never to lie to him. She had given him her word. . . .

A high-pitched scream split the air, and everyone's eyes turned toward the hallway where the servants' rooms were located. O'Hara took off at a run, one word slipping from his mouth.

"Daisy."

Ten

Eve was right behind O'Hara, and Lucien followed her. He turned as he left the kitchen to shake a finger at Nathaniel. "You stay here."

The child, who had been following, stopped in his tracks.

Lucien grabbed Eve's shoulders as he reached the room and saw the horrible scene laid out before them. She turned quickly, and he allowed her to hide her face against his chest as he wrapped his sheltering arms around her.

Ruth dangled at the window, half in the room, half out. One arm and her head had been punched through the glass. Jagged shards of glass had cut her deeply, a long wound on her arm and a smaller, deadlier gash on her neck. She was dead and had been for hours.

Daisy cried, hands covering her face as if she could hide from the truth, and O'Hara stood behind her, obviously wanting to comfort her but not knowing how. He did not touch Daisy. His hands balled into tight fists.

"Why didn't we hear something?" O'Hara asked. "She must've cried out. We should have heard the window breaking. Damn it!"

Daisy cried harder.

"Everyone in the kitchen," Lucien ordered.

"But shouldn't we do something?" Daisy wailed.

"There's nothing we can do," he assured her.

They returned to the kitchen, somber and shaken.

"What happened?" Nathaniel asked.

After considering his answer, Lucien said, "Ruth has had an accident."

"She's dead, isn't she?" Nathaniel asked.

Lucien could not take his eyes from his son's face. Nathaniel was pale, somber, and perhaps a little frightened. Not as frightened as he should be, given the circumstances. "Do you see her?"

Nathaniel shook his head. "No. She's here, but she hides."

Lucien faced the other three. "We didn't hear anything, because we were all sleeping more deeply than usual. Weren't we? There were dreams unlike those we usually have, dreams that took us into a state where we were not able to hear what was happening around us."

Eve placed her arm through his. "I did have a rather unusual dream," she confessed softly.

"And why didn't you tell me when I first asked?"

She looked up at him, not at all wounded by his anger. "I don't know."

"I had a rather unusually vivid dream myself," Daisy said. She tried to sound calm, but again she blushed. And then she took a telling step away from O'Hara.

"So did I," O'Hara said. He turned his calculating eyes to Nathaniel. "Nathaniel woke me and said that a ghost had told him to rouse me from the dream, that if he didn't I would . . . die."

"When I woke up this morning, Thomas was waiting for me," Nathaniel said. "He told me that the ghosts had invaded your dreams, that what you saw was real and yet not real. He said that you were trapped in a world in between and I needed to wake you."

Daisy slapped a hand over her mouth, and her blue eyes went wide.

"How did they get into our heads?" O'Hara asked angrily.

"Ghosts visit in dreams all the time," Eve said.

"Not like this," O'Hara countered.

"Ghosts never come to me in my dreams," Lucien said. "Never. Last night's visitation was an aberration."

"Are you telling me that what I dreamed was *real?*" Daisy asked.

"Only a little," Nathaniel said.

"Nathaniel," Lucien said sternly. "I think you should return to your room."

The boy turned away, obedient as always, but stopped before he reached the door. There he turned and faced Lucien down. "No. I won't go. You can't send me away every time something happens."

Lucien was shocked. So far the child had been meek. He'd obeyed every word. "I'm your father. I can do just that."

"It's not fair," Nathaniel began.

"Fair?"

"I'm not a child."

"Yes, you are."

Take A Trip Into A Timeless World of Passion and Adventure with Kensington Choice Historical Romances!
—Absolutely FREE!

Enjoy the passion and adventure of another time with Kensington Choice Historical Romances. They are the finest novels of their kind, written by today's best-selling romance authors. Each Kensington Choice Historical Romance transports you to distant lands in a bygone age. Experience the adventure and share the delight as proud men and spirited women discover the wonder and passion of true love.

4 BOOKS WORTH UP TO $24.96— Absolutely FREE!

Get 4 FREE Books!

We created our convenient Home Subscription Service so you'll be sure to have the hottest new romances delivered each month right to your doorstep—usually before they are available in book stores. Just to show you how convenient the Zebra Home Subscription Service is, we would like to send you 4 FREE Kensington Choice Historical Romances. The books are worth up to $24.96, but you only pay $1.99 for shipping and handling. There's no obligation to buy additional books—ever!

Save Up To 30% With Home Delivery!

Accept your FREE books and each month we'll deliver 4 brand new titles as soon as they are published. They'll be yours to examine FREE for 10 days. Then if you decide to keep the books, you'll pay the preferred subscriber's price (up to 30% off the cover price!), plus shipping and handling. Remember, you are under no obligation to buy any of these books at any time! If you are not delighted with them, simply return them and owe nothing. But if you enjoy Kensington Choice Historical Romances as much as we think you will, pay the special preferred subscriber rate and save over $8.00 off the cover price!

We have **4 FREE BOOKS** for you as your
introduction to
KENSINGTON CHOICE!
To get your FREE BOOKS, worth up to $24.96, mail
the card below or call TOLL-FREE 1-800-770-1963.
Visit our website at www.kensingtonbooks.com.

Get 4 FREE Kensington Choice Historical Romances!

❤ **YES!** Please send me my 4 FREE KENSINGTON CHOICE HISTORICAL ROMANCES (without obligation to purchase other books). I only pay $1.99 for shipping and handling. Unless you hear from me after I receive my 4 FREE BOOKS, you may send me 4 new novels—as soon as they are published—to preview each month FREE for 10 days. If I am not satisfied, I may return them and owe nothing. Otherwise, I will pay the money-saving preferred subscriber's price (over $8.00 off the cover price), plus shipping and handling. I may return any shipment within 10 days and owe nothing, and I may cancel any time I wish. In any case the 4 FREE books will be mine to keep.

Name _____

Address _____ Apt. _____

City _____ State _____ Zip _____

Telephone (___) _____

Signature _____

(If under 18, parent or guardian must sign)

KN083A

"I'm thirteen years old!"

"Exactly!"

"And I know why you all had those dreams! I'm the only one who knows and you won't even listen to me!"

Lucien stared at his son. "What?"

"There's a potion," the boy said more calmly. "My mother used to make it for a client of hers. She said it was very dangerous, potentially deadly, but that sometimes people who had lost loved ones and wanted to bring them back in a way that was almost real, they would take that risk."

"There is no such potion," Lucien said calmly. "And even if there were, we did not take it."

Nathaniel looked past Lucien, lifted his eyes, and went very still. "Yes, there is, and yes, you did. Thomas says it's so."

Eve placed herself between her husband and the child. "Nathaniel, let's suppose there is a potion." Her own dreams had been so real! "How would it be delivered?"

"I believe it needs to be ingested. Mother tried a formula that could be inhaled as a powder, but it wasn't effective."

"We didn't ingest any potion," Lucien insisted.

Eve turned to her husband. "The tea. That horrid tea Ruth served with dessert. If you will remember, she gave Nathaniel milk instead of tea, which is why he wasn't bothered with unnatural dreams."

Lucien's eyebrows lifted slightly.

"If I can smell the tea, ma'am, I believe I can tell

you if that's the culprit or not," Nathaniel said. "One of the herbs has a distinctive aroma."

"We were not drugged!" Lucien said as Eve began to search for the tea.

When O'Hara and Daisy pitched in, working from opposite sides of the room toward a meeting point, Eve ended her search and went to Lucien. She stood close to him, as close as she dared. "It makes sense that we were drugged, somehow," she whispered. "I dreamed . . ." She swallowed hard. "I dreamed of the child Tommy, as if he were my own. I held him. I rocked him in my arms. It's as if the spirits who haunt this house looked into my very soul, saw my greatest desire, and fed it."

"Your greatest desire is a child?"

"Yes."

She could not deny the ache on her husband's face as he looked down at her. "I dreamed of you," Lucien whispered. "After a nasty visit from one of the twins, I fell back into a deep sleep and dreamed of you. Only you weren't there, Evie. You were always just out of reach, around the next corner, over the next hill. . . ."

Eve turned around to escape her husband's telling glare and almost ran into Daisy. "What about you? What did you dream about?"

"Nothing at all worth sharing," Daisy said, her eyes on the high shelf she could not reach. "Just a dream."

"But I thought we agreed all the dreams were extraordinary in some way," Lucien said.

Daisy blushed. "Well, I did speak with one of the twins, and there was this red dress . . ."

O'Hara turned about abruptly, sending a bowl

near his flailing hands to the floor. It crashed, as the plate he had dropped earlier had.

Eve had never known O'Hara to be clumsy.

"What about your dream?" Lucien asked O'Hara. "Apparently it was quite deadly, as Nathaniel was warned about its potential deadly affects."

"The dream itself doesn't matter," O'Hara said, his eyes flitting to Daisy very briefly. "I would like to understand what Ruth expected to gain by administering the potion, but we might never know."

"She did it for the girls, because they asked her to," Nathaniel said.

"Is Thomas speaking to you again?" Lucien asked testily.

Nathaniel nodded. "Yes, Mr. Thorpe."

Lucien was obviously annoyed. Because Thomas was showing himself to Nathaniel and not him? Or because his son had taken to calling him Mr. Thorpe?

"We should see to Ruth," O'Hara said in a low voice, "and leave the women to search for the potion, if there is such a thing."

"There is," Nathaniel said softly. "That's what killed her; that's what killed Ruth." His eyes took on a misty sheen. "She reached for something that wasn't there; she was walking toward . . . her husband. He died a long time ago, and she misses him, and he seemed so real. Her hand and her face went through the glass, and she cut herself deep. It's not as terrible as it sounds," he said quickly. "There was only a moment of pain. She was ready to die. As soon as the twins move on, she will move on as well. Her husband is waiting for her, a son and a daughter, too."

Daisy had gone pale once again. "I gave Ruth the tea. After she passed out, I gave her cold tea to drink." She swayed on her feet. "I killed her." Daisy's eyes rolled up in her head, and she went limp. As she fell, O'Hara, who stood closest, reached out to catch her so she couldn't hurt herself falling to the floor.

He caught her, quickly lowered her to the floor, and then released her as if she'd burned his hands.

O'Hara and Lucien buried Ruth in the McBride graveyard on the north end of the property. Mr. and Mrs. McBride were buried there, and a single grave was marked for Isabel and Margaret McBride. They were buried together. Tommy had his own small plot, and there was an unmarked grave in one corner. It was the final resting place for the unknown man who had died in the fire, O'Hara imagined.

Only Jim remained to assist them. Everyone else was gone now. Jim's helper and the day girls had been scared away by the ghosts, and now Ruth was gone. O'Hara couldn't help but wonder if Jim would be here, come morning. There was little reason for him to stay.

It was Jim who had built Ruth's coffin, earlier in the day, after Lucien had delivered the news of her passing. It was a fine piece of work. He hadn't just thrown the coffin together, but had made sure the corners fit tight and there were no splinters or rough spots to mar Ruth's final resting place.

As they buried the old woman, Jim was openly emotional. He shed a few tears, shamelessly, and he said little as he threw himself into the work that was required.

O'Hara was glad of the brutal physical activity required for the task of burying the old woman; it almost took his mind off what he'd seen when he'd caught Daisy as she fell.

Impossibly, they had shared the same dream. The flashes of memory he'd seen as he'd caught Daisy were identical to his, only seen from her perspective. Atop him. Taking him inside her body. He knew the sensations she had experienced as he'd entered her body, the way she had shaken as she'd found her pleasure. And in one hand, she had grasped a knife she would have stabbed him with if the dream had run its course.

He wondered if the birthmark was real, and realized he would never know.

Daisy hadn't been alone. In the dream, one of the twins had been with her. *Inside* her. He didn't think Daisy was aware of that. All she remembered was coming to him and the pleasure that had followed.

"I want to send Daisy home—today," O'Hara said as he and Lucien walked back toward the house. They were alone. Jim had returned to the stables, tears in his eyes, after saying a few kind words over Ruth's grave.

"Do you think she'll go?" Lucien asked.

"Send Eve and Nathaniel with her," O'Hara said. "This place is not safe for any of them."

"It's not like the Honeycutt Hotel . . ." Lucien began.

"But they could end up dead just the same!"

Lucien came to a halt long before they reached

the fine house that was laid before them, white and elegant and deceptively deadly. "Do you really think so?"

O'Hara nodded. "I do."

"Without the potion Eve found and discarded, I don't see how there's any physical danger."

Lucien argued about everything! The last thing O'Hara wanted was to lose his temper. "Eve is not herself," he said calmly. "I see that, and I'm sure you do, too."

Lucien's face hardened. "She's been . . . distracted lately. Her problems have nothing to do with the house or the ghosts in it."

"Think of the boy, then. He's much more powerful than you are, Lucien."

Lucien's glare did not silence O'Hara. This was too important; he would not back down.

"He isn't prepared for this," O'Hara said in a softer voice. "He's a very powerful child who has been thrust into a world he does not understand. Would you have been able to deal with this at the age of thirteen?"

"No," Lucien said as he resumed his trek toward the house. "Fine. We'll send them home. There's no snowstorm or Scrydan trapping us here, so there's no reason not to send the women and children back to Plummerville." His nose twitched. "Eve will not like it."

"Daisy will be ecstatic," O'Hara grumbled. That was something else he'd seen when he'd touched her as she'd fallen. She could not wait to get away from him.

* * *

"I won't go." Eve crossed her arms and planted her feet, trying very hard not to show Lucien that she was terrified.

"Why not?" he asked sensibly.

They had retired to the library for a moment of privacy as the others were gathered in the parlor. He said he wanted to tell her first that he was sending her home. Her, as well as Daisy and Nathaniel. "I can't leave. You need me, Lucien; you know you do. Send Daisy and Nathaniel. It's too late today to get them packed and to town before sunset, but to-morrow morning, bright and early, we can get the two of them safely out of the house."

"You're going with them."

"No, I'm not. You need me here!"

Lucien circled around her, studying her as if she were a stranger. "You want to stay because I need you," he said softly.

Her heart leaped. "Yes."

"I don't think that's the reason, Evie," he said. "I think there's something else going on here. You're different. You're hiding something from me."

Out of the corner of her eye, she saw Tommy take shape. She had known he was with her, but it was difficult for him to maintain his form for a great length of time. She turned to look at the child, and he shook his head furiously. "Don't tell, Mama. He won't understand."

"He will," she whispered.

"Who will what?" Lucien asked, losing his patience with her.

She looked her husband in the eye. "Tommy needs me, Lucien. I can't leave him here alone."

Tommy vanished abruptly, perhaps scared now that Lucien knew the truth.

"Tommy is dead," Lucien said in a low voice. "You know that, Evie."

"Yes, of course, but he's so lost and lonely here. He calls me 'Mama,' poor thing, and he needs me. He needs me to be his mother."

Lucien stepped toward her, tilting his face so he could see her more clearly. "Evie, love, Tommy has a mother."

The statement, so hurtful and unnecessary, annoyed her. "Not a very good one! If he has a mother, where is she? Why is he always alone when I see him? Why is there never a mother holding his hand, or asking him where he's been, or making sure he's warm and safe?"

"Because he's dead."

Instinctively, she tried to slap Lucien. He saw the blow coming and caught her hand by the wrist.

"I am all the more convinced to get you out of this place. I don't want to wait until tomorrow."

Eve shook her head. "I'm not leaving. If you put me on a train or in a carriage, I will only get off at the next stop, turn around, and come back."

"Thanks for the warning. I'll make sure you have an escort to prevent such an action. I'm sure I can get Jim to agree to that duty."

Tears welled up in her eyes. Lucien's response was to lean down and kiss her. Gently. Hesitantly. "We have so much to work out," he said, dismissing the immediate problem of whether he would allow her to stay here.

"Yes, we do."

"We can't work through anything while you're irrational."

She jerked her hand from his. "Irrational?"

"Yes, Evie. It scares me that you can't see it."

Her heart began to pound. "You're jealous. He said you would be."

"You think I'm jealous of the ghost of a child?"

"Yes," she whispered.

He traced her cheek with one finger. "I want you out of here and safe."

"I won't leave." She knew Tommy would never be her child. He was, as Lucien so bluntly said, dead. But she could not bear to see and hear him suffer. "If you do your job here and send them all on, if you can reunite Tommy with his mother and send them . . ." Her heart clutched at the thought of Tommy leaving her forever. "If you send them on to a place where they'll be at peace, then I'll leave. With you, Lucien. I won't run. I won't be chased away. We're in this together."

"Daisy and Nathaniel must leave this place," Lucien said. "I know you don't want to go, but I plan to do my best to change your mind before they leave. I want you to go with them, but I won't try to force you."

"I'm not going to change my mind," Eve insisted.

Lucien cradled her face in his hands. "I miss you, Eve. Our troubles began when you decided we should deny ourselves the pleasures of marriage."

"I thought you'd decided you didn't want any children."

Impossibly, he smiled at her. "Only to have one dropped into my life with no warning. Maybe we shouldn't make too many plans. God always has other ideas."

"What are you saying?"

"I'm saying you should stop worrying, then close your eyes and jump into life feetfirst and see where you land. Maybe we'll have a dozen babies; maybe we'll have none. Maybe Nathaniel will become the child you want."

"He doesn't need me."

"He needs you more than a ghost does, Evie. I barely know him myself, but I see that much."

She didn't want to talk about the child Lucien had made with another woman. It hurt too much. But how could she ignore what had been thrust upon them? "Did you love her?" she whispered.

"Zella?"

"Of course, Zella," she snapped. "What kind of name is that, anyway? Zella." She didn't give him a chance to answer that question. There was only one question that mattered. "Did you love her?"

"For a while."

Tears stung her eyes. "She's the other one, isn't she, the one you told me about when I asked if you'd ever been in love."

"Yes."

Lucien insisted on honesty, always. Right now, she wasn't so sure that was a good trait. *Lie to me, Lucien. Tell me you've never loved anyone but me.*

He stroked her cheek. "Don't look at me that way. Remember, I was only four years older than Nathaniel is now when I loved Zella. And it didn't last. In truth, it wasn't real love but more of an infatuation."

"Was she beautiful?"

"Evie . . ."

"Was she?"

"Yes, but not as beautiful as you. No one is as beautiful as you."

Eve wasn't beautiful, and she knew it too well. She was ordinary. Most men didn't look at her twice . . . but Lucien did, because he loved her.

"Maybe we should just talk about the spirits in this house for now." It was a more comfortable subject than Zella. "Have you decided how to send them on?"

"Not yet." Lucien seemed as happy as she to leave the subject of Zella behind. "O'Hara and I are going to examine the site of the fire. Perhaps we'll find some answers there."

"When are you going?"

"Now, I'm afraid."

"I'll go with you."

Lucien shook his head slowly. "That's not a good idea, Eve. You stay here with Daisy and Nathaniel, and help them get packed. We'll speak with Jim while we're out and make arrangements for him to take them to town in the morning. If you change your mind about going with them, you can pack your things as well."

"I won't," she insisted.

"I suspected as much," Lucien said without anger.

He leaned forward and rested his forehead on hers. "You make me wish I was a farmer or a merchant, anything but what I am. You once wished for an ordinary life and an ordinary man. I have tried to give you *ordinary*, Evie; I have, but . . ."

"It isn't in you," she finished when he stalled.

"No, it's not."

She wrapped her arms around his waist and held on for a moment. Maybe he was right. She had been worrying a lot, about something she might not be able to influence! Either she would have children or she would not. All the tears in the world wouldn't change what was to be.

"Have I been terribly difficult?" she whispered.

"No," Lucien answered, his voice as soft as hers. "Only a little difficult."

She leaned forward and rested her head on his chest, where she could feel the beat of his heart and the heat of his skin. After a moment she closed her eyes and took a deep breath.

Lucien stroked her hair. "Glover Manor is not good for you, love. While I'm gone, think about going home with Daisy and Nathaniel. Just . . . consider it, please."

"I'll think about it."

But she couldn't imagine leaving, not until she knew Tommy was all right. As she held her husband and considered his suggestion, as he asked, the scent of caramel drifted to her, and an invisible hand tugged on her skirt.

Eleven

Daisy sat on the settee and gripped her hands in her lap. She really and truly did not want to be in the same room with O'Hara, but she liked the idea of being alone in this house even less.

At the moment, O'Hara and Nathaniel were having a discussion about learning to channel abnormal energies so that the man ruled the power and not the other way around. Nathaniel listened intently, his blue eyes—so like Lucien's—wide and interested.

O'Hara was good with the boy, Daisy observed, as he was most likely good with all children. There was something about him that would appeal to a child, she imagined. His charm, his smile, his easy manner . . . the fact that he was no better than a large child himself . . .

As if he knew she thought about him, he turned his head and laid his eyes on her. Briefly.

That brief glance was enough to make Daisy's heart leap unpleasantly. Yes, she was quite sure she and O'Hara had shared a dream last night. She had not thought such a thing possible, but the way he had reacted to the words "red dress" in the kitchen gave him away.

In the dream she had taken that red dress off for O'Hara, and they had come together in a way more powerful than she had imagined intimate relations could be. She had been bold, demanding, downright forceful, in a way she could never be in real life. It took a brave woman to demand what she craved without reservation. That wasn't like her . . . was it?

When she remembered the dream, which seemed so real still, she quivered.

A segment of the shared dream eluded her, as if a mist formed over the memory. Why could she not remember what it was that danced just out of her reach, when the rest of her memory was much clearer than it should be?

One thing she did remember too well: the ghost who'd visited Daisy had informed her that O'Hara never slept with the same woman twice. Did the ghost speak the truth? For some reason, Daisy thought the answer was a resounding yes. Was this a perversion of some kind? O'Hara didn't seem at all aberrant to her, but she had to admit she did not know him nearly as well as she would like.

Again he turned to look at her, and she jumped from her seat. "I'm going to step onto the gallery for a breath of fresh air," Daisy said abruptly. She would be right outside the French doors, so she would be close to the others. Not really alone. If she saw or heard anything unusual, O'Hara and Nathaniel would be close by to assist her, should she scream for assistance.

O'Hara nodded silently, and Daisy walked to the French doors and opened them wide. It was a cool autumn day, just a touch of the coming winter in the air. She walked onto the gallery and closed her eyes as she took a deep breath of that crisp air. Another year gone. Soon she would be an old maid. No, at twenty-seven years of age, she was surely thought of in that way already. She only had to accept the truth for herself. There would be no children, no husband, no life beyond the little world she had constructed for herself. Her safe, insulated, lonely world.

"Hey, there," a soft voice called.

Daisy's eyes popped open to see not a ghost but Jim, the carriage driver who had delivered them to this place, walking toward her. She'd heard Lucien mention the stable boy more than once. Only Jim and Ruth had been brave or foolish enough to remain behind. Now there was only the stable boy.

Relieved to be confronted with a pleasant-looking young man instead of a haunting spirit, Daisy smiled. "Hello."

He touched a rough hand, the hand of a working man, to his chest. "I'm Jim Harrison. We met a couple of days ago. I work here at Glover Manor, mostly with the horses." He gave her a shy smile.

"I'm Daisy Willard," she said. "I don't believe we were properly introduced."

"No, ma'am," Jim said as he came to a halt there in the grass, a few feet away.

Jim was surely younger than she by a few years, and he was most certainly a good-looking fellow. His dark-brown hair was a little bit too long but wasn't nearly as long as Lucien's. His eyes were a hazel-green tipped in long lashes, and his full mouth smiled easily enough. Daily physical activity kept his long body trim and well muscled.

"Is everything all right?" Daisy asked.

"Yes, ma'am," he said. "I just saw you standing here and thought I'd come over and say hello. You look a little lost, standing out here by yourself."

Lost. That was true enough.

She had money and did not need a man to take care of her. Her father had left her comfortable, if not wealthy. But money wouldn't keep her warm at night; it wouldn't give her children or make her laugh or hold her when she cried. Maybe she'd been going about this the wrong way. Maybe what she needed to do was grab the first willing man who came along and just ask him to marry her. Done. Over. She'd made her life more complicated than it needed to be, waiting for some great love that did not exist.

O'Hara was definitely much too complicated for her. She didn't understand him at all.

One of these days, she'd find a simple man like Jim and make him her husband. That would end all her worries.

"I'm disturbed by Ruth's passing," she said.

Jim's small smile faded. "So am I. Ruth was a good woman. She got me this job after my folks passed away. Sometimes she even made me candy."

"Did she?"

Jim nodded, and for a moment, just a moment, he looked as if he were about to cry.

Daisy lifted her hand to indicate a pair of rocking chairs a few feet away. "Would you like to sit for a moment?"

"If you wouldn't mind keeping me company."

Jim was an easy man to be with, Daisy decided.

He couldn't see anything he shouldn't. He led a simple life and had simple worries.

"Tell me about her," Daisy said as she sat.

Jim spent several minutes singing Ruth's praises. He told Daisy about how she'd cared for him after he moved out to the plantation to work, how she'd doctored him once when he was sick, how she'd cooked for him and some of the others who used to work at the plantation before the ghosts scared them all away. All but him.

"The ghosts didn't scare you?" Daisy asked.

Jim shrugged his shoulders. "A little, I guess. Someone had to stay behind to take care of the animals, and besides, I don't come to the house much. I have my own little cabin near the stables."

"But you're here now."

Jim laid his unflinching eyes on her. No, this was not a man who knew fear. "I saw you standing out here all by yourself, like I said, and I wanted to make sure you were all right."

"How very sweet," Daisy said politely.

"Miss Willard," Jim continued, "you are the most beautiful woman I have ever seen. I didn't know a real woman could be as beautiful as you are. When I saw you at the train station, I felt like something reached inside me and grabbed my heart."

Daisy felt the heat of a blush rise to her cheeks.

"I shouldn't say such things," Jim continued. "I know that well enough. But I figure you won't be here much longer, so . . ." He shrugged his broad shoulders. "What have I got to lose by telling the truth?"

"That's . . . very sweet," Daisy said.

All this time, she'd been afraid of falling in love

and being hurt again. Maybe she'd been going about this all wrong. What she needed was a husband she *didn't* love. Someone who could never break her heart.

"Just the truth, ma'am."

"Call me Daisy. I can't be so very much older than you. How old are you, Jim?"

"Twenty-two."

A few years younger than she, but nothing out of the ordinary or terribly shocking.

O'Hara stepped onto the gallery from the French doors she'd left open. How much of the conversation had he heard? It didn't matter. He'd made it quite clear he had no time for her, except in his dreams.

"Daisy," he snapped. "Please come back inside. Lucien wishes to speak with you." As he spoke to her, he gave Jim a masculine and completely unnecessary glare.

"I'll be right in," Daisy said as she stood. Jim rose, too, politely and quickly. She faced the young man and gave him a smile. "I enjoyed our conversation, Jim. It took my mind off of unpleasant matters for a while."

"I'm glad I could be of help, ma'—Daisy."

She turned away from him and found herself face to face with an angry O'Hara. His eyes were hard, his fists clenched. Blast him, he had no right to be angry! He had no claim on her, on her time or her affections. He wouldn't even touch her . . . not that she wanted him to touch her.

Daisy spun back around and smiled at Jim. "Won't you join us for supper? I'll be cooking myself, so it won't be anything fancy, but we would love to have you." She glanced back. "Wouldn't we, O'Hara?"

"Of course," he said tightly.

Jim nodded. "Thank you. If it wouldn't be too much trouble . . ."

"Not at all."

"I'd be honored."

Daisy nodded once. She smiled sweetly. She didn't turn around until O'Hara said testily, "Lucien is waiting, Daisy, if you can tear yourself away."

She said good-bye to Jim and turned about gracefully to glare at O'Hara. She could thank him for one true gift; he had taught her that love was not for her and never would be. If she didn't give a man her heart, he couldn't break it.

Lucien stood back from the ground where the guest house had once stood. A few remnants of the house still remained, in a corner of a foundation and two crumbling fireplaces. The bricks from those chimneys had fallen here and there, making the path through the site rough and uncertain. The shape and sense of the cottage remained, but the fire had consumed the house and the people in it. He had dreaded coming here for days, but there was no way around it. The sisters and Tommy had died here, seventeen years ago.

O'Hara stood in the midst of the abandoned grounds. "I thought Daisy would be overjoyed at the news she's leaving in the morning," he said absently.

"She seemed rather put out," Lucien said

offhandedly. Daisy's moods were not his problem, thank goodness.

"I know," O'Hara grumbled. "If I didn't know better, I'd think she was smitten with that stable boy." He snorted. "Can you imagine Daisy with a dim-witted stable boy? It's ludicrous."

"Jim didn't strike me as . . ."

"Well, he isn't exactly a genius," O'Hara interrupted. "What does she see in him?"

"If you want to know what's in the girl's mind, all you have to do is touch her," Lucien said.

Again O'Hara grumbled. Then he said in a clear voice, "I can't do that. Should we get started?" Without waiting for a reply, he walked to the crumbling fireplace and very carefully laid a hand there. His eyes closed; his body jerked as if he were in pain, but he did not drop his hand.

Lucien took a step closer. As he dismissed O'Hara and Daisy and everything else that plagued him, he began to see and to hear.

This was where she'd done it. The twin who had resorted to murder—she'd killed those men here. Not five, not ten.

Fourteen.

Lucien felt a clutch in his heart. The ghosts of the twins were not here. Tommy was not here. The three of them resided quite comfortably at the big house these days. Many of the spirits of the murdered men were trapped here, though. Some of them didn't yet understand what had happened.

Lucien's mind was reeling with the sensations of those trapped here. How had she gotten away with murdering so many men? Why had no one noticed? As Lucien reached out to the ghosts of the victims, he began to understand. A peddler passing through town, a gambler, a circuit preacher, an old drunken soldier who'd lost his way, a thief, a man who'd gotten lost on his way to another town . . . men who would not be missed—and if they were, there was nothing to lead anyone here.

She had chosen her victims very carefully.

Not all the victims had become trapped spirits, but many had. One by one Lucien spoke to them. He called them by name when he could. He told them they were dead, then told them it was time to move on, and that he would do his best to find justice in their names. The woman who had murdered them was dead herself and beyond earthly justice, but the truth had to be made known. Some spirits went more easily than others, but they did go. Brightly, surely, and with relief, they moved on.

Lucien didn't pay O'Hara any mind as he worked. He was alone with the spirits, comforting them, touching them in his own unique way. But when his task was done, he looked about and saw that O'Hara had not moved. The psychic stood at the crumbling fireplace still, hand in place, face paper white.

"O'Hara?" Lucien picked his way across the uneven ground that was littered with bits and pieces of the twins' lives. No one had bothered to clear the land properly. Perhaps the spirits Lucien had just sent on had prevented such an activity. Broken glass crunched beneath his feet; the remnants of charred wood surrounded by wild weeds threatened to trip him as he approached O'Hara.

O'Hara didn't move until Lucien laid his hand on the man's shoulder. At the light touch, he jumped like he'd been shot. "This was a bad house," he whispered.

"Yes, I know."

O'Hara dropped his hand. "She was fine, some days, but there were other days when she walked the roadway searching for the men who raped her, with a knife in the pocket of her apron. Whenever a man stopped to help her, she made herself believe he was one of them. Inside she wanted to scream, but she didn't. She wanted revenge, so she pushed her fear deep." O'Hara shuddered, as if he felt that fear himself.

"She pretended to be lost," he said in a lowered voice, "and asked the men she found to help her find her way home. They did, and somewhere along the way she made it very clear what their reward for their kindness would be." The psychic laid a hand over his own face, as if he could hide from what he'd seen. "She took the men who'd tried to help her into her bed, and when she was finished with them, she . . . killed them."

"Why not just kill them before?" Lucien asked. "On the road, or in the woods between the cottage and the road. She took a great risk in bringing them here. Why?"

"She wanted her baby back," O'Hara said in a low voice. "The one she lost when she fell down the stairs. No—she didn't fall. Over the years she tried to convince herself that she'd fallen, but she knew the truth, deep inside. It wasn't an accident that took her baby. She purposely threw herself down those stairs, wanting not only to kill the baby but to die herself."

O'Hara glanced around the ruins as if he saw the

past. Lucien's eyes followed. He had seen the spirits that were trapped here. O'Hara had seen the past.

"Seeing her sister's child every day ate at her heart in a way she had not expected," he continued. "It hurt so much, she pretended Tommy was hers, but deep in her heart she knew he was not. With every kill she grew angrier and angrier, because she did not become pregnant again. She suspected losing the baby had damaged her in some way. And she was correct. She was unable to have another."

"How did she get away with it?" Lucien asked. "Surely she didn't have the strength to dispose of the bodies on her own."

"She had help."

"Ruth?"

O'Hara nodded. "And her sister. The three of them buried the victims together. Ruth tried to make them promise it wouldn't happen again. She didn't know which sister was the culprit, or if both were guilty."

"Did both sisters kill?"

O'Hara stood very still for a moment; then he shook his head. "No, just one."

"But the other sister covered for her twin."

"Yes."

Lucien walked around the cursed ground. He should not be surprised by what people were capable of, but sometimes the reality struck him hard. It was Eve's fault, he suspected. She made him see the good in people, especially women. Unfortunately, sometimes there was no good to be seen.

"Who set the fire?"

"I don't know." O'Hara nervously raked a hand through his hair. "I didn't see."

"The man who died here that night, was he the latest victim?"

"I don't think so."

"Then who was he?" Lucien asked.

"I don't know."

Lucien looked toward the house. The sisters could have seen their old home from here. They were reminded every day of what had happened to them there. "I need a name, O'Hara. Which sister killed?"

"I didn't see that, either. I can try again tomorrow, but there are no guarantees."

They walked away from the grounds and toward the big house, but neither of them walked very fast. Their work was draining. Exhausting. Some days Lucien felt like his calling sucked the very life out of him, a year here and a year there. He and O'Hara stopped along the way to sit on a fallen tree trunk and catch their breath.

O'Hara was more exhausted than Lucien, and Lucien felt a weakness in his knees and a shudder in his spine.

"Why do we do this?" O'Hara asked. "We can't make a home; the fees we collect don't exactly make us wealthy; the work is fatiguing and thankless and . . . hard. It's hard, Lucien."

O'Hara was not Lucien's favorite person, for many reasons, but in this one aspect they shared something very few would ever understand. "We have no choice. Have you ever tried your hand at a normal job?"

"Once." O'Hara shuddered. "All was well, for a

week or so, and then I started to have terrible dreams."

"Spirits calling you."

"Yes. Besides, I could still see inside people when I touched them. It's not as if I can shut the ability off at will. Not for long, anyway. The longer I try to put a damper on the ability, the more insistent it becomes."

Lucien nodded. "I have had the same dreams. Nathaniel will have those dreams if I do not prepare him for what is to come."

"He already does," O'Hara revealed gently.

Lucien stood abruptly, filled with the need to see his wife. His wife and his son, a son he didn't know, a child who needed him in the very way he did not want to be needed. Could he protect Nathaniel from what was to come?

"Wait," O'Hara said when Lucien took a step toward the house. "There's something else, and I can't possibly discuss it with the others around."

"What?" Lucien asked impatiently.

"I need to tell you about my dream," O'Hara began, but he did not get to the point quickly. He stammered and stuttered. Something about Daisy, Lucien could tell that much.

As he waited for O'Hara to get to the point, a deep voice whispered in his ear. "Run, Lucien. He wants her to die. *Run.*"

Daisy and Nathaniel were in the kitchen, preparing the evening meal. Stew, Daisy had informed Eve as she'd made her way down the stairs after packing most of her clothes in preparation for tomorrow's travel. Biscuits, too, the way Ruth had taught her to make them.

Eve tried to ignore the observation that Daisy had somehow changed. Her smile was not as bright; her movements were different, in a subtle way only a good friend might notice.

There was no time to ponder on Daisy's life at the moment. Her problems had something to do with O'Hara, Eve was certain.

Eve stared at the wardrobe in her room. Lucien wanted her to leave. Perhaps she should consider the idea. Like it or not, Lucien was correct when he said she was no longer rational where this house and the ghost of Tommy were concerned. Should she pack?

Deep in her heart, Eve was certain that if she left Glover Manor with Daisy and Nathaniel, she'd be deserting not only her husband but a child who needed her as he needed no other.

The scent of caramel preceded Tommy's arrival, as usual. She turned to find him sitting on her bed, cross-legged and somber-faced. "Don't leave me," he wailed. "Please, don't leave me, Mama."

His pleading broke her heart.

It was her husband who had the gift that had brought them here, but in this case Tommy came to her, not to Lucien. It was a more difficult transition for him, to appear to her and hide from Lucien, but something made it possible. Her craving for a child, perhaps. A need so deep she could not shake it.

"I'm not your mama," she whispered.

Tommy's lower lip trembled.

"You have a mother. We need to find her for you. We need to bring the two of you together."

"I want *you*," the child said softly. "I want a mama who will never leave me. A mama who will love me." His dark eyes grew wide. "You do love me, don't you?"

"Of course I do."

Tommy shook his head and leaped from the bed. He did not leap like a real child but flew up off the covers and headed for the door. "You don't love me! If you did you'd stay!" He went through the door, and the scent of caramels faded.

"No!" Eve chased the specter into the hallway, throwing open the door and holding her breath when she found the child—looking so real, she was sure that if she touched him she'd find him warm—standing just a few feet away, in the center of the long hallway. "Don't be upset. I only want what's best for you."

"You don't." Tommy pouted. "If you leave I won't have anyone to play with, not ever again. No one will hold me." He took a step back.

Eve followed the ghostly child. "It was wrong of me to try to take your mother's place," she said. "Even for a short while. Lucien can help you, if you'll let him."

The child sneered. "He wants to kill me."

"Tommy, sweetheart, you're already dead. You know that."

He turned and ran, crying, wailing, and Eve gave chase. She'd been too blunt, too uncaring. "Come back!" she shouted.

Tommy glanced over his shoulder. "You can't catch me, Mama. You can't."

Eve ran harder, faster, her eyes on the child who ran straight ahead.

She didn't know anything was wrong until her foot found air instead of solid ground. All at once the scene was clear. Reality bombarded her. Tommy floated above the stairs, arms outstretched. The long stairway that descended into the entry hall loomed before her. Someone shouted her name; Tommy smiled.

As she fell, she caught sight of something else. Lucien, vaulting onto the bottom of the stairway with his hair flying around his face and his arms outstretched, much as Tommy's were.

As Eve tumbled, she wondered . . . who would catch her?

Twelve

They met with a thud, there on the stairs. A running Lucien wrapped his arms around a tumbling Eve, and he sheltered her with those arms as she knocked him off his feet and they fell, together, down the stairs and into the entryway. The breath left him as they landed, but he didn't release her.

His heart pounded as he gently laid his unconscious wife on the cold floor. "Evie?"

She didn't move, not even with so much as a twitch of her eyelid. Lucien cupped her head in his hand and felt the sticky warmth of blood against his palm. There wasn't a lot of blood, thank goodness. The cut he found on the side of her head was small.

O'Hara arrived. Daisy and Nathaniel, called by Lucien's shout and the startling sound of the fall, were right behind him.

Lucien placed two fingers at Eve's throat, easily finding her pulse. Her heartbeat wasn't as strong as he would have liked, but it was regular.

"She's bleeding," Daisy whispered.

Once again Lucien touched the small cut on the side of Eve's head. Already a small bump had formed there. If he hadn't sheltered her for the last half of the fall, if she had landed in the entryway alone . . . He looked up at O'Hara.

"Tell me she's all right," he commanded.

O'Hara knelt beside Lucien and reached out very gently to take Eve's limp hand. He closed his eyes and held that hand for a minute that seemed like an hour.

"She's in between," O'Hara whispered.

That wasn't what he'd wanted to hear. "What do you mean, she's in between?" Lucien shouted.

"Between this world and the next," O'Hara explained. "She might wake up and she might not. I'm sorry, Lucien," he said in a softer voice. "But I won't to you and tell you she'll be fine when I don't know that to be true."

Lucien dismissed O'Hara and the others who watched, and touched Eve's face with gentle, blood-stained fingers. "Come on, love. Wake up."

"It's the boy," O'Hara said. "He tricked her into falling, disguised the stairs before her so she couldn't see."

"He's in her head?"

"I'm afraid so."

"Then he'll be doing his best to make sure she doesn't wake up."

Would Eve choose the child she had bonded with over him, if she truly had that choice? Would she fight for life in order to come back to him, or would she gladly walk into death and embrace the child?

"Mr. Thorpe?" Nathaniel said softly.

"What?" Lucien didn't mean for his voice to be impatient, but at the moment he didn't have the time or the patience for anything but his wife.

"I might be able to help."

Lucien took a deep, stilling breath. Nathaniel was his son, a part of the family. He would have to learn to find time and patience, no matter what the circumstances. "It's nice of you to offer, but I'm afraid there's nothing any of us can do."

"That's not true, sir."

Lucien turned his head to look at his once-obedient son. "What do you suggest?"

"First of all, you should take her to bed and make her comfortable." Nathaniel sounded almost grown up. Almost, but not quite. "Whatever you do, don't leave her alone."

As if he would.

"Talk to her," the child continued solemnly. "Even if she does not respond, she does hear you."

"That's true," O'Hara agreed.

Nathaniel took a deep breath as Lucien gently lifted Eve from the floor. "Before she died, my mother spent years working on a spell that would repel spirits."

"You're not giving Evie any damned potion Zella dreamed up!" Lucien insisted. Eve rested limply in his arms.

"Mother was trying to perfect the spell so that I might have time to myself. Time without the spirits. It's not ingested, sir, so it can't be called a true potion. The powder is scattered about the person for whom protection is intended, as an incantation is spoken."

Lucien stared at the boy. His son was a witch, as well as a medium. That would likely not make things easier in the years to come.

"You said she was working on this spell," Daisy said. "Does it work?"

Nathaniel looked at Daisy, wide-eyed and much too young for such a conversation. "On occasion."

Daisy nodded. "I'll help, if I can."

Lucien carried Eve up the stairs as Daisy and Nathaniel made their way to the kitchen. He kept expecting Eve to come to, to smile at him, to tell him everything was going to be all right.

But she didn't move at all, not even as he placed her on their bed and lay down beside her.

He rested the length of his body along hers. "Stay with me, Evie," he whispered. "I need you. I can't do this without you." He couldn't do *anything* without her. "Nathaniel needs you, too. And Daisy. All of us, we are not the same without you here."

She didn't move.

"You know I love you," he said softly. "No one, living or dead, needs you more than I do, can love you more than I do, will care for you as I do." His heart pounded too hard, and anger mingled with the fear. "If you die, Evie, if you dare, I will call you back from the dead. You will have no rest until the day I die, do you hear me?"

It was a curse, a promise, a vow. One he meant to keep.

Eve stood in a meadow, alone and at peace. There were no more worries about children or Lucien or Tommy. She was happy, in a simple way. Content.

Lucien shouted her name, much as he had as she'd been falling down the stairs. He sounded frantic. Eve turned her head and smiled at him. He was so far away . . . and still she heard him whisper in her ear, not at all agitated, *"I love you, Evie."*

She smiled, because she knew without doubt that those words were true.

"Mama!"

Tommy called as frantically as Lucien had, and from just as great a distance. Eve shaded her eyes and tried to make out Tommy's indistinct figure. A small hand waved her over, and she took a step in that direction. The deep voice in her ear whispered, *"Don't leave me. Don't make me live without you."*

Eve stopped. It was an important choice. Tommy or Lucien? They both needed her; they both loved her. And she loved them. Tommy shouted again. So did Lucien.

And Eve sat herself down in the meadow and lifted her face to the sun. Some decisions should not be rushed.

O'Hara knocked softly and entered even though there was no response. Lucien lay on the bed with Eve, his face turned to hers, his arm around her.

"No change," he said without turning to face O'Hara. "She should have come to by now."

"Yes, she should have."

O'Hara stepped to the opposite side of the bed and reached out to take Eve's hand again. He hadn't liked what he'd seen the first time. Indecision. A craving for something she feared she might never have. The certainty that without this something she would never be a complete wife to Lucien, or a complete woman for herself.

"She's holding her own," he said as he gently laid her hand back on the bed. "She loves you," he added.

"Enough?"

"What's enough?"

Lucien didn't answer but continued to hold his wife tenderly. Every now and then he whispered in her ear, words so soft that not even O'Hara, who stood so close, could hear them.

"The bleeding has stopped," O'Hara said as he studied Eve's head.

"I know," Lucien said absently.

The portrait in the corner caught O'Hara's eye, and he turned to study it. Watching a desperate Lucien and an unconscious Eve was just too painful to bear.

"This is them, I suppose."

"Yes. Eve found the portrait in the attic."

"The attic I have been warned to steer clear of."

"The very one."

The McBride twins looked perfectly harmless. Neither of them appeared to be a cold-blooded killer.

"One of them is here now," Lucien whispered. "The one in red. She finds this all very amusing, and damn it . . . I can't make her go away."

O'Hara nodded, but he had no answers for Lucien. "I never did finish telling you about my dream."

"It doesn't matter," Lucien grumbled.

"I think it does."

For a thirteen-year-old boy, Nathaniel knew his way around the kitchen quite well. He was quite comfortable with Ruth's collection of herbs and spices, at least, and he worked diligently as he gathered the ingredients for his spell.

A chill danced up Daisy's spine. A spell! Maybe when she chose her ordinary man for a loveless marriage, she would move to a place where no one knew her, and where she didn't have to be reminded that there were such things as ghosts and witches. Until a year ago, she'd been blissfully ignorant of such things.

"Are you sure this will work?" Daisy asked as she crept up behind Nathaniel.

"No, but it might."

"You've done this before."

Nathaniel nodded as he took a pinch of some greenish-yellowish herb and dropped it into the bowl where the rest of the ingredients lay dormant. "Mother tried to teach me, so I could make my own when I needed it. The problem is, the more often it's used on a particular person, the less effective it will be."

Daisy nodded, trying to act as if she understood.

"And sometimes it explodes," Nathaniel added as an afterthought.

Daisy took a step back. "So, your mother used this for you?"

"A few times. We tried to use it when things were really bad, when the ghosts came and came and wouldn't stop." He took a deep breath. "I can still use it, but the effects are not as strong as they were the first few times, and it doesn't last as long."

Nathaniel was so grown up for thirteen. It wasn't right.

With his unusual gifts, O'Hara had probably been forced to grow up quickly himself. It was difficult to be so very different from everyone else, to see and hear and know things others were blinded to. She pushed aside any sympathy she might feel for O'Hara. She needed to harden her heart, as he had hardened his.

"Stand back," Nathaniel whispered.

Daisy took another step of retreat, just as Nathaniel closed his eyes, muttered a word Daisy didn't understand, and tossed in a pinch of the final ingredient. He squeezed his eyes tight and wrinkled his nose as a loud pop and a puff of smoke came from the bowl.

When the smoke died down, Nathaniel opened one eye and peered into the bowl. After a brief inspection, he grinned. "It looks good, just as I remember."

"Will it work?"

"There's only one way to find out."

Even though it was a pleasant afternoon, she was tired of lying in the sun. Eve lifted her head slowly and studied her surroundings. Grass. Flowers. A clear blue sky. Lucien waited to her right, so far away she could barely see him. Tommy stood far away, too, to her left. They no longer shouted at her, but waited silently. Patiently.

Eve stood slowly and turned her head to the left. Tommy looked so small there, so lonely. She couldn't see his face, so why was she so certain that he cried?

She turned her head once again. Lucien was just as far away, not so small but just as lonely. He had Nathaniel, though, and all his friends. If she left

him, he would find and love someone else, someone who could give him the children he did not
want but should have around him.

Eve took a step toward Tommy and stopped. Tall
grass danced in the wind at her feet and around the
full skirt of her dress. A soft voice, a familiar voice,
whispered, *"I love you, Evie."*

Eve shouted at Tommy. "I'm sorry! I can't stay
with you! I don't belong here!"

He screamed and began to run toward her. In an
instinctive move, Eve turned her back on the ghost
and ran toward Lucien. Child or no child, she belonged with him. She was his wife. She loved him
with all her heart.

She ran hard, and after a moment he did, too.
Tommy's voice grew distant, less real, as Lucien
came closer. Eve smiled. Everything was going to be
all right. Not always easy, perhaps, not always pretty.
But they would be all right.

When she was close enough to see the stubble on
his face and the worry in his eyes, she threw herself
at Lucien and held on tight.

She woke so suddenly, Lucien was startled. Eve
took a deep breath and sat up fast. Too fast, judging by the way she laid a hand to her head and
groaned.

"I ache all over," she said as she dropped back to
her pillow.

Lucien placed a soft hand on Eve's face and
kissed her, not paying O'Hara any mind at all. "You
came back."

"I didn't go anywhere," she insisted with a gentle half smile.

"Do you remember what happened?"

Her smile faded; her eyes met his. "The stairs."

"He lured you to the stairs."

"I'm sure he didn't intend—"

"I don't think you're the first," Lucien interrupted.

The maid who had fallen down the stairs and still haunted this house—had she been tricked? Had there been others they didn't know about, spirits who had made the transition in spite of their violent deaths?

Eve didn't want to believe that Tommy would lure her to her death, any more than she wanted to believe that he could be responsible for previous deaths, but she did. "He's just confused."

"Yes, I know," Lucien said gently.

"But I don't belong with him. I belong with you."

He smiled. "Yes, you do."

The door opened slowly, and Daisy poked her head in. Lucien could not help but picture the young woman as O'Hara had described her from his dream. He'd withheld some details, Lucien knew, but the gist of the dream was clear enough.

Daisy would have killed O'Hara if the dream had continued to the end. They had to get her out of this house as soon as possible. Lucien turned his eyes to the darkening sky. Not tonight. It was too late.

"You're awake!" Daisy said with a wide and innocent smile.

Eve nodded. "My head aches, but I'm awake."

Nathaniel followed Daisy into the room and

closed the door behind him. In his hand he carried a small wooden bowl.

"Thank you, Nathaniel," Lucien said as he sat up. "But that won't be necessary."

"Unfortunately, it is," he said.

Stubborn child! "As you can see, Eve is fine."

Nathaniel stepped into the room. "The child wants her, and he knows you plan to send her away. He'll be back, tonight, to finish what he started."

"I'll be ready."

"He can hide from you."

"I know, but . . ."

"And he's killed before."

Eve did not raise her head from the pillow, but she turned her head to look at Nathaniel. "What is that you have there?"

"It's a spell," he said in a gentle voice. "One meant to keep the spirits away, for a time. I would be happy to make this room safe for you for the night. It will not keep them away forever, but for a while . . ." Nathaniel straightened his spine and lifted his chin. "I don't know you very well, Mrs. Thorpe, but you seem like a kind person. I just buried one mother. I have no desire to bury another so soon."

Lucien started to protest once again. He didn't want Eve surrounded by one of Zella's blasted potions! But before he could utter a word of protest, Eve laid a stilling hand on his arm. "I would be very happy if you'd do that for me, Nathaniel," she said.

"Come along." O'Hara herded Daisy back to the door, without touching her. "Let's leave the Thorpes to their business and see about making dinner."

"You're going to help me cook?" Daisy asked incredulously.

The door began to swing closed. "I'm starving," O'Hara replied.

Nathaniel approached the bed, and Eve smiled up at him. "Since we're family, I suppose you should call me something besides Mrs. Thorpe."

"What do you suggest?" Nathaniel asked formally.

"I'm not your mother, and I suppose you would feel uncomfortable calling me by that name. But Mrs. Thorpe is simply too stodgy. We'll think of something fitting, I'm sure."

Nathaniel leaned toward the bed and Eve. "If you don't mind, when it's just"—the boy's eyes flickered to Lucien and back to Eve—"just us, might I call you Evie?"

Eve smiled. "If you'd like."

"I hear him call you Evie sometimes, and I believe it suits you."

Him. No name at all. Lucien suspected he was still Mr. Thorpe. He couldn't be angry, not when Eve smiled this way. "Evie it is, then."

Nathaniel began the ritual, sprinkling some of the powder in each of the four corners of the room and before the window, muttering under his breath as he went about his business.

"Latin?" Eve whispered.

"Greek," Lucien replied as he watched his son closely. There was something graceful about the boy's movements, something much older than thirteen about his eyes and the set of his mouth.

His worst fears had come true, without warning. Could there be proper warning for such a situation? He now had a child he could not protect in his care. No matter what Lucien did to insulate and train his son, Nathaniel would always be haunted. He would always feel the pain of those long dead, answer their cry, try to help.

And sometimes he would not be able to help but would bear the pain of failure forever.

Forever.

When the ritual was finished, Nathaniel stood at the end of the bed. He laid those old eyes on Lucien. "Did it work?"

Lucien glanced around the room. All was quiet. Still. He was alone with his family. "Yes, it did."

Eve closed her eyes and sighed. "I will sleep without haunted dreams tonight, thanks to you, Nathaniel. Thank you so much."

Nathaniel smiled, more brightly than usual. "You're welcome, Evie." He turned and headed for the door. "There's some powder left. I think I'll see if Miss Willard would like me to put the spell on her room as well. She hasn't actually said so, but I don't think she likes ghosts very much."

When Nathaniel was gone, Lucien once again reclined beside his wife. "That's my son."

"Very much so," Eve answered softly. "He's so much like you. Are you scared?"

He didn't need to ask why she asked such a question. It hadn't been so long ago that he'd revealed his fears about bringing a child into the world. Until a few days ago he hadn't even known of Nathaniel's existence . . . and still he had an undeniable urge to protect his son at all costs.

"Terrified."

Eve snuggled against him. "I still want a child," she whispered.

Lucien threaded his fingers through her hair, being careful not to touch the bump on her head. "I know."

"But you were right when you said we can't always make plans. That would take all the fun out of life."

"We certainly didn't plan for Nathaniel."

Could he take his own advice and jump in with both feet? "He calls me Mr. Thorpe."

"Well, you can be intimidating, darling."

"He can't call you Evie and me Mr. Thorpe. It's not right."

"Give him a little time."

Lucien nodded and glanced around the room. It remained quiet and free of spirits. He couldn't remember the last time he'd felt such a sense of peace. Evie was alive and in his arms, he had a son, and the ghosts who haunted him were absent . . . for tonight.

Thirteen

O'Hara was not a happy man. He'd suggested that in light of the circumstances Daisy should withdraw her dinner invitation to the stable boy. She'd refused, saying to rescind the invitation at such a late hour would be rude. Rude!

Nathaniel had taken a tray of stew, biscuits, and untainted tea to Lucien and Eve. Neither of them would be leaving their room tonight.

The dining room table was set for four, as if they were hosting a dinner party. The food they had prepared wasn't fancy, but Daisy took great care to see that the meal was presented in a fine, elegant fashion. There were even freshly picked autumn flowers on the table.

Jim arrived right on time. O'Hara added *punctual* to his list of the young man's faults. Determined to prove the stable boy a liar and a conniving sneak, O'Hara offered his hand to Jim almost immediately.

"Nice to see you under happier circumstances," O'Hara said with a smile. Even though Ruth had been buried just that afternoon, it seemed that unhappy event had taken place days ago. So much had happened since then.

Their dinner guest offered his hand at the greeting, and O'Hara took it. In an instant, he knew the man well. Jim was open, easy. There was no attempt to hide or disguise who and what he was. The stable boy who was so taken with Daisy was a simple man, raised on a small farm and happy with his simple life. He wanted nothing more than a little piece of land to call his own, a wife, and a few kids. And while he admired Daisy for her beauty and her charm, he did not think for a moment that such an incredible woman could ever be his.

O'Hara sensed no jealousy in Jim, no artifice, no hate, no schemes of any kind. As if he had been burned, he dropped the hand he had so eagerly taken. Damn it, Daisy would be much better off with a man like Jim than she would ever be with him.

Dinner proceeded smoothly, in spite of O'Hara's worsening mood. He didn't have to touch Daisy to know she was trying to make him jealous. She directed all her smiles and most of her conversation to their guest. Jim was flattered to be the object of Daisy's attentions, as any man would be.

Nathaniel remained silent throughout the meal, and he did not eat as well as a thirteen-year-old boy should. Daisy noticed it, too. She laid her eyes on the child often, and when she did so, her smile dimmed slightly. Not so much that anyone would notice . . . but O'Hara noticed.

When there was a lull in the conversation, she asked, "Nathaniel, do you feel well?"

"Not particularly, ma'am."

"What's wrong?" O'Hara asked.

Nathaniel kept his eyes on his plate. "They're mad at me," he whispered.

"Lucien and Eve?" Daisy asked incredulously.

"The ghosts," O'Hara said.

Nathaniel nodded and glanced up at O'Hara with wary eyes. "They're mad because I protected the room. Tommy is mad most of all," he said in a quick voice, "but one of the women, she's mad, too, because my . . . because Mr. Thorpe is protected."

"Remember what we told you," O'Hara said. "Close the doors. Shut the spirits out."

"I'm trying," he whispered.

"We should get Lucien," Daisy said, obviously concerned.

"No!" Nathaniel's head shot up. "Leave them be for tonight. I'll be fine, and . . . they need a few quiet hours, some time without the spirits coming at them."

"Can't you try the powder for yourself?" Daisy asked.

Nathaniel shook his head. "No, ma'am. I've used it too often in the past. It no longer works well for me. It will keep the ghosts out of your room tonight, though. I promise you that."

Jim contributed nothing to the conversation except for a suddenly pale face and a fascination for his biscuit.

O'Hara was impressed with Nathaniel, more than he'd expected he could be with a child so young. The kid was determined to protect those he could, at any price, even if it meant suffering himself. He was his father's son, apparently.

In all his life, O'Hara had never thought himself a noble man. Never. He did not sacrifice for others. He did what he did because he had no choice, not because he felt this to be the most efficient and benevolent use of his talents.

No, he was not noble. But the best thing he could do for Daisy Willard would be to walk away. He had never much cared for what was best for anyone but himself, but in this instance . . . what choice did he have?

None. None at all. "Daisy," he said calmly as he rose to his feet, "why don't you serve Jim dessert in the parlor. Nathaniel and I are going to head off for bed."

She stood. "So soon?"

"Nathaniel needs to get to sleep. I'll watch over him until he dozes off." He looked down at the somber kid. "You did say they don't come in your dreams, right?"

The kid nodded. "Once I get to sleep, I'll be fine for the night."

O'Hara smiled at Jim, and it hurt like hell. This was the kind of man Daisy deserved. Good. Uncomplicated. And he would adore her if she gave him half a chance. "I'm glad you could join us for dinner."

Jim stood. "It was nice of you all to ask me. I've never eaten in the big house before. Not in the dining room, anyway. Ruth, she used to let me eat in the kitchen now and then."

The mention of the woman they had buried that day put a damper on the already melancholy mood.

"Come along." O'Hara motioned for Nathaniel to stand. After taking a moment to close a few doors of his own, he placed his arm around the kid's shoulder. "Let's get you to bed."

He turned his back on Daisy as she very softly said, "Good night."

Jim spoke of ordinary things as they sat in the parlor and sipped ordinary tea. Daisy had taken special care to see that the tea was untainted tonight.

The man who sat in a chair facing the settee where Daisy perched talked about the weather, his family—all gone now but beloved still—his favorite horses, and his fond memories of Ruth. Daisy tried to pay attention, but her mind wandered on occasion. It wandered to last night's dream, the way O'Hara had stared at her over dinner, and to the doorway where he might appear at any moment.

Daisy knew it was best that she leave Glover Manor in the morning, as Lucien and O'Hara had suggested. She did not have Eve's dedication, or Lucien's fearlessness, or O'Hara's curiosity. Yes, that was best, for so many reasons.

A part of her insisted that she should not have come here at all, but another part was glad. She knew now that there was no chance for her and O'Hara. Had there ever been? If the spirit who had come to her in her dreams was correct, O'Hara was a dreadful scoundrel, a man who never lay with the same woman more than once. Did women bore him? Did she?

She should not think of dreams! Her heart leaped in her chest. Last night's dream had seemed so real; O'Hara had seemed so solid and warm, and . . . and just because they had experienced a similar dream, that didn't mean there was anything real about the encounter.

She had not climbed atop him and taken him inside her body; he had not touched her without fear. The dream had ended abruptly, while he was still inside her, and she had awakened feeling . . . empty.

In any case, best to get out of here and take the next step in her life, whether that be embracing spinsterhood or settling for a man who would not make her feel this way, as if she were being shredded inside.

Eventually, she quit watching the doorway and tried to give Jim her full attention. O'Hara wasn't coming back, not tonight. He had been so cordial to Jim tonight, had wished them well as he'd left the dining room with Nathaniel, as if he were handing her over to another man, as if he were saying, *Take her, she no longer interests me.*

Ghosts were probably present, but she didn't see them. She did not see them the way Lucien and Nathaniel did, the way O'Hara sometimes did. The one she had seen since coming here always came when she was alone in bed, in the middle of the night, when there was no light to illuminate reality, and no other person present to share her horror with.

She suspected Jim had never seen a ghost and never would.

When he glanced around the room, she began to wonder if he did see something, after all.

"I've heard so many stories about this house," he said in a deep, masculine voice that was tinged with wonder. "They say it's haunted. I didn't believe that for a long time, but I guess it could be true, given what I heard tonight."

"I'm surprised you didn't bolt from the table," she said with a forced smile as she remembered what Nathaniel and O'Hara had said over supper.

Jim looked right at her, with clear eyes and a face so honest, she imagined he shared Lucien's distaste for lies of any kind. "Normally I would have run," he said. "I have no desire to go up against a haint."

"And yet, here you are."

He hesitated before saying, "I might never again have occasion to sit down and talk to a woman as beautiful and kind as you. You're leaving in the morning. I'd be a fool to miss this rare opportunity on the chance there might be ghosts about."

Men had told her she was beautiful before, but never in such a heartfelt way. The woman Jim married would be very lucky indeed. It would not be her, though. Like it or not, she was in love with another man. A man who didn't want her. A man who would never love her.

"You're a lovely man, Jim," Daisy said as she rose to her feet. "I have very much enjoyed the evening." It was a polite but clear dismissal.

Jim stood slowly. "I'll see you in the morning, then. Mr. Thorpe, he said I was to drive you and the boy to town. Shortly after dawn, he said, so you can catch the noon train."

"I'll see you then."

Jim nodded his head politely. If she offered her hand, he would surely kiss it, but Daisy kept her hands at her sides, untouched.

"I hope it doesn't rain too hard tonight," he said casually.

"Is it going to rain?"

He opened the French doors, allowing the night breeze to circulate in the room. "Can't you smell it?" he asked.

Jim turned to look at her, and she shook her head slightly. After a polite "Good night," he left by way of the French doors, rather than walking through the entryway and to the front of the house to make his exit.

For a moment Daisy stood in place, watching the doors Jim had closed behind him.

"He's a fine young man."

Daisy spun to find O'Hara lounging in the doorway, easy as you please, as if he had been standing there all night. "What are you doing here?"

O'Hara stepped into the room. "Nathaniel is asleep. It's too early for me yet."

"Are you sure Nathaniel won't . . . dream?" She felt the blush rise to her cheeks.

O'Hara ignored her reaction. "Apparently since he and Lucien see the ghosts so clearly in their waking hours, they are spared in their sleep. It's as much a gift as their ability to see, I imagine. Otherwise, how would they survive with their sanity intact?"

She nodded.

"I imagine you'll be glad to get out of here in the morning," O'Hara said casually.

Daisy began to nod again, but in order not to look like a simpleton with a bobbing head, she said, "I will."

An awkwardness hung in the air between them. There was so much to be said. So much they couldn't say. For a moment, just a moment, Daisy wished she could be as bold as she'd been in last night's dream.

"It's not an easy life," O'Hara said abruptly. "Traveling from haunted place to haunted place, feeling the trouble of others, solving the problems of the dead when your own problems are impossible to solve."

Was he talking about Lucien, or trying to explain to her why they had no chance?

"You could find another job, I imagine," Daisy said gently. "If the life you lead does not agree with you, that is."

"No," he said quickly. "I could not. It's not that easy." He walked past her, leaving the space between her and the door clear for her departure. "I've tried, Daisy, I truly have. Lucien has tried, too. We all have. You can't turn your back on a calling. You can't dismiss the distress of people who cry out for help, not even if they've been dead a hundred years."

"I understand that, but does it mean that you can't have a life of your own?" After all, Lucien and Eve were trying to make it work for them. Daisy ignored the fact that they had serious problems of their own.

O'Hara turned to look at her. "I know what you want," he said in a lowered voice.

"You have no idea . . ."

"You want a home, babies, a husband who's home every night. You want safety and security and . . . and flowers." His brow furrowed at this last.

"Doesn't every woman want those things?"

"I don't know," he said angrily. "I only know what *you* want."

She took a step back. "You haven't touched me. . . ."

"Apparently I don't have to," he interrupted. "I feel you everywhere. In everything I touch. In your letters, in a plate you held, in a chair you sat upon, in the very air you breathe."

"I didn't know your abilities were so sensitive."

"They're not," he said sharply.

Like it or not, she was in love with O'Hara, and he wanted nothing to do with her. A niggling bit of doubt made Daisy's head swim. If he didn't love her, why was there so much pain in his eyes?

She took a single step toward him. If she could be bold in a dream, why couldn't she be bold in real life? "Do I want too much?"

"Yes."

"Does that scare you?"

"Absolutely."

She had no paranormal abilities; she was an ordinary woman with ordinary hopes and dreams. And still, she saw so much of this man. She saw, in an instant, what he was afraid of. "So it's better to run than to risk failure."

"Not failure," he said in a lowered voice. "Disaster. Catastrophe. Damn it, Daisy, you don't even like the way I dress, and still . . ." He caught himself before saying anything more.

"And still . . ." she prompted, taking another step toward him.

O'Hara didn't move. He could run or simply take a single step back. That would be message enough, that one step he did not take. "And still, you see me all wrong."

"Wrong?"

"I'm not a gentleman, Daisy, I'm no white knight."

"I never said you were."

"No, but in your dreams . . ." He stopped, perhaps deciding it best not to mention dreams at all. "In your plans for the future, you see me as a man without faults, as the perfect husband and the perfect father, and Daisy, I am so far removed from perfect that I would disappoint you before a year was out."

Daisy moved toward O'Hara another step, holding her breath as she reached for the part of herself she had found last night. She could be daring if she chose. She could take what she wanted without hesitation, without constant worry.

"Is that why you didn't come back to Plummerville?" she asked. "Because you were afraid of disappointing me?"

"In part," he admitted.

"And the other part?" She had to know, before she turned her back on him one last time . . . or continued moving forward.

His hands balled into tight fists. "I can't live the rest of my life with a woman I feel so deeply there's no rest from it," he said gruffly. "I can't shut you out, no matter how hard I try. I touch a letter you penned, and all the hopes and fears rush through me. I lay my hand on a table your fingers brushed against, and I *taste* you. I press my palm to the wall, knowing you sleep on the other side, and I feel every desire, every doubt." He shook his head. "I can't live that way. It's impossible."

Knowing why he'd turned his back on her shattered what little bit of hope she had left. "I'm sorry."

"It's not your fault." He lifted his hand but did

not touch her. As if he had surprised himself by reaching for her, he dropped the hand abruptly.

"I guess I shouldn't write you again after I return to Plummerville."

"Probably not."

"It was never my intention to hurt you."

"I know that."

But she couldn't just walk away and leave it like this. There was so much unsaid and undone. "If you know me so well, then you know what I want most of all."

He nodded.

"Is what I want impossible?"

He thought about her question for a moment, then shook his head.

Daisy tilted her head back and leaned in a bit closer. She held her breath in anticipation. She had waited so long for this. O'Hara's hands drifted away from his body and up as he tilted in and down to meet her, so that there was no chance he might accidentally touch her with those powerful hands.

Daisy's eyes drifted closed moments before their lips touched. She had wanted this kiss for such a long time that her eyes stung with unshed tears as O'Hara kissed her. Only their mouths touched, mouths that moved gently against each other, that tasted and teased.

The kiss stirred her, deep and certain. It was everything she had imagined, and more. Mouth to mouth, breath to breath, the kiss was intimate, unlike anything she had ever experienced before. And she knew, as her lips teased and tasted him, that she wanted so much more than a kiss.

How could O'Hara walk away from this? Daisy's

lips danced over his; she was entranced by the taste and feel of him, by the way his very touch excited and warmed her. Her entire body reacted to the kiss, and with every second that passed, she wanted more. The kiss deepened, and still only their mouths touched.

It was O'Hara who ended the kiss, backing away and taking a long breath as if the contact had surprised and affected him as much as it had her.

Daisy opened her eyes. She should run, she supposed, but there was no true escape from O'Hara. He was already so deeply embedded inside her, there was no shaking him loose. The woman she had become would run from these feelings. The woman she wanted to be would stand her ground and fight for what she most desired.

"It isn't fair that you see everything in my heart and I see nothing of yours."

"Perhaps there's nothing to see."

"I don't believe that," she whispered. If she turned her back on O'Hara now, it was over. He wouldn't run to her, not ever. He wouldn't seek out another kiss, or more. She would have to be the one to push him, to make him understand.

"You know that I love you," she said. "You know that if you asked me to be your wife I would gladly say yes." She nervously licked the lips he had just kissed. "And you know that if you asked me to lie with you, tonight or any other night, I . . ."

"Stop," he commanded. "I can't marry you, and I won't treat you the way that . . . that other man did."

"Is that what stops you from loving me?" she asked. One of the tears escaped and dripped down her cheek. "Knowing that I was fool enough to give myself to another man when he promised to marry me?"

"No!" O'Hara reached out as if to wipe her tear away, but stopped well short of touching her face. "You were a child, and in love. He is to blame, not you. I would never blame you."

Daisy wiped away her own tear.

"I never said I didn't . . . care for you," O'Hara said, his voice low as he made the confession.

O'Hara had been so careful not to lay his hands on her. There was no reason why she could not touch him. Daisy lifted one hand and laid it on his chest. "You've seen my heart, now tell me what's in yours."

He hesitated, looked deep into her eyes. "Sorrow, lust, anger . . ."

"Anger?"

"Anger that I'm not the man I should be."

O'Hara continued to hold his hands to the side, away from his body. He worked very hard to control those hands, to keep them away from her.

For her sake or for his own?

"You're nothing like that man from my past. You've never made false promises, you've never pretended to be someone you're not in order to take something that wasn't yours to claim."

"It doesn't matter if I tell you pretty lies or the ugly truth, the fact remains that I can't marry you. I can't be a part of your life. One night would only . . . it wouldn't change anything."

"I know that," Daisy whispered.

"And I won't take the chance. . . ."

Daisy grasped O'Hara's hand so quickly, he was

taken by surprise. When she guided that hand to her body, the fingers twitched and curled.

"Touch me here," Daisy whispered. She placed his palm against her belly, low, where she throbbed and ached. Could he feel her desire? Of course he could. "You see so much of me. Everything, you say." She held his hand in place and lifted her head to look him in the eye. "If we lie together tonight, will we make a child?"

His hand relaxed. He licked his lips and swallowed hard. "No."

"Then nothing can stop us. Nothing but you."

He narrowed one eye suspiciously. "Daisy, are you . . . alone?"

She blinked quickly. "Alone? No, I'm with you."

"Are there ghosts about that I don't see?"

She smiled, understanding the question at last. "You think this boldness unlike me."

"Yes."

"Then perhaps you do not know *everything* about me, after all."

She rose up on her toes and kissed him, and she did not release his hand. It remained pressed to her belly as they kissed. "If you can truly feel me, as you claim, then you know how much I want you," she whispered, her mouth close to his. "Surely with your hand there where I tremble, you can feel my passion for you, my emptiness. And you also know that I will leave you behind, if that is what you truly desire, and you will never be bothered by me again." She kissed him once more, more deeply this time but just as briefly. "No more letters, if they disturb you, no more surprises when you arrive at a haunted house thinking you'll only have the dead to battle with."

"Daisy . . ."

"I have a bedroom above stairs that is free of ghosts for this one night. You're welcome to share it with me, if you dare."

He threaded his fingers through hers and led her toward the doorway. "I'm going to regret this," he mumbled.

Daisy practically had to run to keep up with O'Hara's long, impatient strides. "I'm not," she whispered.

Fourteen

O'Hara guided Daisy into her bedroom and quietly closed the door behind her. A touch of moonlight kept them from complete darkness.

He didn't need a brighter light to illuminate this moment. Touching Daisy's hand, he could see her yearning and her love . . . and even her determination to walk out of his life when this night was over, because she didn't want to hurt him.

He couldn't believe that he was here in Daisy's room, her hand in his and her bed waiting just a few feet away. But he was here, and it was no mistake. He didn't need to ask Daisy if she was sure. She was.

She dropped his hand and took a step back. "I don't want to hurt you. Maybe we should try this without you using your hands too much."

He grinned as she began to unbutton her gown. She was worried about hurting *him*. Had anyone ever worried about that before? No. Only Daisy.

"I don't think so."

"If laying your hands on me causes you distress, then we shall be very careful about how often, and . . . and where you touch me," she said as she continued to undress herself.

"What I experience is not distress," he told her as

he gently took her wrists and moved her hands aside so he could have the pleasure of undressing her himself. "It's an assault of sensations."

At the moment, those sensations were delicious, not at all disturbing. In the dark, he managed to find all the buttons and ties and hooks and eyes on Daisy's gown. He found most of them himself, but once or twice she had to guide his hands to the correct fastening. He could not block her, but he could concentrate on her passion and her love, and do his best to bury the bittersweet knowledge that this would be their only night together.

Daisy wanted him to think that she was as detached as any man might be about a casual encounter. That she could enjoy this one night and then walk away with no regrets. She would walk away . . . but there would be regrets. She was not a cold woman who could approach a night like this one with indifference.

But she wanted it, and so did he.

When Daisy's voluminous gown and her finely crafted underthings had been removed, he ran his hands long her bare body, from neck to breasts to thighs. As he studied her silky flesh with his hands, it struck him that it was a shame to cover such a body with bows and frills and so much fabric when, in this form, natural and without any artifice at all, she was so absolutely perfect.

It was more than the feel of her in his hands and the vision she presented by moonlight that affected him so deeply. Daisy quivered at his touch, and deep inside she clenched and unclenched. She needed him. She was empty without him. And she did love him.

Daisy undressed him, as he had her, fumbling in the dark. She had never undressed a man before. Each button, each tie . . . it was all new to her. But he did not help her. She wanted to do this on her own; she found a pleasure in the simple task, and he would not hurry the chore along because he could not wait to press his naked body to hers.

When he was as naked as she, Daisy began to tremble. But she did not stop, she did not back away. She caressed and studied him, as he had done to her. O'Hara let his hands fall from her body. Palms upward, he held those hands to the side so he could experience the sensation of her hands on him without interference of any kind. Her hands were gentle, curious, and loving.

He wanted so much to be able to touch Daisy the same way, to feel skin without being assaulted by her thoughts and her past and her emotions. It was such a simple desire, and yet it was impossible. That would never, ever happen. He could not touch Daisy without seeing more than he should. More than any man should.

As if testing him, she crushed her body along the length of his. His erection pressed into her soft belly, his hard chest met the sweet softness of her breasts. With his hands to the side, he should not be able to sense anything of Daisy but the physical, and yet . . . he breathed her in, he felt her heartbeat, he felt the quiver of her body against his.

"Can we lie down now?" she whispered.

O'Hara tossed back the covers on her bed, and she scooted to the center of the big mattress. Moonlight touched Daisy, and for the first time he saw her very clearly. He quickly searched for the birthmark he remembered from the dream. It should be there on her side . . . he knew exactly where. But there wasn't enough light for him to see the pale mark, if it did exist at all.

Sitting on the bed, naked and anxious but unafraid, Daisy removed the pins from her fair hair and let the thick strands down. Golden waves, wild and soft, fell, one thick strand at a time. As she let her hair down, she tossed her hairpins toward the bedside table. Some found their mark; others fell to the floor.

She was exquisitely beautiful, an angel, *his* angel.

Hair loosened, she lay back so that her head rested on a pillow, and O'Hara joined her on the bed. Touching the bed Daisy slept in gave him a jolt, but he tried not to let his response show. It was startling to be so close to another person, to know another so deeply. Daisy had dreamed here, slept here, worried here.

But she was not worried now.

He tried not to touch Daisy with his hands, reclining beside her with his mouth searching for hers and quickly finding the kiss he craved. He didn't dare to lay his hands on her, but she freely touched him. Gently, as they kissed and savored the sensation of flesh to flesh. More boldly, as the kiss drove them both toward the pleasure they craved.

One night, that was all he had, and it would not be a short one. He wanted to taste Daisy, make her moan, give her a night she would never forget.

He moved his head lower, kissing her throat, her chest, and finally taking a nipple into his mouth. She inhaled sharply, and as he suckled, she moaned deep in her throat. He wanted to bury himself in her now, hard and fast, but she deserved more. She deserved ecstasy, and he was going to give it to her.

She shuddered along the length of her body, and O'Hara returned his mouth to hers. He kissed her deeply while he parted her thighs with his hands, while he touched her intimately, stroked her and felt her grow wet and ready for him.

Yes, she would leave in the morning, but she wouldn't stop loving him. She wouldn't write any more letters; she wouldn't tag along with Lucien and Eve on these expeditions in order to see him; she wouldn't cry about what they could never have. She might even, one day, marry a man who would care for her.

But she would never love anyone but him. She would carry the memory of this night to her grave, a treasured secret.

The night was dark and velvet, a riot of sensations soft and heady. O'Hara felt as if he'd drunk too much wine, as if Daisy had gone to his head. She felt the same way, he knew that, too. He listened to every breath she took, every soft moan, every gasp of surprise when she found another small pleasure.

Her legs spread, and his fingers stroked her intimately. Easy, then harder. She rocked against him, each small move instinctive. In moments everything within Daisy faded but her need for him. This was a physical need he could satisfy, unlike the wishes of a woman's heart, which he could not.

O'Hara rolled atop Daisy, guided himself to her, and thrust to fill her. Her body adjusted to his gradually, making way for him, opening and inviting. Daisy arched her back, wrapped her legs around his, and pulled him closer, deeper. He felt her shatter. Her release came the moment he was buried fully inside her, and it came on waves as she whispered his name and clung to him.

Holding himself inside her, he leaned down and kissed Daisy as she tried to breathe deeply. Hot and tight around him, she continued to quiver, but he did not allow himself the release he wanted and needed. Not yet. This was too fine a moment to rush.

He wanted to know what she felt at this moment, if she was as satisfied as the expression on her face told him she was. With one finger he traced her jaw.

And felt only warm, smooth skin.

It was surely an aberration. He placed his palm against the side of her breast and felt the give of her tender flesh. Nothing more.

"Daisy," he whispered as he moved inside her, slowly out, slowly in again. "I can't . . . I can't see you."

She smiled. "You don't need to see me. Can you feel me?"

"I feel your body but not your mind or your heart."

She did not seem at all surprised as her hips thrust up to meet his gentle movements. "Feel my body, then, and I will tell you what's in my mind and my heart."

He rocked above and into her. One hand held his weight from her, but the other caressed her skin. Face, neck, breast, hip. He could not get enough of that touch. Flesh, warm and silky, gave beneath his fingers, but there were no jolting images in his mind.

"I love you," Daisy whispered as they danced slowly and surely. A sway, a thrust, a coming together of his body and hers. "And I did not expect it, but I want

you still. Again, that is. I want you again." She smiled
and lifted her hips. Her hands rested on his hips, and
her fingers fluttered. "I feel like I'm falling, falling
but flying. Shaking and tingling."

"Flying," he whispered.

"Flying." There was wonder in her voice. "I have
no control over my body. It's yours. All yours. And
I'm . . ." She inhaled sharply as he drove deeper
than before. "Oh, I can't talk anymore. Don't ask
me to tell you how I feel, just . . . just love me."

He did, fast and hard, frantic with the need to
feel Daisy tremble beneath and around him again,
to feel her climax with a power that left her breathless. She did just that, shaking and moaning while
she cleaved to him. His own release came while she
shuddered around him, and he held her close
while he joined her.

He held her, and all he felt was pleasure and
warmth and love.

Sated and breathless, he continued to cling to
her. His fingers stroked, his hands explored. Their
bodies were joined still, and he could touch her
without his gift assaulting him with images and
words.

"I can touch you," he whispered.

"All night, if you'd like," Daisy murmured quietly.

"No, you don't understand." He lifted his head
and smiled down at her while one hand cupped a
full, warm breast. "I feel your skin, your heat, a
tremble so faint it is barely perceptible, but I do not
see inside you. Isn't that remarkable?"

"Perhaps. Perhaps not." She lifted her hand and
touched his face. "At this moment, we are one. Do

you sense your own emotions when you lay one hand in the other?"

"No."

"Are you assaulted by memories of your own past when you touch your clothes or your bed?"

"No."

"I am a part of you," she whispered.

He had bedded women before, and while the release was necessary, he had never lost his gift in another woman's body. Which meant that like it or not, this joining went beyond the physical. He and Daisy were one to their very souls.

"I don't want to leave you."

She hooked a leg around his. "Then don't," she said softly.

"I want to stay inside you all night."

He saw her hint of a smile in the moonlight, and it tugged at his heart. "Then do."

They lay there, still and not so still, kissing and touching with less haste than before.

As he caressed Daisy's breast once again, she said, "I did not know it was possible to enjoy such pleasure twice in one night. I was overcome with the throes of passion two times, in case you didn't notice."

He grinned down at her. How could she be so passionate and yet so innocent? "I could tell."

"Could you?"

"Yes, dear Daisy."

She smiled. "Dear Daisy. That's very sweet. Perhaps I should call you my darling Quigley."

"Please don't. You'll ruin the mood."

Her smile faded. Was she worried about tomorrow? He didn't know.

Daisy's hands roamed, they explored and ca-

ressed and aroused. Impossibly, he began to grow
hard again. Daisy rocked her hips and moved
against him with a gentle undulation. "If twice is
possible, then three times would be . . ."

O'Hara leaned down and suckled at her breast,
drawing a nipple deep into his mouth.

"A given," Daisy finished in a whisper.

Eve lay back and listened to the rain come, as Lucien slept deeply beside her. She ached all over
from the fall, and both she and her husband
sported nasty bruises. Her head hurt a little, but
not so much that it had kept her from sleep.

But now she was wide awake. She wanted to talk
to Lucien, but he was sleeping so soundly she
didn't have the heart to wake him.

She might have died, falling down those stairs.
Her life could have ended in an instant, and all because she had become obsessed with a child. She
couldn't blame this incident entirely on Tommy;
her obsession had begun long before she'd arrived
at Glover Manor.

If Lucien hadn't caught her . . . she didn't want to
think about what might have happened. She wasn't
ready to leave Lucien, and she never would be.

Nothing else mattered. Not the ghost of a child
who was not hers, not babies that might or might
not ever be. She had been captivated with a child of
the past and children of the future . . . when all that
really mattered was *now*.

And how often would she and her husband have
a night truly and entirely to themselves? No ghosts.
No spirits. Just the two of them.

She rolled onto her side and whispered into Lucien's ear, "Are you awake?"

He rolled toward her. "No," he mumbled.

"That's too bad. I'm cold. I was rather hoping you'd keep me warm."

Lucien opened one eye. He was sleeping naked, as usual, and all Eve had to do was shimmy out of her linen nightgown and toss it over the side of the bed—which she did.

"A chilly woman taking *off* her clothes," Lucien said in a deep, sleepy voice.

"You know what that means," Eve said as she wrapped her arms around Lucien's neck and slipped one leg through his. It felt so good to hold him. She couldn't believe she'd been avoiding him for two weeks.

"Yes, I do."

Eve laid her mouth on Lucien's neck, kissed him once, twice, then flickered her tongue against his throat. He was instantly hard, his erection pressing into her flesh.

She had never doubted that Lucien wanted and loved her. Had he doubted her? She didn't want her husband to doubt her love for him, not now, not ever.

His hands caressed her gently and in the easy way that only a man who knew her well could. Lucien knew where to touch her, how hard, how soft . . . in just the right way to make her want him so much she could no longer think clearly. That was all right. She'd been thinking too much lately.

"I've missed this," she whispered.

"So have I."

"No matter what happens, we belong together. I know that, if I know nothing else."

Lucien rolled her onto her back, parted her legs with his knee, and nudged against her waiting flesh. She closed her eyes as he entered her in one long thrust.

They fit together the way a man and wife should, as if they had been made for each other. No, not *as if*. They had been made for one another; Eve knew that. She had known that from the moment she'd first seen Lucien Thorpe. She was his, in more ways than she had known were possible. It had taken them so long to get here, to find their own happily-ever-after.

Lucien loved her hard, fast, their bodies spiraling together toward completion. He was no longer gentle, and she didn't ask for gentleness from him. Breathless and wanting, she wanted him this way; primal and without restraint. They climaxed together, clinging to each other and shaking with release.

She came back to earth gradually, winded and sated. Lucien kissed her, slowly and deeply, as she found her breath. "It hasn't been two months, you know."

"I know." She draped her arms around his neck. "Are you sorry?"

"No," she said quickly. "Never. I got so wrapped up in my plans that I forgot how wonderful this is. It's just us, Lucien. That's all that matters."

He lifted up slightly and looked down at her. "Is it?" he whispered. "Is it enough?"

She pushed a length of long dark hair away from his beautiful face. "Yes."

He grinned at her. "Did you get any sleep at all, love?"

"I did. I feel quite well rested."

"Good." He lowered his mouth to her neck. "You won't be getting any more sleep tonight."

The rain had begun early in the morning, dripping on the roof at first, then pouring. It poured still. Daisy cuddled against O'Hara and smiled. She hoped it rained all night, so much so that the roads would be impassable in the morning and she would have no choice but to stay here. Here in this bed, here in O'Hara's arms.

They were no longer physically joined, and still he could touch her without pain and flashes of memory that were not his own. For tonight O'Hara was just a man, and she was his woman.

Neither of them wanted to waste the night sleeping.

"I wonder if it's the spell." O'Hara said, his voice low and very near her ear.

"I don't think so. How could that be?"

"How could this be?" He raked his hand down the length of her body until his fingers delved between her legs.

This could not be, Daisy thought as she closed her eyes. She couldn't want him again with the stroke of a finger! It didn't make any sense at all. But then, nothing about this night made any sense, so she just relaxed and enjoyed the pleasure that shot through her body when O'Hara touched her.

"I do know one way we can find out." She rolled away from O'Hara and left the bed, and she grabbed his hand as she came to her feet. He held on tight, savoring for a while the sensation of touch without the power he had lived with all his life.

"Come," she said, taking a step back as O'Hara left the bed.

"What are you doing?"

"We're going to see if this extraordinary event is caused by the spell Nathaniel cast, or if it goes much deeper than that."

He didn't know what she was doing until she reached behind her and opened the French doors. The chill of the wind cooled by rain washed over them, but even as she stepped onto the gallery and past the edge of the room where Nathaniel had cast his spell, she felt no rain on her bare flesh.

"In case you have forgotten," O'Hara said as he followed her, "we are both naked."

"I haven't forgotten," she said with a smile. "No one will see us here. The clouds hide the moon and the stars. I can barely see you, even from this short distance. Besides, who would be up at this hour to see anything?"

She stopped halfway onto the gallery. Here a few drops of rain had dampened the floor, and the occasional droplet landed on her warm skin, cooling her. She smelled the rain, the crispness of the night combined with the scent of her lover's skin when she leaned in so close she could press her nose to his chest.

O'Hara's fingers threaded through hers. "What do you feel?" she whispered.

He reached out and touched her shoulder, then trailed those lovely fingers to her breasts. "I feel you, Daisy. Just you."

"Then it wasn't the spell Nathaniel cast."

"No, it wasn't."

He sounded a little uncertain, as if he almost preferred the explanation that a witch's spell had dampened his powers.

She knew he had been with women before, though she tried not to think of what the ghost had told her last night. "Has this ever happened to you before?" she asked as O'Hara wrapped his arms around her and held her close.

"Never."

According to the ghost, O'Hara had never been with the same woman more than once. Was he frightened of what he saw when he touched a woman? Was he still afraid of her?

He didn't touch her as if he were afraid. He touched her as if he truly loved her, with tender hands and a wicked mouth.

A warm bed awaited them inside her room, just beyond curtains that whipped in the nighttime wind. But O'Hara didn't lead her inside. Her skin was chilled by the wind, but inside she burned. O'Hara's hands were never still. He caressed her, kissed her, aroused her, until her skin burned as well and the throb of her desire increased to a point where she wanted to scream.

Instead of screaming, she took O'Hara's length in her hand and stroked, arousing him as he aroused her, taking him to the edge and then pulling back so that they were lost in a sea of exploration and growing, gnawing need.

If this was all they could have, she wanted to make it a night to remember. She didn't want to have any regrets when she rode home to Plummerville and returned to her solitary life. She would dream about this night in years to come. She would dream about O'Hara, and love him, and curse him for being so stubborn.

But she would not curse him tonight.

O'Hara lowered her to the gallery floor. The floor was cold against her back; he was hot above her. Daisy closed her eyes and waited for him to guide himself inside her, but he didn't. He touched her, raking his hands over every inch of her skin, kissing and licking and sucking on her skin, arousing her until she felt nothing but his hands and his mouth and the raging need that grew with every passing second. Perhaps the rain and the wind continued, but she did not feel them. She felt only her lover. His hands. His body. His own need for her.

"Now," she whispered.

"Not yet." O'Hara ended the refusal with a flick of his fingers between her legs and an equally talented tongue on an already hard nipple.

"But I need you."

"Don't be impatient, Daisy," he teased.

She reached out and laid her hand over his heart. He was so hard and warm, so alive and delicious beneath her fingers. "If you do not make love to me *now*, I will tell everyone I meet that your name is . . ."

He rolled atop her and guided himself to her, quickly entering with a long thrust.

"Quigley," she finished with a whisper and a smile.

Fifteen

The rain continued. It wasn't stormy out, but the rain fell hard enough for Lucien to be sure Daisy and Nathaniel would not be leaving today. He should be annoyed, but he felt too good at the moment to be bothered by anything. There was nothing to be done about the weather, so he'd might as well not concern himself.

He rolled over, kissed his sleeping wife, and left the bed as quietly as possible. It was later in the morning than he usually left the bed, but he was no more bothered by his tardy rising than he was by the rain. Last night had been an unusual night, and he felt like Evie was fully his once again. His mood had been affected.

Maybe everything would be all right after all, and he'd been worrying for no good reason. He and Evie would work out the baby-or-no-baby problem. Actually, that problem would probably work itself out, sooner or later. They would learn to handle the fact that Lucien had a son, and they would make Nathaniel a part of the family and learn to live with a thirteen-year-old witch who talked to dead people, like his father did.

The spell Nathaniel had cast had worn off. As he

dressed quietly, Lucien caught sight of a number of spirits who hovered just out of reach. He wouldn't leave Eve to sleep much longer, knowing the spirit of Tommy could enter the room again, but he'd let her rest a while longer. She was truly exhausted.

Dressed for the day, a smile on his face, Lucien left the room. The house was strangely quiet, but for an unexpected sound from downstairs. A jingling. A clink.

He hurried down the stairs, more curious than alarmed. What was O'Hara up to?

The noise he'd heard as he left his room came from the parlor, Lucien noted as he reached the end of the stairway and turned in that direction. It was even louder from this vantage point. Maybe O'Hara and Daisy were having breakfast in the parlor, instead of eating in the dining room. He couldn't quite figure those two out. Did they like each other or not? He couldn't tell.

He stood in the parlor doorway and looked in on a seemingly empty room. But again he heard a noise. What he heard sounded suspiciously like metal on metal, a scraping and a muted thunk. Lucien stepped into the room and to the side, so he could see around the settee.

Nathaniel sat on the parlor floor, a rug beneath him, his little face very serious and intense . . . the pieces and parts of the disassembled specter-o-meter spread around the boy as if it had exploded.

Lucien's good mood vanished. "What is this?" he asked quietly.

Nathaniel's head popped up; his eyes grew wide. He paused to swallow before answering. "I just wanted to see how it works," he explained, jumping

to his feet and dropping . . . *dropping* . . . the com-
ponent in his hand. "Sir!" he added as he stepped
on a small metal spring. "Everyone was sleeping
late, and I thought I'd take the device apart to see
how it works and if any improvements could be
made and . . . and . . ." As the boy stared at Lucien,
his face paled. "I'm sorry, Mr. Thorpe. I thought it
would be simple to reassemble, but . . ."

"You took it apart," Lucien said softly.

Nathaniel didn't move. It didn't look as if he
even breathed.

"On purpose," Lucien added incredulously.

"Yes, sir," the child answered in a small voice.

Lucien pointed a long finger at the boy's feet.
"You're standing on the mainspring."

Nathaniel jumped aside. And landed on a coiled
wire that was an integral part of the device.

"Would you look where you're stepping!" Lucien
shouted.

Nathaniel very carefully picked his way around
the pieces of the specter-o-meter. His head remained down as he gave the ruined device a wide
berth. "I can fix it," he said.

"You cannot," Lucien said darkly. "It's ruined."

"I'm sorry." The kid bolted, running past Lucien,
into the entryway and up the stairs.

When Nathaniel was gone, Lucien sighed. Ecstatic one moment, distraught the next. Heaven
help him, he no longer knew what to expect from
his own life.

He gathered the pieces of the contraption together, examining each part and assessing the
wreckage. A few components had been irreparably
damaged, but most of them could be reused when

he put this specter-o-meter back together again. He very carefully laid the pieces on the table by the window.

What on earth could possess the child to take the specter-o-meter *apart*? It must've been an act of defiance. A statement of Nathaniel's displeasure at his new circumstances.

As Lucien lined up the last of the pieces of the device, Evie walked into the room. She'd dressed in a blue skirt and a white blouse, simple but lovely, and she'd twisted her hair back. It was the curve of her lips and the glow in her cheeks that made her so beautiful he couldn't help but smile. A little.

"What's going on down here?" she asked. "I heard shouting."

Lucien stepped aside and gestured to the mess on the table by the window. Surely Eve would be as outraged as he was. "Nathaniel decided to take the specter-o-meter apart to see how it works."

Instead of being shocked, Eve smiled. "How clever of him."

"Clever?"

"Yes. He has his father's inquisitive mind."

Was she suggesting that the child had inherited his troublesome behavior from *him*? "I would never do such a destructive thing, Evie."

She walked toward him. "When you were Nathaniel's age, if someone had plopped that contraption in front of you, you would have done exactly the same thing."

She knew him too well. "He's old enough to know better."

"Oh, he is not. He's just a child, and no matter how difficult these new arrangements are for us, you can be assured they're ten times worse for Nathaniel. You yelled at him, didn't you?" Eve asked as she reached him and placed her arms around his waist.

"Yes."

"I'll make us some breakfast, and you go find Nathaniel and tell him you're sorry."

"I will not—"

She silenced him with a kiss. "You're a father, Lucien," she said when she took her mouth from his. "That was the easy part. Now it's time to learn to be a papa. Tell Nathaniel that you're sorry, tell him he must not touch your things again without permission, and then make him help you put the contraption back together."

She was right, of course. "How did you get to be so smart?"

"I'm a woman married to a difficult man. It comes with the territory." She kissed him again and headed for the dining room and the kitchen beyond. "Go!" she shouted as she disappeared from view.

"I'm not difficult," Lucien muttered as he left the parlor. He had heard the boy run up the stairs, so that was the route he took.

Apologize! Nathaniel had been wrong, and wasn't it his duty as the boy's father to make sure he understood when he was wrong? Lucien went first to the closed door to O'Hara's bedroom, the room where Nathaniel had been sleeping. He knocked softly, then opened the door.

No one was in the room, not even O'Hara. The pallet on the floor, where Nathaniel had been sleeping, was unoccupied. The blankets had been neatly folded at one end. O'Hara's bed was rumpled but also empty.

Lucien glanced up and down the hallway. It was very quiet this morning. No O'Hara, no Nathaniel, no Daisy . . . and no ghosts. Not one. He walked to Daisy's door and knocked. He did not dare to open this door without permission, but he did lean close to listen for an answer.

"Yes?" Daisy asked sleepily.

"Is Nathaniel in there?"

"No!" She sounded horrified by the prospect.

One by one, Lucien examined the remaining rooms on the second floor. They were all deserted. There was no sign of Nathaniel *or* O'Hara. From his own room, Lucien walked onto the gallery. Rain had dampened the floor, but the overhang kept the rain from touching him as he circled the deserted gallery.

Again, all was quiet. The kid had not disappeared! Lucien returned through his room, after making a circle of the house, and stood in the quiet hallway with his hands on his hips and his jaw twitching. Nathaniel was hiding from him. How childish and unnecessary.

A sound, a mere scrape that sounded like a shush or a whisper, caught Lucien's attention. His head snapped up. *The attic.*

He ran to the end of the hallway and the closed door there, threw it open, and looked up. The door at the top of the stairs was closed as well. No wonder there were no spirits wandering the hallway this morning. They were all up *there.*

"Nathaniel?" Lucien knew what horrors awaited him in that room, and still he ran. Damn it, he had told the boy to stay away from the attic! The very idea of a child being bombarded with the images and sounds from the past was enough to make his heart skip a beat. The fact that the child in question was *his* only made matters worse, in a way he had not expected.

Maybe it was a mouse he had heard, or a ghost, or . . . dear God, let it be anything but Nathaniel.

He threw the door open and braced himself for what was to come. And memories not his own did come, in a wave that threatened to knock him flat. Ghosts, trapped and tortured, filled his mind with vivid remembrances of their most horrific days. He couldn't stop the assault, but Lucien didn't hesitate as he ran to the boy who sat in the middle of the floor. Nathaniel's head hung, and his thin body shook.

It was impossible to block out anything so horrendous as the events that had taken place in this room, but Lucien tried. The screams grew inside his head. Loud. Endless. Blood covered the floor, so real that he was afraid he'd slip in it. Blood covered his hands, blood he knew was not really there. And still he tried to wipe the offensive blood away. In his heart he felt not only his own fear but theirs. Pain. Pleading. Disbelief.

Lucien lowered himself to the floor and wrapped his arms around Nathaniel as if he could protect the child in that simple way. He could not, he knew it. The child shook even harder with his father's arms wrapped around him.

When Lucien glanced at his son's face, he saw tears on pale cheeks and lips that trembled, and in that moment he knew he would do anything, anything at all, to take away this child's pain.

"You shouldn't be here," he said hoarsely

Nathaniel didn't respond. His eyes were glazed, and they stared not at Lucien but at the window and the gray light beyond.

Lucien closed the doors in his mind, one and then another, forcing the images back so he could function. It wouldn't do Nathaniel any good at all if they were both paralyzed. He stood and lifted Nathaniel, trying to shield the child with his arms as he carried him to the door and down the stairs. Above and behind them the attic door slammed shut, and a distant ghostly scream followed.

In the hallway Lucien dropped to his knees. Nathaniel continued to shake; his eyes were still too bright and fixed on a point far beyond this physical world.

The pain Lucien had experienced in that attic had sliced through him like a thousand knives. Nathaniel's gift was greater than his—O'Hara had said as much—and he was a *child*. He should never be made to experience such agony, to relive and taste and see an anguish he could not possibly comprehend.

Lucien took the child's face in his hands and forced Nathaniel to turn his head. Somehow he had to drag the boy into the present, away from the past. His own world awaited him, but at the moment it was out of reach. Lucien tried to catch and hold Nathaniel's gaze, but those eyes, so much like his, remained unfocused.

"Look at me," Lucien commanded softly.

Nathaniel's breathing was too fast and shallow,

and he would not stop shaking. If anything, it seemed he was getting worse.

"Look at me!" Lucien said in a louder voice.

The child's face was so pale, and the dark circles under his eyes hadn't been there as he'd puttered with the pieces of the damned specter-o-meter. And no matter how forcefully Lucien commanded it, Nathaniel's eyes remained firmly fixed on the past.

Frustrated and growing more desperate as the seconds ticked past, Lucien lifted his head and shouted at the top of his lungs, "Evie!" When nothing else made sense, he could turn to Eve. She'd be here in a minute, and she'd know what to do. She always knew what to do.

Nathaniel's body convulsed, jerking hard. Lucien's response was to hold the boy tighter. He couldn't help but think of the long minutes he'd spent scowling over a damned piece of equipment, the lazy way he had searched the house, once Eve had commanded it. He should have moved faster, he knew that now. He never should have left Nathaniel alone in this house. Not for a minute. Not for a single second.

"Heaven above, how long were you in that room?"

"Long time," Nathaniel whispered. "Very, very long time." He did not look directly at Lucien, but he had heard the question and understood.

Eve ran up the stairs. Lucien heard her approach, and his heart reacted. A door off the hallway opened, and other footsteps joined Eve's. Lucien did not look up. He kept his eyes on Nathaniel's face. "They can't hurt you," he whispered. "What you saw and felt was in the past, it all happened a long time ago."

"No," Nathaniel whispered. "Now. It's happening *now*. Don't let them hurt me. Please, don't let them . . ." He began to shake more violently, and Lucien pulled the child's head to his shoulder and held on tight.

"What happened?" Evie asked as she dropped to her knees beside them. A half dressed O'Hara, feet bare and shirt unfastened, and a disheveled Daisy in a wrapper were right behind her.

"Nathaniel went into the attic," Lucien said. He would not cry. He absolutely would not! Still, his eyes stung. He blinked twice, very fast. "I don't know how long he was up there."

"Long time," Nathaniel whispered again. "I thought no one would ever come. Not ever."

"We're here," Eve said gently.

"He won't stop shaking," Lucien said softly. "And his eyes . . . he can't see us. He still sees *them.*"

Eve remained calm as she wrapped her arms around them both. "We're here, Nathaniel. Everything's going to be all right."

It was a lie, Lucien knew that—a pretty lie delivered in an angel's voice. No matter how he wished it, nothing was ever going to be all right!

"O'Hara," Eve said, her voice remaining gentle. "Would you please take Nathaniel's hand?"

O'Hara didn't hesitate. He knelt on the opposite side and took a small, limp hand in his own. Immediately, his body jerked. But he didn't let go. He raised his other hand, and Daisy took it without hesitation or instruction.

And so they all surrounded and sheltered

Nathaniel in the hallway of this damned haunted house.

"Nathaniel, darling," Eve said. "I want you to give us everything inside you that hurts. Push it away. Send it to us. We will take all that grief from you and send it far, far away."

The child shook his head. "Can't."

"Yes, you can." Eve stroked his hair with one hand. "Release it."

Lucien felt the expulsion in the way Nathaniel's body jerked. He himself didn't take on the pain that left his son's body, and neither did Eve, but O'Hara jumped as if he'd been burned, and so did Daisy.

Nathaniel's shaking subsided, changing in an instant into a gentle all-over tremble. The kid hid his face against Lucien's shoulder. No one let go. No one stepped away. Lucien held his son close, Eve's arms were wrapped around them both, and O'Hara continued to grasp Nathaniel's hand, just as Daisy held his.

"Better?" Eve whispered.

Nathaniel nodded but did not lift his head.

Daisy dropped O'Hara's hand, then O'Hara dropped Nathaniel's hand and stood. "I thought you told him to stay out of the attic."

"I did."

"Then why. . . . ?"

"It's my fault," Lucien interrupted. "I . . . I was a jackass." Over a piece of equipment that could be repaired or rebuilt, over a *thing*. "It's my fault."

Nathaniel lifted his head and looked Lucien in the eye. He was not completely himself, not yet. Would he ever be? But his eyes were no longer fixed on a long-ago horror. They were fixed on a present-day terror—his own father.

"I'm going to be sick, sir," Nathaniel said in a soft voice.

"Go right ahead." He didn't want to move from this spot.

Daisy took another step back, and Eve whispered, "Lucien!"

"I . . . I think I can make it outside," Nathaniel said softly.

Lucien stood, and Eve did, too. He didn't release Nathaniel but held the kid in his arms and carried him toward the nearest room and the French doors Eve opened for them. Once they were all on the gallery, Lucien placed Nathaniel on his feet . . . and still he didn't let the kid go. Not even when Nathaniel leaned over the railing and retched repeatedly.

"If you're all right for a moment, I'm going to get a damp cloth and some tea from the kitchen," Eve said.

Lucien nodded. "I'll take Nathaniel to our room when he's done here."

Eve left quickly, and when she was gone, Lucien let the tears that had been stinging his eyes fall. He'd been right all along. He was a terrible father. He couldn't protect his son, or any other child he and Evie might have, from pain. Would Nathaniel ever be the same?

The retching finally stopped, and Nathaniel swiped a hand across his mouth as he stood straight and stared away from the house without moving. It was almost as if the child didn't breathe. Lucien ran his hand through Nathaniel's tangled hair, and with a subtle and almost unconscious movement, the boy shrugged off the gesture.

Lucien let his hands fall. He wanted to hold the child again, to make sure he was better, that he had begun to forget. At the moment, it was all he could do. But as he reached out, the boy shrugged off his father's hands in a more forceful manner. It was not an unconscious movement, not at all.

"How many days was I up there before you thought to look for me?" Nathaniel asked in a low, accusing voice.

"Days?" Lucien repeated in horror as he backed away a single step. "No, it was . . ."

"Didn't you hear me screaming?"

Lucien shook his head. "You were . . ."

"Didn't you hear me shouting for them to *stop?*"

Nathaniel turned to run, but he was too weak to get past Lucien just yet. This time, he would not allow the child to shrug him off.

"You were up there for minutes, Nathaniel, not days." The fact that it had seemed like days to the boy sent chills down Lucien's spine.

Nathaniel struggled, but Lucien did not let go. "Why did they do it?" he cried. "I don't understand."

"Neither do I," Lucien admitted in a soft voice.

"I can still feel it," Nathaniel said as he fought against Lucien's grasp. "They're in my head and they won't go away. Not now, not ever."

"They will go away."

Nathaniel shook his head quickly, and then he became very still. A shudder racked his frail body, and he fainted. Lucien caught and lifted his limp son.

* * *

O'Hara followed Daisy into her room and closed the door behind them.

"You shouldn't be here," she whispered.

"Why not?" He kept his voice as hushed as hers, even though no one was likely to hear them.

"Someone might see you."

"I need my shoes."

She began to search the floor for his shoes, looking more beautiful than ever in her pale green wrapper, with her hair going this way and that and her cheeks flushed pink.

He would enjoy the sight more if he didn't still see and feel what Nathaniel had seen and felt in the attic. The boy didn't understand everything he'd experienced, and the memories that were not his own were already beginning to fade. Maybe eventually he would forget it all. O'Hara prayed that would be so; no child should ever be forced to endure the kind of agony Nathaniel had experienced.

Daisy found his shoes—one under the bed and the other beside a chaise—and she retrieved them, along with his jacket and his socks. He was supposed to leave now, he imagined. The night was over. And what a miraculous night it had been.

If anything would take away the remnants of the horrors that lingered in his mind, it was Daisy. Daisy, with her love and her hope and her impossible dreams. Last night they'd been together, in a way he had never experienced before, and he had not been able to read her thoughts. But the night was over, and he needed to drink her in to take away the ache of knowing she would never again be his.

When she handed him his clothes, he didn't try not to touch her but allowed his fingers to brush against hers. He waited for the assault of emotions. . . . Had she been as thrilled by last night as he had? Had her love for him survived? Did she want him still?

Nothing.

He shuffled the things she'd handed him into one hand and grasped her hand in his. Nothing. Not a tremor of emotion or a single memory.

"What's wrong?" she asked.

"I can't read you."

"Last night . . ."

"I didn't think it would last until morning," he interrupted, dropping her hand and leaning in to kiss her gently. "Very strange," he said as he took his mouth from hers.

"Strange indeed." She gave him a halfhearted smile. "Maybe not so strange. At least, no more strange than the rest of my life has become."

How could she simply accept this? Without question, without a single hint of doubt?

"Will Nathaniel be all right?" Daisy asked, her half smile fading away.

"I don't know. I hope so."

"It must be very difficult, to be . . . different."

"On occasion." He placed his hand over hers, expecting the sensations he always experienced when he touched a person to streak through him. Again all he felt was Daisy's hand, her warmth. . . . "All I feel is your skin. It's very nice."

She sighed and threaded her fingers through his. "I don't suppose it will last."

He shook his head.

He had never promised her anything more than a single night. Why did he feel as though when he walked out of this room he was leaving a piece of himself behind?

She drew her fingers from his reluctantly. "I really should help Eve. Nathaniel will need a bit of care today, I believe."

"Yes."

"I don't imagine we'll be leaving just yet, with the rain and Nathaniel's incident."

A few more hours, perhaps a few more days. That's all the time he had left. "Probably not. Though I'm sure I could get Jim to escort you to town if you're anxious to get back to Plummerville. You'd probably have to travel on horseback, but it's not . . ."

"No."

She sounded so adamant, and in truth he wasn't ready to say good-bye either. Yet at the same time, he feared for her safety in this house. "You shouldn't be here."

"I have a feeling none of us belong here," she said with a shudder. "Glover Manor is a bad place, O'Hara. Even I can feel the badness here. And it isn't getting better. It's getting worse."

He didn't want to admit as much, especially not to Daisy, especially not now . . . but she was right.

Sixteen

Eve found Lucien and Nathaniel in her bed. Nathaniel lay on his back in the center, white as a sheet and terribly still, eyes shut and chest barely moving. Lucien reclined on his side, close to his son, one hand on Nathaniel's chest, his eyes on the boy's pale face.

She placed the tray she carried on the dresser. Nathaniel didn't need tea at the moment, but the damp cloth might make him feel better. Eve sat on the mattress beside the boy and very delicately wiped his too-warm face with the cool linen.

"I was right," Lucien whispered.

"About what?"

"I shouldn't have children."

Her heart broke a little, but she tried not to let her reaction show. "It's a little late for that, don't you think? Better than thirteen years too late."

"I've known Nathaniel for two days. Two days, Evie, and if I could, I would take the pain out of his body and store it in mine forever. I hurt because he hurts, and I can't do a damn thing to take his pain away." Lucien rose up and placed a hand on Nathaniel's forehead. The other remained on the boy's chest. "Why can't I do that? Why can't I just suck what he saw out of his mind?"

"The desire to do so only proves to me that you're going to be a good father."

He finally took his tortured gaze off Nathaniel and looked at her. "If we have a child, he or she will very likely be born with the same curse that Nathaniel and I share."

"It isn't a curse," she insisted.

"Tell that to Nathaniel when he wakes up. *If* he wakes up." Lucien shuddered. "I shouldn't have told him not to go into the attic. Tell a young boy not to do something and that's exactly what he's going to do. I should have known that."

Eve lay down beside Nathaniel herself, facing him and Lucien, so that the boy was bracketed by his new parents. "He's going to be fine."

"No, he's not."

"You often forget what you see," she reminded him. "You remember more of what you experience now because you have trained yourself to remember. Nathaniel is young. He won't remember what happened to him today."

"Can we be sure of that?" Lucien looked at her with haunted eyes. "And even if you're right . . . this is not the last time Nathaniel will experience someone else's pain. How can you say that's not a curse? He will always see ghosts wherever he turns, and they will hound him until he gives them what they want. There's no escape. There's no peace."

"Are you telling me that you've never known peace?"

Lucien's eyes held hers. "You know that's not what I meant. The best days of my life have been with you." He pushed fine strands of dark hair away from Nathaniel's face. "He believed he was up there for days, screaming for help, and I ignored him. He thinks we left him up there to suffer alone, day and night, screaming for us to come . . . and he's a baby. He's just a baby, Eve."

She leaned over and kissed Lucien's cheek. "He's going to be fine."

"You don't know that to be true."

"We'll make it so."

She moved closer to the sleeping boy, snuggled against him, held him close. Nathaniel was not her child. In fact, he was living, breathing proof that Lucien had once loved another woman. More than that, he was evidence that if she and Lucien did not have babies, it was because she was defective in some way.

And yet . . . she could love this child. He needed her every bit as much as he needed his father.

Daisy stood on the gallery off the parlor and watched the rain fall. There were already huge puddles of water here and there. The trees were heavy, the limbs and leaves soaked and dripping.

She heard O'Hara behind her, even though his step was soft. "How are they?"

He stepped up to stand beside her, and in an easy, familiar way, he laid his hand at the small of her back. The way he allowed that hand to linger . . . she knew he could still not see her thoughts.

"Lucien and Eve are going to stay with the boy until he wakes," O'Hara said, his eyes on the dreary landscape before them.

"Will Nathaniel be all right?"

"I don't know."

"You didn't . . ." Her heart skipped a beat. "Touch him?"

"Lucien wouldn't allow it." The hand at her spine rocked gently, easily, the fingers tender and yet not at all shy. "I don't think I've ever seen him so scared."

Daisy nodded. "I can't even imagine." She wondered: if O'Hara had children, would they inherit his gift of sight? How difficult would it be to raise a child from whom there were no secrets, a child who would suffer the way Nathaniel suffered now?

She couldn't very well ask. He'd made his intentions more than clear.

The ghost who had visited Daisy told her that O'Hara had never slept with the same woman twice. Did that count several times in one night? Should the proper wording have been more than one *night*? Again, it was a question she could not ask.

His hand skated up her back, palm pressing against her spine. He enjoyed touching her, being able to caress her without seeing more deeply into her. But how long would that last? He seemed to be surprised that the phenomenon had lasted this long.

Daisy ached all over, and yet if O'Hara asked her to lie with him again, she would. No doubts, not a single second thought. Last night had been the most extraordinary night of her life.

A gentle voice whispered in her ear. *"He doesn't love you."*

Daisy's head snapped to the side. She searched for the woman who had spoken to her, but she saw nothing. No one was here but her and O'Hara.

"What is it?" he asked.

"Nothing," she said softly. She didn't see any ghost. Perhaps the whispering voice had been her own imagination, her own fears rising to the surface to taunt her.

O'Hara laid his wandering hand on her hip and pulled her closer to him in a proprietary way. She wanted to believe that she was different, that she was not one of many women, in O'Hara's mind. She wished she could borrow his gift just for a moment, so she could know what was in his heart.

"Does he have a heart?"

Daisy flinched.

O'Hara pulled her closer. "Are you getting chilled? Perhaps we should go inside."

"I'm fine," Daisy said. Her eyes scanned the deserted gallery, the rain-soaked landscape, and even the man beside her. She did not hear ghosts; she had rarely seen them . . . so what was that whisper in her ear?

"There is a way to know," the breathy voice cooed distantly.

How? How could she know if O'Hara truly cared for her?

"Will he bleed?" The hushed tones persisted. *"Will he bleed for you, Sister?"*

Daisy took a deep breath and jerked up to find herself sitting on the settee in the parlor, a gently smiling O'Hara beside her. He held her hand. The rain continued.

"Where . . . where am I?"

"You fell asleep," he said gently. "And you looked so peaceful, I couldn't bear to disturb you."

After taking a moment to still her rapidly beating

heart, Daisy glanced down at their joined hands. "You can still touch me without . . ."

"I can't read you. That probably won't last long, so I intend to enjoy the anomaly while it lasts." His thumb raked across the palm of her hand.

She grasped his hand tight. "Nathaniel?"

O'Hara's smile faded. "Still sleeping. Lucien and Eve are going to stay with him until he wakes."

Daisy's heart hammered again. This conversation was turning very familiar. "Will he be all right?"

"I don't know."

She waited for a hissing voice in her ear, but all remained silent. "You didn't . . ." Her heart skipped a beat. "Touch him?"

"Lucien wouldn't allow it." O'Hara lifted her hand and kissed it tenderly. "Honestly, Daisy, I don't think I've ever seen him so scared."

"I can only imagine," she whispered.

O'Hara laid his free hand on her shoulder and brushed a thumb against her throat.

"When will your ability to read my thoughts return?" she asked.

"I don't know."

At the moment, Daisy was glad he couldn't see the disturbing dream she couldn't shake. "Hasn't this ever happened to you before?

He shook his head. "Never."

But there had been other women, she knew that. Had he told them pretty lies to make them love him? Had he made them feel as if he loved them, even if he wouldn't say the words?

Did he have a heart?

* * *

Lucien refused to leave the bed. He reclined beside his son, as if his presence could give the child strength.

"He should be awake by now," he said, his voice rasping. "It's been hours."

"He finds peace in sleep," Eve reminded her husband. "There are no ghosts in his dreams."

"No, but there could very well be memories of what he saw this morning."

"Maybe I should collect O'Hara—" Eve began.

"No," Lucien interrupted.

Eve reached across the sleeping child and placed an easy hand on Lucien's stubbled cheek. He had not shaved this morning, he had not eaten. "I know there are times when you dislike O'Hara," she said gently. "But he might be able to help us."

"I don't trust the man."

"Ridiculous," Eve said. "You've worked with him often enough to know that he's dedicated and honest—"

"He's a scoundrel," Lucien interrupted.

She really shouldn't argue with him when he was in such a state. "Some days that's true."

"He was in Daisy's room last night," Lucien said in a lowered voice.

"I know."

"He's a scoundrel who cares for no one but himself, and I won't have him touching my son again."

Was Lucien angry because O'Hara had taken advantage of Daisy? He was not usually so gallant, but he had his moments.

But it would be silly to turn their backs on a power that could help them. Like it or not, they had to stick together. "If Nathaniel doesn't wake soon . . ."

"He will," Lucien insisted. "He has to."

The rain had stopped at last, but the day remained gray. Twice Eve had caught a glimpse of Tommy, but she'd closed her mind to the ghost, in a way Lucien had often described to her.

The ghostly boy had come to her clearly in the past because she'd wanted him to. Tommy had become the child she craved, and she had almost lost a part of herself to the call of a long-dead child.

"We should leave this place," she said. Her hand joined Lucien's on Nathaniel's chest. "The roads are probably too muddy for the carriage, but we can go on horseback. I want us all out of this house, Lucien. We can't leave here soon enough to suit me."

He nodded agreeably, to her surprise. She knew why he was so agreeable when he said, "The two of you, and Daisy, are getting out of this house as soon as Nathaniel wakes up. As for O'Hara, he can do whatever he wants. Stay or go—I don't care."

"And you . . ."

"I'm staying," Lucien said gruffly.

Eve's heart fluttered. Lucien had worked alone before, he would work alone again. But not here, not now. "No. You can't help these spirits. They don't want your help. They'll only hurt you."

Lucien brushed Nathaniel's hair back, trailing his fingers along a pitifully pale forehead. He touched the boy often, as if he could offer strength in that way. Perhaps he could. "They're not evil," he said softly. "They deserve to be set free. Only I can do that, Evie."

"How can you say they're not evil after everything

that's happened here? After everything you've discovered?"

"They're angry, and confused, and . . . lost. They're lost souls, love—even the twin who murdered all those men. What happened to them was wrong, and I can't go back and change the past. But I can end their suffering now if I can release them."

She knew better than to argue with Lucien on this subject. "And how do you plan to do that?"

"I have to give them what they want." His eyes were hooded, deep and sad. The sadness was not for himself or for Nathaniel at the moment, but for the souls he had come here to save. "Thomas wants the woman he loves set free from this trap. Tommy wants a mother who loves him. The mother he should have had. The sister who gave birth to Tommy wants to move on with her life, to claim her child and the man she loves and forget the past, but her twin won't allow that to happen."

"And the twin who murdered fourteen men?"

"She's the most desperate of all, Evie," Lucien said softly. "In her heart, she wants the child she lost and the peace that was violently taken from her. She killed those men in a sadly misdirected revenge, yes, but also . . . she's searching for something to the depths of her soul. Love, maybe. Forgiveness, certainly."

"After what they've done to Nathaniel, how can you have sympathy for them?"

"They weren't the ones who did this to Nathaniel, Evie. Margaret and Isabel lived the horrors that put him in this state, that tore at his mind and his heart until time had no meaning and there was nothing in their world but pain and fear."

She glanced at the portrait across the room. Did the innocent girls they had once been still live deep inside the sisters?

"I'm so afraid," she whispered.

"I'm sure he'll be fine, as soon as he's rested." Lucien said the words, but Eve was certain he didn't believe them.

"I'm afraid for you, Lucien," she confessed. "I won't leave you here."

"But . . ."

"Daisy and Nathaniel should get out of here, I agree with you on that point, but I will not leave you here. Don't ask me to desert you."

He threaded his fingers through hers, and their clasped hands rested over Nathaniel's heart.

Daisy carried bread and hot tea upstairs late in the afternoon, insisting that Lucien and Eve needed to eat. She twittered about, as she often did when she was nervous, and she didn't often look O'Hara squarely in the eye.

Hours had passed since the night had ended, and still he could touch her. He had never before experienced such a miracle, not even for a short while, and he had expected that he would eventually be stunned with a jolt of emotion or memory when he touched Daisy. So far, that had not happened.

So he enjoyed the freedom while it lasted. He had never been able to touch a woman, or anyone else, without working to put a barrier between his

mind and theirs. With Daisy, he was free to concentrate on the silkiness and warmth of her skin.

No woman had ever responded to him the way
Daisy had last night, so quickly and intensely that
watching and feeling her response was an aphro-
disiac unlike any other. He wanted that again: to
watch her surrender completely and shudder
around and beneath him until . . .

In the past he had walked away from the women
he'd been intimate with, because after a short time
he knew them too well . . . and he didn't like what
he saw inside them. Daisy was different. She was
good and pure, with a fine heart and a world of
love to give.

They had most of the house to themselves, and
nothing could be done about the ghosts until Lucien was ready to continue. This particular
haunting was far more than O'Hara could handle
on his own, so there was nothing to be done until
then.

He could seduce Daisy, perhaps in the parlor or
in the kitchen or . . . anywhere. It didn't matter.

There was one small problem with that plan. Last
night he had been able to lay his hands on Daisy
and know she would not conceive a child. But if
he could no longer read her, he could not guaran-
tee that their joining wouldn't lead to a child, a
baby who might have his curse, as Nathaniel had
Lucien's.

He wouldn't walk away from Daisy knowing he
might leave her in that situation, and he couldn't
marry her.

Daisy returned from her chore empty-handed.

"Any change?" he asked as she headed for the kitchen.

"No." She didn't look at him. "I think I might make some stewed apples. I believe I saw all the ingredients in the kitchen, and I desperately need something to do. When Nathaniel wakes, he will want something tasty to eat. I can make biscuits and stewed apples."

O'Hara jumped up from the chair and followed her. "I'll help."

"That's not necessary, truly," she said, sounding desperate to be rid of him.

"There's nothing else for me to do," he said, following her doggedly.

"Can't you do something about the ghosts so we can leave Glover Manor once and for all?" she asked testily.

"Not alone. I'm afraid I've done all I can do, for now."

She didn't look at him as she began to gather her ingredients and set them on a long worktable: apples, a large bowl, spoons, spices, sugar, a paring knife. Once everything was assembled in an orderly manner, she began to peel the apples.

"I could ask Jim to take me to town, I suppose," she muttered beneath her breath. "There is a boarding house, I saw it when we came in on the train. I could stay there until the others are ready to go."

"That's not a bad idea," O'Hara said. "I could take you to town, though. You don't need to ask Jim."

Like it or not, he was jealous of the simple man who was exactly the kind of husband Daisy needed and wanted. Maybe he did have to walk away and leave her to some other man. That didn't mean he wanted to watch. Jim was much too interested in Daisy for O'Hara's liking. How selfish of him. He knew Jim to be a good, kind fellow.

"I'm sure you're needed here," Daisy argued.

"A couple of hours . . ."

She lifted her head sharply. "I don't want you to take me!"

He crossed the room and took her face in his hands. For once, he wished he *could* know what was in her mind. "What's wrong?"

"I'm confused," she whispered. She dropped the apple she'd been peeling, and it rolled across the worktable a few inches. "I did want last night, and it was lovely, but . . ."

The power to see into Daisy was coming back, apparently. A flash of white-hot anger shot through O'Hara, through his hands . . . and then it was gone. "I would never do anything to hurt you, Daisy. You know that. Don't be angry."

"I'm not," she insisted. And in truth, he didn't see hate in her blue eyes—just the confusion she'd confessed to.

He couldn't tell her that he loved her, that he wished he were a different man, that he wanted so much for her and for himself. "I want to touch you," he whispered. "While this lasts, I want to lay my hands all over you."

"And can you tell me, as you did yesterday, that if we lie together we won't make a baby?"

"No. We can't be together the way we were last night, but . . ." Best to show her rather than tell her. Best to demonstrate what he could not say.

O'Hara caressed one full breast through the fabric of her gown, and she responded with a sharp intake of breath. He laid his mouth on her throat and kissed her there until she closed her eyes and sighed.

He could make her shudder, even if he could not be inside her as he longed to be. There was no rush, no hurry, and he wanted to feel her bare skin, touch her, taste her. While he kissed and sucked on her sweet neck, he unfastened the buttons down the front of her dress. When it was unbuttoned to her waist, he laid the palm of his hand on her chest, then fluttered his fingers to one bare breast. The nipple hardened at his touch, Daisy sighed.

It happened again. A jolt of fear and fury shot through him, as it shot through Daisy, and he pulled his head back. His hands no longer caressed her but remained still and benumbed. The emotion he'd experienced through her had come and gone in a heartbeat.

But this time, the emotion had lingered just long enough for O'Hara to know the anger was not Daisy's. It came from a spirit who called herself "Sister" and "darling" and hid her true self deep, beneath the rage. She had a liking for red and a longing for blood. His blood.

Daisy did not possess the strength for a lengthy possession, but the spirit of the bloodthirsty twin was obviously flitting in and out. No wonder Daisy was confused. How long had this been going on?

O'Hara glanced down briefly. "Daisy, dear, perhaps you should put down the knife."

Seventeen

If sheer will could command healing, Nathaniel would be awake by now. Lucien had never wished so hard for anything, not once in all his years.

What if the boy never awoke? What if the excruciating experience he'd suffered in the attic were his last lucid moments in this life? So many things in life were not fair, but this . . . Lucien wished a little harder.

He wished for a chance to know his son well, to show the child how to fix the specter-o-meter he had taken apart, to control his abilities. With a little work and a lot of help from Evie, he and his son might find a way to have an ordinary life, along with the bizarre moments their gifts would bring them. Maybe one day they could even go fishing. Lucien had never been fishing, but he had heard other men mention the pastime with some fondness. Maybe Buster would be willing to instruct them.

Nathaniel woke with a start, taking a deep breath and sitting up straight in the bed, his eyes wide and his face pale.

Lucien kept his hand on the boy's chest. "It's all right. We're here."

It took a moment for Nathaniel to realize where he was, but when he did, he calmed down visibly, his eyes clearing and a hint of color returning to his cheeks. A quick glance at the window would tell the child how many hours had passed since he'd gone into the attic to hide.

"You stayed with me all day?" Nathaniel asked.

Lucien nodded.

The boy looked at Eve. "Both of you?"

"Of course," Eve said. "It's good to see you looking so much better."

No one wanted to ask what Nathaniel remembered of his trip to the attic, if anything. Not yet.

They stayed where they were, warm and oddly cozy. No one rushed to leave the bed. It was very nice, Lucien noted, to be resting here all together. The three of them. His family.

"I'm sorry," Nathaniel said gently.

"There's no need to apologize for anything," Lucien said quickly. Not for the specter-o-meter, not for disobeying his orders to stay away from the attic . . . not for accusing his father of abandoning him in that cursed place.

"I hated you for so long, and I know now that I shouldn't have."

That was not what Lucien had expected to hear. Perhaps his expression gave away his surprise, because the boy continued quickly.

"I thought you had deserted us, Mother and me. It wasn't until after she was dead that she told me the truth, that you didn't even know about me."

"If I had known . . ." Lucien began.

"I know that now."

He wanted to be angry with Zella, but she had probably only done what she thought was best.

"I hated you, too, because you gave me the affliction that Mother called a gift. I never wanted it."

"Neither did I," Lucien confessed in a lowered voice.

"Did your father give it to you?"

The way the child asked that question, you'd think their ability was a dreaded disease. "I don't know," Lucien said honestly. "He died before I was old enough to understand that not everyone saw the things I saw."

"What you can do is a gift," Eve insisted in her gentle voice. "Not an affliction. You are two extraordinary men, and I intend to take very good care of you both."

She would; he knew that. One day soon Nathaniel would know it, too.

A muted sound caught Lucien's attention. A thump. A distant wail.

"Something's wrong," Nathaniel whispered.

"No," Eve said gently. "Everything's fine now. We're here, and you're awake, and . . ."

Nathaniel shook his head and turned his eyes to Lucien. Lucien could see full well that his son had not forgiven him. The lingering anger was not for the trip to the attic or his short temper, but for cursing him with this ability. "Don't you feel it?"

Lucien had blocked out everything about this house as best he could, wanting to give the child his undivided attention. Nathaniel deserved that much. But something had changed. He lowered what remained of those shields and let the spirits talk to him again. More whispers, concern, and excitement joined what he had already begun to see and hear.

"We must hurry," Nathaniel said. Lucien nodded his head in agreement.

The three of them left the bed and, still disheveled, headed for the hallway and the stairs. Almost unconsciously, Nathaniel lifted his hand to Eve. She took that hand and held on tight.

"O'Hara!" Lucien called as he descended the stairs. "Daisy!"

There was no response. None at all.

"What's happening?" Eve asked as they made their way into a silent and deserted parlor.

"I'm not sure." Lucien's eyes swept right past the remnants of the specter-o-meter.

"It's Isabel," Nathaniel said softly.

Lucien turned and looked down at his son, who continued to hold Eve's hand tight. So tight, his little knuckles were white. "You can tell the twins apart?"

Nathaniel nodded. I couldn't before but now I can. "Isabel is angry. She's very angry."

An understatement, but true enough.

"How do you know it's Isabel who's angry?" Eve asked. She leaned down slightly to place her face close to Nathaniel's.

"Deep inside, they always knew who they had been." Nathaniel's blue eyes were wide, innocent. "Deep, very deep. They forgot, some days, but the truth was always inside them." He had seen too much today. Would he remember? Or would he be blessed with forgetfulness? "They buried that part of themselves because it hurt too much to know they would never be the same."

"Is Isabel here now?" Eve asked.

"No." Nathaniel closed his eyes. "She's in the kitchen."

Lucien ran in that direction, cutting through the dining room. He heard Eve and Nathaniel following, but his eyes were ahead. Spirits urged him to hurry. Thomas, the other twin—Margaret—and a weaker spirit who had to work to make herself known. Ruth.

Too late, a voice inside his head insisted as he ran into the kitchen. *You're too late.*

Lucien had never been overly fond of O'Hara, but to see him prone on the kitchen floor, blood marring his white shirt and atrociously bright green vest, his eyes closed and his body motionless, was a shock.

Daisy stood over O'Hara, a knife in her hand and a shocked expression on her face. Her dress was askew, buttons undone and her normally perfect appearance marred by twisted fabric and tiny specks of blood. She lifted her head as Lucien came into the room. Tears streamed down her face.

"I don't know what happened," she whispered hoarsely. "I was peeling apples, that's all. And then . . ."

The spirit of Isabel hovered around Daisy, trying to force her way in. For a moment the spirit's form was misty but human: red dress, dark hair, angry face. Then she transformed into a ball of white light and shot toward Daisy. Daisy's expression changed.

Lucien took a step forward. Isabel would not be able to stay inside Daisy for long. The innocent woman who didn't want or deserve to be a part of this didn't have the strength to maintain the connection. Fortunately, neither did Isabel.

"Drop the knife," he said.

Daisy's grip on the weapon changed, and there was no more fear or confusion in her eyes as she looked at Lucien, ignoring Eve and Nathaniel completely. She even smiled. "I don't think so." She stepped around O'Hara. "Do you have a heart, Lucien?"

When the spirit was forced from Daisy's body, expelled in a rush of white light, he took that opportunity to lurch forward and wrest the knife from her hand. There was blood on the knife and on Daisy's hand, and he took the weapon from her easily.

She began to tremble.

"Evie, see to O'Hara," Lucien commanded. He gripped Daisy's wrist and placed the knife she had wielded on a shelf out of her reach.

While Eve knelt beside O'Hara, Lucien held Daisy tight and looked deeply into her pale blue eyes. "A spirit has been using your body," he said gently. "You must learn to keep her out."

"How?"

"Doors," Nathaniel whispered.

"Yes. Close the doors in your mind, Daisy. Keep Isabel out."

"I don't have doors in my mind," she insisted.

"Yes, you do."

The spirit tried once again to enter Daisy's body. For a split second she succeeded. "I am not Isabel," Daisy said in a husky voice. "There is no Isabel."

The ghost was forced out, and once again Lucien held a very frightened Daisy.

"Isabel doesn't want anyone to have love," Nathaniel said in a soft, uncertain voice. "Not Daisy, not you. Not even her own sister."

The spirit turned its anger on the boy. "Doors, Daisy!" Lucien insisted as he released her and turned to his son. "Leave him alone." Once again, he was confronted with the twin in red. She was so clearly visible to him, and to Nathaniel, but it seemed that Daisy and Eve did not see her at all. "Leave him alone, Isabel."

The ghost turned from Nathaniel and glared at Lucien, hovering before him. Her anger gave her power. Made her visible, strong. Almost tangible. "I told you, *there is no Isabel!*"

Eve and Daisy leaned over a prone O'Hara, unable to see what Lucien and Nathaniel saw. Eve had unbuttoned O'Hara's shirt and vest and was busy trying to stop the bleeding with a clean linen towel. Daisy didn't move. She just knelt there, staring at the damage she'd done.

Lucien heard Eve whisper, "He's not dead." At that news, Daisy began to cry softly.

He listened, but Lucien kept his eyes and attention on Isabel. Since she continued to concentrate on Nathaniel, he went to the child's side and stood there. Since Nathaniel had taken Eve's hand, maybe he'd take the hand of his father. Lucien gripped Nathaniel's hand in his, and the kid held on tight.

Unexpectedly, the power of Lucien's gift increased. Perhaps the same thing happened to Nathaniel. The child's entire body lurched, but he did not release his father's hand.

"Thomas was there," Nathaniel said softly. "In the attic."

As if Nathaniel had spoken magical words, Isabel vanished.

O'Hara managed to open his eyes halfway. He was somehow sure that if he opened them fully, the pain in his chest would increase tenfold.

Daisy's tear-streaked face hovered close to his. He flinched, remembering the quick and powerful way she had stabbed him with the paring knife. Twice. She would have stabbed him a third time if he hadn't managed to grab her wrist and stop her attack. Then he'd passed out.

"Everything's all right." Eve's voice was close, clear, and comforting, and still, all O'Hara saw was Daisy. "She's gone."

"The sister who . . ." O'Hara began.

"Yes," Eve finished when he faltered.

"I'm sorry," Daisy whispered. "It wasn't me, I swear. One minute everything was fine, and the next I was standing there with blood on my hands and you were on the floor bleeding and I thought you were *dead.*"

He was in pain from head to toe, probably from falling to the floor, but it was his chest that hurt most. Even though he understood what had happened, he still couldn't believe it. Daisy had stabbed him, with fury on her face and a question for him. *Do you have a heart, O'Hara?* Thank goodness Daisy had been holding a paring knife and not a butcher knife!

Two pretty heads hovered over his, blocking out everything else. Eve and Daisy, his friend and his lover. Eve was intent on her work, which was centered on his chest, and Daisy held his hand and sobbed.

"Don't cry," he whispered.

She sniffled loudly. "I thought . . . I thought . . ."

He knew what Daisy had thought, but not because she held his hand and not because she had already told him, tearfully and quietly. She'd been afraid, at least for a while, that she had killed him.

"The blade was short, and apparently either my heart is very small, or you have a blessedly bad aim."

She shook her head gently. "Darling, your heart is not small."

O'Hara ignored Eve. He didn't think he was going to die, but there was a lot of blood, and those who had gathered around him appeared to be concerned. Eve shifted, and he caught a glimpse of Lucien standing above him, so high it seemed as if he were miles away. Even Lucien looked worried!

Even though the wounds were shallow, what if he did die? What if Eve couldn't stop the bleeding?

He squeezed Daisy's hand as tightly as he could. It was not nearly tight enough. "I love you," he whispered. There was no way to tell Daisy how he felt without the others hearing, but what difference did it make?

She shook her head quickly. "You're only saying that because . . ."

"No. It's the truth. I didn't want to love you, I truly didn't."

That news made her frown.

"I didn't want to love you, because I know that in the end I'll hurt you somehow. I'll disappoint you, Daisy, I'll never be the man you want me to be."

"I just want you to be . . . you. That's all."

It wasn't that simple. He had seen the images Daisy dreamed, the desires she kept warm in her heart. Children, a home, a wonderful and simple life. There were no hauntings in her dreams, no attacks by those who saw his talent as a gift of the devil, no reliving past pain over and over again in order to free a spirit or solve a mystery.

In Daisy's dreams, there were none of those long, bad nights when he could not make the images that bombarded him fade.

Daisy thought this disaster was her fault; O'Hara knew it was his. This was what happened when you dragged a woman who did not belong into a world where some days nothing made sense. Where vengeance and hate lived on even after death, where a woman as open and innocent as Daisy could become a pawn for those spirits who would use her.

She threaded her fingers through his. "If you can feel me again, then you know that's the truth."

He shook his head as much as he could. "No. You're still . . ." Eve and Lucien didn't know what had happened last night. Did they? How much had Daisy told them while he'd been out? "Maybe it will always be that way. Maybe I will never again be able to know what you think and what you feel."

Lucien dropped down to his haunches. "Welcome to the real world, O'Hara. From now on you can struggle through trying to figure out what women want, along with the rest of us."

It sounded as if Lucien expected him to survive. And if he could trust that assurance from anyone, it was Lucien Thorpe.

"It was Isabel," Lucien said in a low voice.

"Isabel? Are you sure?"

"Yes."

"How is that possible? I thought even they didn't know who they had once been." Daisy certainly didn't have the strength or the ability to discern which of the sisters had possessed her for a short time. She barely understood what had happened to her.

"Nathaniel was able to discover the sisters' true identities," Lucien explained.

O'Hara tipped his head back and smiled wanly at the boy who stood slightly behind his father. "Ah, I see you're finally awake."

"Yes, sir."

He had lost some blood, and though the knife had been small, it had also hurt like the devil. O'Hara had never been cut before; it wasn't pleasant, and the experience had left him oddly weak. But he did have the strength to lift his hand and offer it to Nathaniel.

"Not now," Lucien said, his refusal kinder than it had been earlier in the afternoon.

"I can help," O'Hara said, his hand remaining lifted even though holding his hand in the air was an effort. He wanted to lay that hand on his chest and drift back into oblivion. "If Nathaniel saw so much of the twins that he can now tell which is which, then it's possible there's more information locked in the back of his mind. Things he does not see or understand." O'Hara tried to catch and hold Lucien's gaze. "That's why I'm here, isn't it?"

Lucien glanced at his wife, eyebrows lifted in

silent question, and Eve responded. "He'll be fine. The wound is nasty, but it's not deep."

"It's not Mr. O'Hara's time," Nathaniel said. "Ruth told me so when I got worried."

"You were worried about me?" O'Hara managed a smile for the kid.

"Yes, sir."

The feeling was mutual. O'Hara needed to discover not only what Nathaniel knew about Isabel and Margaret, but what the boy would remember of his encounter in the attic, in the days and years to come.

Lucien finally nodded, and Nathaniel dropped to his knees and offered O'Hara his hand. Their hands joined, clasped together tightly, and O'Hara closed his eyes.

The kid was stronger than he'd been this morning. Somehow. Some way. It was as if in fighting off the terror, he'd strengthened his gift. O'Hara didn't sense the horror he'd experienced this morning when he'd touched the kid. The memories, the terror, had faded. Nathaniel no longer remembered most of what had transpired in the attic. He knew he had been frightened and sickened, but the images themselves were gone. O'Hara breathed a sigh of relief. No child should have to carry those memories.

He turned his mind to the ghosts themselves. "Thomas is the key," he whispered.

"Thomas," Lucien scoffed. "Why didn't he warn me when Nathaniel went into the attic?" he asked angrily. "I could have gotten there sooner. . . ."

"He stayed with Nathaniel," O'Hara said. His eyes remained closed, and Nathaniel held his hand tight. The child was not afraid to touch a man who could see inside him, the way so many were. "Thomas tried to shelter the child, the same way he tried to shelter . . ."

The doorway between the kitchen and the dining room slammed shut, pushed closed by an angry, invisible hand.

"Thomas is the key," O'Hara said as he released his grip on Nathaniel. "Thomas is the key."

Darkness fell too quickly to suit Eve. Things in this house had turned from bad to worse very quickly. She wanted her family and her friends out of this place!

But this was her life. A part of it, at least. When she'd married Lucien, she'd taken on not only him, but his vocation as well.

They had returned to the parlor for the remainder of the night. O'Hara was resting comfortably on the floor. The settee was too short for him to get comfortable there, and he really shouldn't be sitting. Daisy had made a pallet for the injured man and fussed over him constantly.

Perhaps O'Hara could, with some assistance, make it up the stairs and to bed, but it appeared that no one would be getting any sleep tonight.

Something had happened when Lucien and Nathaniel had joined hands in the kitchen. Either of them alone was remarkable, but together . . . Lucien had sworn their heartbeats were connected, as well as their hands and their minds.

There would not be another séance, as such. Not tonight. Daisy sat on the floor beside O'Hara. Her dress had been refastened, but she remained pale and shaky. She'd tried to wash away the tiny blood splatters, but small brown stains remained. Changing clothes would require leaving O'Hara, and that was something Daisy refused to do. She was still so shaken, it wouldn't do for her to participate in any séance. And Eve imagined that even if Lucien asked, Daisy would refuse.

Tonight only Lucien and Nathaniel joined hands. They sat in matching chairs in the middle of the parlor, facing each other, both hands clasped. They formed their own circle.

Eve watched from several feet away. All she could do was worry. She worried for O'Hara and Daisy, and her concern had nothing to do with a knife wound that would heal in time. She worried for Nathaniel, who should have a few days to recover from his ordeal before being subjected to this kind of test.

And she worried for Lucien, who took the weight of the world on his shoulders.

"Are you ready?" Lucien asked kindly.

Nathaniel nodded his head.

Eve didn't have powers as Lucien, Nathaniel, and O'Hara did. But she had experienced so much in the past five years that her mind was opened to all possibilities. That's why Tommy was able to appear to her now.

But tonight he could not hide from Lucien. Nor from Nathaniel.

"Mama," Tommy said as he took shape near the fireplace. His voice drifted, reaching toward her as if the child shouted from a long distance.

Tonight Eve could smile at him and say, "Sweetheart, I'm not your mama."

Tommy's lower lip trembled. "You don't love me anymore. You're going to leave me."

"Yes, I'm going to leave," Eve said calmly. "But when I go, you won't be here anymore. You and your real mama are going to a very nice place. Together."

"I can't find her."

"She's going to find you," Eve assured him. "She's been looking for you for a very long time. Her name is Margaret, and she'll be here soon."

The figure of the ghostly child faded, but Eve felt certain he did not leave.

Lucien and Nathaniel stared not at the fireplace or at her, but at each other.

"Thomas is the key," Lucien said, repeating O'Hara's words.

"Yes. He was in the attic," Nathaniel whispered. "He was there."

"This morning . . ." Lucien gripped his son's hands tight. "Thomas was with you this morning."

"Yes. But he was also there . . ." The kid swallowed. He trembled once but did not release his father's hands. "Then. Thomas was there *then*."

Eighteen

Lucien grasped Nathaniel's hands tight. He felt stronger than he ever had before, and he wasn't draining the child. Nathaniel grew stronger, too.

Isabel, dressed in red and shimmering with fury, took shape. In an instant, she was so distinct she looked almost solid. But not quite.

"Yes, Thomas was there," the angry shade said. With his heightened power, the ghost appeared so real, Lucien could see the sheen of dampness in her eyes and the horror that lurked behind the tears.

"He tried to stop the others, didn't he?" Lucien whispered.

"But he didn't!"

"He couldn't," Nathaniel added. "He tried, but there were too many of them. They . . . they hit him and they tied him up, and he couldn't get free."

Lucien's heart rate increased, and he knew, somehow, that this happened because Nathaniel's heart began to beat too fast. He tried to slow his racing pulse, to find calmness amid the madness, in hopes that if he could find calm, so could Nathaniel.

"We would like to talk to Thomas." Lucien stared at Isabel, but out of the corner of his eye he saw the other spirits. They were not fully formed; they were afraid. Afraid of Isabel. "Only he can tell us what his part in your assault was."

"Assault," Isabel whispered. "Is it easier for you to say that we were assaulted than it would be to speak the truth? We were raped and tortured. We begged for mercy, but the soldiers had none. No mercy. No heart." Lucien saw more than fury. He saw the spirit's pain. "All the while I screamed for my mother, and she *didn't come!*"

Thomas took shape several feet away. He was not as strong as Isabel, and he remained frightened of her. But he did come. "She didn't hear you."

Isabel spun on the spirit. "How could she not? I screamed at the top of my lungs. So did Sister. We screamed until our throats were raw and we could scream no more. You know. You were there!"

"Your mother was ill. One of the men gave her a drug to make her sleep. She couldn't hear you, I swear."

Isabel's form shuddered. "You're lying."

"No, I'm not." Thomas lifted a hand, but he remained several feet from Isabel. "I didn't know what they were like when I agreed to ride with them. I was just . . . tired of war. Sick of death. I wanted to get away. I didn't know what they would do."

"More lies," she whispered.

"No."

"Thomas," Lucien called the spirit's name, and the ghost faced him. "Are you Tommy's father?"

"No! I never touched her, I never touched either of them. Not until . . . much later."

"No, he didn't touch us. But he abandoned us," Isabel explained with a smile. "He told us he was so sorry for what had happened, that he would have stopped it if he could, and then he left us in a puddle of blood, riding off with his fellow Yankees. Deserters. Renegades. Bad, bad men who had no hearts. We had no one left but one another. Mother was dead." Her expression softened. "But Ruth was here. She took care of us. She tended to us as if we were her own, and I . . ."

"You loved her for it," Lucien finished.

"No," Isabel said abruptly. "I didn't love anyone. Not ever. No one but my sister."

Margaret took shape behind Thomas. Dressed in white and barely perceptible, it was almost as if she hid there.

"Thomas had no choice," Margaret whispered. "He couldn't stop the soldiers, and if he had tried to stay behind to help us, they would have killed him."

"If your precious Thomas couldn't stop them, then he should have killed the soldiers for their crimes against us!" Isabel thundered.

"I did!" Thomas answered, his own voice just as loud and insistent as Isabel's. "All of them," he said in a softer voice. "It took years, but I did kill them all. They split up after leaving here, afraid someone would hear of what they'd done and give chase. I hunted them down, each and every one, and I killed them."

"More lies," Isabel said.

"I made sure they knew why I took their lives, before they died," Thomas explained. "I made sure they knew they had to pay for what they'd done."

"That's impossible. You didn't kill them," Isabel insisted. "I did."

"You killed innocent men," Thomas responded.

Isabel neatly ignored that statement. "Thomas returned to us as if he had a right to do so." She turned her attention to Lucien. "He had been gone for years, but when he came to our door that afternoon . . . I remembered his face, just as I remembered all their faces. I wanted to kill him, but Margaret wouldn't allow it." She glanced toward her sister, the pain of betrayal in her eyes. "Sister said she would tell about the others if I hurt Thomas. She said she loved him, that she remembered how he had tried to help us. She remembered how he held her and comforted her when it was *too late.*" Dark hair began to float around Isabel's head, and her skirt danced, too, as if a wind tried to lift her. It was rage that made her dance.

"But he didn't hold you," Lucien said.

"I wouldn't allow it!" Isabel screamed. *"He was too late. He was too late!"*

"Isabel killed them all," Nathaniel said. "She killed her sister, and Thomas, and Tommy, while they were sleeping. And when that was done, she set the house on fire and went to her own bed to die."

Isabel spun on Nathaniel. "They were going to leave me!"

"I'm sorry you had no one to love," Nathaniel said softly. "Not your mother, who truly did die without knowing what had happened to you and Margaret. Not your sister, who survived without surrounding her heart with hate. Not a child . . ."

"I didn't want that child," Isabel insisted. "I'm

glad he died." The sheen in her eyes and the tremble of her form gave her away.

"He didn't die," Nathaniel whispered.

Other spirits moved closer and gathered in a circle around Isabel. Around her and still separate. She kept them from coming too close, with her fury. Margaret, Thomas, Tommy . . . all of whom she had killed. Tommy clung to Margaret's white skirt, and she rested a gentle hand in his hair. The truth had brought them together at last.

A woman who appeared to be older and weaker came. The twins' mother. And then there was Ruth, who somehow held them all together.

"I took him," Ruth said. "You were so determined not to have a child, and I was afraid of what you would do if you knew the baby had survived your fall and the difficult birth that followed. It's true. He lived, and I gave your son to a husband and wife who desperately wanted a child. I did it for you, and for him."

Isabel turned her attention to Ruth. "He lives?"

Ruth nodded.

The news somehow dented Isabel's anger. "And you never told me? You never spoke of it to anyone? More lies," she whispered. "Lies spoken to confuse me. I would have heard if you'd ever whispered a word of his existence. I would have known. . . ."

"After I placed the baby with a good family, I never again referred to him or even thought of him as your child. I was afraid if I did I would have second thoughts, that I would question what I had done. If I had known the truth would heal you, I would have told you he lived."

Isabel shook her head. "I don't need to heal. I *want* to hurt so I will never, ever forget."

"None of us will ever forget," Ruth said with a shake of her head.

"My baby truly lives?"

Ruth nodded.

"Where?" Isabel whispered, her face softening.

Ruth, as dignified in death as she had been in life, lifted her chin defiantly. "Your son is happy, and he is blessedly ignorant of the ways of his conception and birth. His life will be better if he never knows."

Isabel accepted this silently, and without another flash of anger.

"He is a good man," Ruth whispered. "You should be proud."

Tommy continued to cling to Margaret's skirt. If Eve saw the ghostly child, she paid him no mind. At least, no more mind than she paid the others. What did she see? Not everything, he knew. Not everything he and Nathaniel saw at this moment.

"This is your mama," Lucien said, his words directed to the boy.

Tommy smiled and nodded.

"Her name is Margaret." Lucien looked at Margaret, and for the first time he could see the serenity that was so much of the portrait above stairs. "You tried to protect her," he said.

Margaret nodded.

"You went so far as to allow her to call your son her own, because she needed to believe that her child had survived. You even . . . pushed your old identity down, when it tried to resurface, because you didn't want to leave Isabel behind."

"I would have done anything to protect Isabel,"

Margaret said. Her expression was somehow serene and anguished at the same time. She was so close to letting the anguish go and embracing the peace she so desperately needed and deserved. "I did terrible things to keep her safe."

"You helped her cover up the murders."

Margaret nodded again. "She promised me so many times that it wouldn't happen again, that she would stop. . . ." She glanced up at the man at her side. "I never suspected Sister might kill us, too."

"You were going to leave me, all three of you," Isabel moaned. "One night, when you thought I was asleep, I heard you talking about *leaving.*"

"We would have taken you with us, Sister," Margaret said. "You and I, we belong together. Then and now. We will still take you with us, if you will come." Margaret offered her hand.

Isabel shook her head. "It's too late."

"Come with us, Isabel." Margaret's hand remained aloft, and her shape began to change. She was as solid as her twin. As strong, in her own way.

Isabel shook her head. "I can't. You can't forgive me, you don't know . . ."

"I do," Margaret said.

Isabel stepped shyly forward, her own hand lifting slowly. When the twins' fingers touched, they began to glow. Both sisters smiled as they vanished. The other spirits faded with them.

Nathaniel squeezed Lucien's hands tight, even when all the spirits were gone.

Even O'Hara, who did not see ghosts the way Lucien and Nathaniel did, knew Glover Manor had quieted. Still, they all remained in the parlor, and likely would all night. Nathaniel slept on the settee, exhausted and looking very childlike, after his latest experience.

His own bed was rather hard, but comfortable enough. Daisy sat beside him. She said little and often reached for his hand in a way no one else ever had.

Lucien sat on the floor in front of the settee, as if he could protect his sleeping son, and Eve sat beside him. Close, the way a wife could.

Lucien had done his best to explain everything that had happened after he and Nathaniel joined hands. They had all seen and heard some of the ghostly commotion, but only the two Thorpe men had seen and heard it all.

"I think I understand," Eve said softly, so as not to disturb the sleeping child, "but I don't understand the last exchange between the twins. What was it that Isabel thought Margaret didn't now? What did she think her sister would not forgive?"

Lucien glanced back at Nathaniel, as if to assure himself the child was still sleeping. "Isabel tried to go to Thomas and make him think she was the sister he had fallen in love with. She wanted to . . . treat him as she had the others. She wanted to lie with him and then kill him. In her mind, that would have been justice, not only for herself, but for Margaret."

Eve sighed. "He knew, didn't he? He looked at Isabel and he could tell she wasn't the woman he loved?"

Lucien nodded. "At that moment, Isabel felt the beginning of a permanent separation from her sister. Even if they hadn't planned on leaving the area, the fact that Margaret was making a life for herself, that she was able to love, proved to Isabel that everything in her life was about to change. She was going to be left behind, and she couldn't bear the thought. And when she realized that Thomas could tell them apart . . . it terrified her."

"So she killed them all, including herself."

Lucien nodded, then leaned over and kissed Eve on the forehead. "I have work to do. If I don't get this done tonight, we won't be able to leave here in the morning."

"I thought they were all gone," O'Hara said.

Lucien looked his way. "Only the nasty ones," he said with a crooked smile. "There's still a lost soldier and a maid who fell down the stairs."

"Did Tommy . . . ?" Eve couldn't finish the question.

Lucien kissed her again and then stood. "Yes, love. I'm sorry. Tommy tricked the maid into falling, just as he tried to trick you."

"But he's all right now," Eve said.

Lucien smiled at her. "Yes, love. He's just fine."

While Lucien searched the room for spirits the others could not see, Eve decided to turn to O'Hara. His wounds needed her attention, she said. Since he suspected she needed to keep busy, he didn't argue.

"I can't wait to get out of here," O'Hara said as Eve sat on the floor beside him and lifted the thick bandages to check the injuries to his chest.

"Neither can I," she said without looking him in the eye. "I wish you and Lucien could do . . . something else," she said in a lowered voice. "Open a shop, perhaps."

"I wish for that, too, sometimes," he said. "So does Lucien, I imagine."

"Maybe they could become a mayor and a judge," Daisy said wistfully.

Eve laughed.

With his free hand, O'Hara touched Eve's arm. With his shields down, he felt her as strongly as he ever had. Whatever it was that was blocking his ability to see Daisy, it affected only her.

But even with Eve there was something different. Something . . . new. It took a moment, but he finally realized what he sensed inside her.

"Congratulations," he said weakly. "Do you want to know if it's a boy or a girl?"

Eve's hands trembled, but she didn't stop working at his damaged chest. "You're suffering from delusions," she said softly.

"No, I'm not. You're going to have a baby."

She couldn't wait to get out of this house! Eve packed almost frantically as the sun came up, her mind on everything but the news that O'Hara had so calmly delivered. A baby. It was what she wanted, what she had always wanted. So why was she terrified?

Lucien walked into the room and closed the door behind him.

"Where's Nathaniel?" Eve asked without looking at her husband.

"Sitting with O'Hara."

O'Hara really shouldn't travel yet, but he didn't

want to stay in this house any more than the others did. They would make a bed for him in the back of a wagon, and as soon as everyone was packed and ready to go, they were leaving Glover Manor for good.

Lucien crept up behind her and placed his arms around her waist. His capable hands rested over her belly, low and warm. He had accepted the news so calmly, so . . . so like a man!

"You really don't want to know if it's a boy or a girl?"

Her heart leaped. "O'Hara could be wrong. He was rather badly hurt. I still think delusions brought about by loss of blood are to blame."

Lucien didn't move. "Perhaps. I imagine we'll know soon enough."

Eve stopped packing and just stood there. She rested her hands over Lucien's and said, "You told me you didn't want another child."

"I did, didn't I?" he said without heat of any kind.

"And now here we are. . . ."

Lucien very gently turned her about and laid his hands on her shoulders. "Here we are, four instead of two. A family instead of a couple, all of a sudden. I don't think it will always be easy, and if this child has the gift, too, I can't imagine . . ." He shook his head at the very thought of what awaited them.

"I thought living with one medium was a challenge, but *three?*" She tried to feel the child inside her, if indeed O'Hara was correct, but she sensed nothing out of the ordinary. "How do we protect this child from the kind of horror Nathaniel experienced in the attic?"

Lucien's jaw tensed, and his eyes went hard. "I don't know that we can. But we can try."

"Nathaniel . . ."

"Will be fine," Lucien said. "O'Hara said the boy remembers very little of what he experienced in the attic. He knows it was painful, and he remembers being scared. But most of what he saw and felt there is gone."

"When did O'Hara . . . ?" Eve wrinkled her nose. "Oh, I remember." So much had happened last night, it was impossible to keep up with it all! "He saw this in the kitchen, when he touched Nathaniel to see what he remembered about the twins?"

Lucien nodded. "Yes. I asked O'Hara what he saw, as soon as we had a moment alone. Which, by the way, didn't happen until Daisy decided she needed to freshen up and change into clean clothes for the trip. I had to know, Evie," he whispered. "I had to know if Nathaniel would carry that agony with him forever."

"He won't."

Lucien shook his head. "No, thank goodness."

Eve laid her head on Lucien's chest. "I have a feeling our life is going to be very exciting."

"Perhaps we'll be lucky and have a few dull moments here and there."

She smiled. Her husband was many things, but dull was not one of them. "Do you want to know if the baby is a boy or a girl?" she asked.

"You no longer think the child is a delusion?"

"No." A shiver danced down her spine. "I think it's very real."

Lucien held her head to his chest, his fingers raking through her hair. "Maybe we should be surprised, as other parents are when their families grow."

She nodded gently. Her dearest wish was coming true: Lucien's child, a baby that was already growing inside her. She had not known there would be such fear mixed with the anticipation.

"I do love you."

"I know," Lucien responded, his voice touched with wonder. "And I love you. I love Nathaniel, too. And this one." He pulled her closer, as if by doing so he would be able to feel the child inside her. Not yet, but soon.

There would probably always be times when she wished her husband and her children could be perfectly ordinary, that their only gifts might be for math or art or music. But this was the man she loved, and she would take whatever came her way.

"We might not be at all ordinary," Eve said with a smile. "But I have a feeling our life is going to be very interesting."

O'Hara was sleeping again. Daisy sat beside him on the parlor floor, her hand resting very gently on his chest, over the bandage that covered the wounds she had inflicted.

Dressed in a clean blue gown fit for the autumn weather and the return trip to Plummerville, she sat on the edge of the carpet with her skirt swirling around her. Nathaniel was fiddling with the pieces of one of Lucien's contraptions, as if he were trying to figure out a complicated puzzle. Eve and Lucien were upstairs, packing. It was likely the last moment she would have alone with O'Hara, at least for a while.

"I know why you can't feel me," Daisy whispered. O'Hara did not respond, but his breathing remained steady and strong. "Whether you like it or not, I am a part of you. I will always be a part of you, whether you take me into your life or not."

There would be no mediocre husband for her, no matter how much sense that possibility made! She would not ruin a man's life by making him her husband while she loved another. And she would always love O'Hara. Quigley Tibbot O'Hara, with his abundance of charm and his horrible taste in clothes, with his talent and his demons and his penchant for trouble. She could make his life so much better, if only he would allow her to do so.

"You are such a stubborn man," she whispered.

She wondered if there was anything she could do different to make O'Hara love her more. He said he loved her, but he didn't love her *enough*. Enough to stay. Enough to risk the pain that sometimes came with love. One of the twins—had it been Margaret or Isabel?—had suggested that Daisy dress more provocatively, more like a *woman*. Daisy glanced down at the ruffles on her bodice. Were her gowns too childlike, as the spirit had suggested?

As much as she wanted to find a simple answer, she suspected her style of dressing would make no difference to the man she loved. Besides, O'Hara didn't dare to judge her based on her clothing, when his own was so often appalling. No, their problems went much deeper than the clothes they wore.

He would make a wonderful mayor.

When Jim walked in through the open French doors, Daisy lifted her head sharply.

"Mr. Thorpe tells me y'all are leaving today."

"As soon as we're packed," Daisy said without rising or taking her hands from O'Hara.

Jim nodded, not commenting on the situation.

For a moment, Daisy stared at him. Jim had told her he was twenty-two years old. Ruth had gotten him a job here; she had taken a special interest in him and even made him candy on occasion. Goose bumps popped up on her arms. Dark hair, dark eyes, though they were hazel rather than brown. And the shape of his face! If he were to stand beside the portrait upstairs, the resemblance would be clear for everyone to see.

Jim was Isabel's child. It all made sense. Had Ruth gotten him a job here so she could watch him grow? So she could always be assured that one member of the ill-fated family had survived and was well?

It was in Jim's best interest that he never know the truth.

"You've been a great help to us," Daisy said.

"Not really." Jim shuffled his feet. "Just doing my job, that's all." He looked suspiciously around the room. "Are they gone?" he said. "Are you all leaving because the ghosts are finally gone?"

Daisy nodded, and Jim's response was a smile. He was obviously and openly relieved. "That's great. I'm going to get the wagon ready." He glanced down at O'Hara. "Are you sure he can travel? Mr. Thorpe said Mr. O'Hara had an accident, but I didn't expect he'd look so poorly, all laid out like that."

Daisy's heart lurched. "He'll be fine, and I'm sure he's well enough to travel."

Jim did not seem convinced, but he left the same way he had come, through the French doors. When he was gone, Nathaniel turned his attention to Daisy. Of course, he had been listening.

"It would be best for Jim if he doesn't ever know who his mother is."

Daisy nodded. "How did you figure it out?"

"Ruth told me, but she also said my father shouldn't know. He would tell. He hates lying."

"I know. So . . . you're going to keep the truth from your father? That's not a great way to get started with your new family."

"I have no choice," Nathaniel said, much too pragmatically for a child. "I'll tell him once we're in Plummerville," he said as he again began to sort through parts that looked like a collection of junk to Daisy's eyes. "He will be very angry for a while, but he will forgive me, eventually. I hope."

"You're very much like Lucien," Daisy observed. "I'm sure he will forgive you very soon. Perhaps he will even understand."

"What if he doesn't? What if he . . . hates me?"

"He won't."

"But what if . . . ?" Nathaniel stopped, as if he'd choked on a word.

Daisy managed a gentle smile. Perhaps it wasn't wise to try to reason with a thirteen-year-old. "Then you will come and live with me, and we will have cake for breakfast every day and pie for lunch and candy for supper."

He glanced at her suspiciously.

"You will never be without a home, Nathaniel,"

she said in a more serious tone of voice. "Lucien and Eve will be wonderful parents, I just know it, but if you ever have a bad day you can turn to me. We haven't known each other very long, but surviving a few days in a haunted house makes us rather like . . . like soldiers who have survived a battle together. We're family."

He seemed to relax, as if knowing he had another ally in the world was a comfort.

"I'm glad you don't hate me."

"Of course I don't hate you!"

"When people find out that I'm different, sometimes they hate me."

"In that case, they are not good people."

"There are a lot of people in the world who are not good."

Daisy looked down at O'Hara. He was different and always had been. Had he butted heads with people who were "not good" too many times? Of course he had. Was that why he was so determined not to be a part of her life?

"I love you," she whispered.

It was Nathaniel who answered, "He knows."

Nineteen

Eve took a deep breath of the autumn air as she stepped away from the train station. It was always good to come home, but after a job like the one at the Glover Manor, the little town was especially welcoming. It was home, after so many years of wandering.

O'Hara was able to walk on his own, but he certainly didn't need to walk far. He stood in a strangely canted way, as if that position were less painful for him. Daisy kept a hand on him always, as if she could catch the man if he fell.

Lucien left them waiting at the train station while he went to the livery to rent a horse and buggy. They were normally able to walk everywhere they needed to go, but as they had a mound of baggage and a wounded O'Hara for this homecoming, another form of transportation was called for.

O'Hara and Daisy sat on a bench facing the main street of Plummerville. O'Hara seemed grateful for the opportunity to rest there, and his eyes scanned the street almost suspiciously. He should remember the place from his trip here in January. Plummerville hadn't changed since then, not at all. Eve suspected she could live here fifty years, and it would not change.

That was a good thing, in her mind. She knew the people well, the good and the not so good. She knew the small shops and their owners, and the local law, and the women who arranged the occasional celebration. Plummerville was a good place to raise a family.

Nathaniel was very close beside her before she realized he had been scooting in her direction. He stared at the street before him as skeptically as O'Hara.

She would soon have to explain to everyone in this small town that Nathaniel was Lucien's son. Perhaps she wouldn't have to tell anyone. They looked so much alike. Not only that, they moved in the same way on occasion. Yes, people would look at Nathaniel and know he was Lucien's child.

The first few days, maybe weeks, would be awkward, as everyone asked questions and the gossip flew about town at full speed.

Eve draped her arm around Nathaniel's shoulder. No matter how awkward the situation was for her, it was much worse for the child. He'd lost his mother too soon, and been forced upon the father he had hated all his life—unfairly, of course—right in the middle of a nasty haunting. And now he was being plopped down in a new home, which he would share with that father he did not know and a brand-new mother.

"I know it doesn't look like much," she said as her own eyes scanned the street, "but I think you'll like it here. I understand the new schoolmaster is demanding but fair, and on Saturdays the boys often play ball right here in the street."

"I've never played ball," Nathaniel said in a low voice.

"Well, that will be remedied shortly," she said pragmatically.

Lucien approached, driving the horse and buggy that would take them all home. "He's going to be a good father," she said in a voice so low that no one but Nathaniel could hear. "He loves you already, and the two of you are so much alike, I'm sure you'll become close in no time at all."

Nathaniel said nothing, but he remained skeptical.

"I'm glad you're here," she said. "Lucien needs you."

The boy glanced up in surprise. "He does?"

"Of course he does," Eve said logically. "Now, why don't you go help him with the bags. O'Hara," she called in a louder voice as the wounded man began to rise, "you sit yourself down until Lucien and Nathaniel finish loading the luggage. You're not to lift anything, do you hear me?"

O'Hara glanced her way and grinned. "Yes, ma'am. When did you get to be so bossy?"

"Trust me," Lucien said as he jumped from the buggy's seat. "She's always been bossy." He threw a grin her way and winked.

Nathaniel and Daisy assisted O'Hara into the conveyance when the bags were in place. He tried to move as if he didn't hurt, but it was all an act. She'd have to put him in the spare bedroom, she supposed. But what about Nathaniel? A pallet in one of the other rooms, until O'Hara was well enough to leave. Maybe she should just purchase another bed. It would take a while to obtain the bed, but she had a feeling she'd need it even after O'Hara was gone. After all, they would have company on occasion, and Nathaniel would want his own room.

And if O'Hara was right about the baby she carried, she'd need a cradle, too, in order to transform the fourth upstairs room into a nursery.

It was everything she'd wanted for so long. A family. A home. And at the center of it all, Lucien. No matter what happened, as long as they had one another, everything else would be fine.

They stopped at Daisy's house, and Lucien began to grumble about her luggage. Again. Nathaniel offered to help, his voice brighter than it had been at the train depot. When they had unloaded all her bags, Daisy pointed to another, smaller case.

"And that one," she said sweetly.

"Daisy," O'Hara said, "that's my bag."

"I know that." Standing beside the buggy, she pulled herself up to her full height of five foot one and looked at O'Hara, who remained seated in the buggy, in the eye. "You're staying here."

O'Hara shook his head. "No. I couldn't possibly . . ."

"I'm going to take care of you, Quigley Tibbot O'Hara. You might as well get used to the idea."

"Daisy," Eve began calmly, "you're not . . ."

"I know all the arguments," Daisy interrupted. "We're not married. I live alone. My reputation is at stake. People will talk. Eve, I don't care about any of that. I'm the one who hurt him . . ."

"It wasn't you," O'Hara argued.

"I'm the one who hurt him," Daisy said more calmly, "and I'm going to fix him."

"No, it's not right." O'Hara looked as if he had no intention of leaving the buggy, and then Daisy lifted her head and looked him in the eye.

"Please, don't leave me here alone."

For a moment, O'Hara didn't move. When he began to struggle to leave the buggy on his own, Lucien hurried over to assist.

Lucien, rushing to aid O'Hara so the psychic wouldn't hurt himself any more than he already had. Would wonders never cease!

"You're just as bossy as Eve, in your own way," O'Hara said as Daisy wrapped her arm around his waist and offered her support.

"Am I?" Daisy smiled brightly. "Why, thank you, O'Hara."

When he'd agreed to come to Daisy's house a week ago, he'd had every intention of saying good-bye and making his way to the boardinghouse in Plummerville to heal on his own. He didn't want to intrude on Lucien and Eve's homecoming, and he certainly didn't want to blacken Daisy's reputation by staying here.

And yet here he remained. In her bed, where he'd slept alone for the past seven days.

Daisy had insisted upon nursing him back to health herself, gossip be damned. She blamed herself still for the injuries he'd suffered, refusing to place the blame on Isabel, where it belonged.

A week in bed, frequent visits from Lucien, Eve, and Nathaniel, and the most tender loving care any man had ever received helped to heal O'Hara. He was almost completely well now. There was no reason why he couldn't travel. In truth, he could have left days ago, but leaving Daisy behind for a second time was going to be so damned hard.

What was he going to do? He couldn't give Daisy the life she wanted, but he absolutely could not imagine leaving her behind and never looking back.

"You're awake," she said as she walked through the door, a silver tray laden with a bowl that steamed enticingly and a plate of biscuits in her hands.

"I've slept quite enough lately, thank you," he said as he very slowly and gingerly sat up.

Daisy's smile faded. "Be careful. You shouldn't be moving without help. You might start bleeding again!"

"I'm fine," he assured her. "The wounds are healing nicely, and they weren't very deep."

She placed the tray on the dresser, and as she turned to him, she bit her lower lip. "I could've killed you."

How many times in the past week had she said those words? Too many. Somehow, he had to make her understand that she was not at fault. "It wasn't you."

They'd had this conversation often in the past week, but they'd never finished it. Daisy left the room, or he went to sleep. It was long past time to finish this particular argument.

"Come here," O'Hara commanded.

Daisy, beautiful as ever in a warm fall gown, crossed the room and stood beside and over him.

"Is everything all right? Do you hurt? What do you need?"

He grabbed her wrist, and with a tug she joined him on the bed. She sat hard, bouncing beside him. He held her wrist in his hand, and all he felt was her skin, her heartbeat, her heat. It was everything he'd ever wanted, and still . . .

"You would never intentionally hurt anyone," he said softly. "I know that as strongly and surely as I have ever known anything."

"You can see inside me again?" she whispered.

"No." He had accepted that he never would. "But that doesn't mean I don't know you better and more distinctly than I've ever known anyone. Damn it, Daisy, what are we going to do?"

She leaned forward and kissed him. Her lips molded to his, and after a moment those lips began to move.

He couldn't think when she kissed him like this. It was as if she teased him with everything he wanted and could not have.

"Are you well?" she whispered when she took her mouth from his.

"Yes, but . . ."

He got no further. Daisy had already begun to unbutton her dress, and watching her . . . he could not speak. He could only see wonder and beauty in her wanting for him. She was a miracle. His miracle.

"Daisy, I can't lay my hands on you and tell you that we won't make a child if we . . ."

"*When* we, not *if*," she said, not even slowing down as she continued to undress.

"I would die before I'd hurt you."

"I know that." She stripped down to her chemise, removed a wealth of pins from her golden hair so that it fell loose, and then she reclined beside him on the bed. Without a moment's hesitation, she laid her hands on his chest. "I know so much about you, O'Hara. I believe I know you more completely and wholly than I have ever known anyone."

"You only think—"

"You're a good man," she interrupted. "Better than you will allow anyone to know. Only a truly good man would be afraid that he would never be able to give me what I want from life." Her soft hand rose to his face, where it rested on a stubbled cheek. "You're afraid of so many things, and there's no reason for your fear."

"I'm not afraid of anything."

She responded with a smile. "You can't fool me. I see too much. You're afraid you'll hurt me. You're afraid we won't be happy. You're afraid we'll have babies who are like you. I know you love me. You can't hide that from me."

He looked into Daisy's blue eyes, so close and honest and real, and the truth hit him with a jolt. "My God. I not only can't read you, you can read me, now? How is that possible? It's not possible. It's . . ." *Magic.*

Daisy's grin widened. "I can see inside you because I love you, O'Hara." She unbuttoned the chemise, revealing the swell of her breasts and the nipples that had already peaked. Bolder than she had once been, she lifted his hand and placed it there. "And you can see me in the same way, you know. If you try hard enough, you will see that I love you, and that love will be enough to help us get past everything else."

When her clothes had been shed, she began to work on his. Fortunately, he didn't wear much.

This was real, it was right, and in a few minutes he would be inside her and he would not be able to hide anything else from her, not ever again.

"Marry me," he said as a very naked Daisy laid her lips on his throat.

"Of course," she whispered.

"You don't even sound surprised!"

"I'm not. Eve and I have already been discussing what we'll wear to the wedding."

"You're psychic, aren't you? I somehow transferred a fragment of my power to you. I didn't know that was possible, but that must be what happened."

Daisy climbed up and atop him, her legs spread to straddle him. Skin pale and perfect but for a small, milky birthmark, gold hair loose and just a little wild, she was the kind of sight that might take any man's breath away.

"Darling," she whispered, "I know you well because I adore you. Because love truly does conquer all, because I am not a separate being but a part of you, in your very soul."

"That's true," he said. And it was a wonder. A true, breathtaking wonder.

"And besides," she said as she drifted down to lay her mouth over his, "you talk in your sleep."

"I hate Halloween," Nathaniel said sullenly. "There is no rest on All Hallow's Eve."

"This year will be different," Lucien insisted. "Have you been doing your exercises?"

"Yes."

They had already reassembled the specter-o-meter, making a few improvements along the way. Lucien and his son were fiddling with The Damned Thing. The name had been changed, since a child was now involved with the development of the mechanism. Evie had dubbed it the Thorpe and Son Psychic Evaluator. That would do for now.

"Then you'll be fine. There's always a hullabaloo in Plummerville on Halloween." Lucien couldn't help but frown. He'd never had a liking for the day himself, so he understood Nathaniel's concerns. The walls between the living and the dead were always thin on that night. "Games and cakes and such nonsense," he said under his breath. "Most of the children seem to enjoy it."

They'd been home a month. Evie was indeed with child, a fact that thrilled and horrified them both. Nathaniel had become a part of the family much quicker than any of them had imagined. Lucien had decided he would not shelter his child as Zella had. Protect, yes; conceal, no. Nathaniel went to school like any other boy might, and he had already made a few friends. Exercising his power to shut the spirits out for a time had helped in that matter.

Nathaniel glanced beyond Lucien. "Grandmother says everything will be fine," he said, as if he didn't quite believe the ghost.

"Zella's mother?"

Nathaniel shook his head. "No. Yours."

Lucien felt as if someone had pulled the rug out

from under his feet. His world tilted. "You're mistaken."

"No," Nathaniel said calmly.

"My mother doesn't . . . come."

"Yes, she does, Father. I've seen her several times. She isn't earthbound, so she visits no more often than Mother does, but she does come. Don't you ever see her?"

Lucien turned his head and stared at a blank wall, where Nathaniel's eyes were fixed. "No."

"Oh." Nathaniel bent over his task. "Then I suppose you don't see your father, either."

Someone, a mischievous spirit perhaps, was playing a trick on his son.

"I didn't even know my father. He died when I was two."

"That doesn't mean he doesn't know you," Nathaniel argued without so much as lifting his head. "Sometimes he and Grandmother are together, but on other occasions they come separately."

A trick, Lucien decided with a thud of his heart. An ugly trick.

"You don't understand," he said calmly. "Zella was far from perfect, but your mother loved you dearly. She protected you from those who would . . ." Lucien stopped speaking. *Those who would torture you the way my mother tortured me.* "From those who didn't understand your gift. My mother never understood."

Nathaniel lifted his head. "She understands now," he said.

"Then why can't I see her?" Lucien asked testily. "You don't see her, either," he reasoned. "This is some kind of mischievous spirit interference, or one of Zella's nasty tricks, or a thirteen-year-old's joke, or . . ."

"Your heart doesn't want to see her, that's what she says." Nathaniel lifted two metal connectors. "Is this right?"

"No!" Lucien stood quickly, just as the boy touched the two metal clips together. The shock made a popping noise, and Nathaniel jumped out of his chair and dropped the components. "Are you all right?" Lucien took Nathaniel's hands in his own and studied them, looking for burn marks on delicate skin. He saw none.

"I'm fine."

"We'll test the device on me and on O'Hara until we're sure it's working properly, do you understand?"

As Lucien dropped Nathaniel's hands, the boy smiled. The smiles were rare, but they did come more often these days.

"Grandmother says you are always trying to prove that your gift is real, when the proof has always been within you."

"I'd like proof others will accept," Lucien said brusquely.

"It doesn't matter if others accept or not," Nathaniel said. "It only matters that you know the truth. Those who are blind to miracles will always be blind."

Again, Lucien looked at the blank wall. Perhaps he saw a glimmer there. Perhaps it was his imagination. "I wanted *her* to understand."

"She understands now."

"Too late." But was it? He had always been so sure his mother never visited, because he didn't see her.

That made him no better than those who didn't believe in ghosts at all, because they did not see. "Tell her . . ."

"You tell her," Nathaniel said. "Grandmother does hear you, even if you can't see her. I'm going to get my coat. It's almost time to leave." The boy left the parlor and headed for the stairs, leaving Lucien alone.

He stared at the almost bare wall. Yes, a light glimmered there. "I always thought you hated me," he said softly. "Now that I have a child of my own, I don't see how that's possible."

Suddenly he knew, without words, that his mother had loved him. She had just been afraid of what she didn't understand. For a moment she was inside him, strong, loving, and full of pride and wonder. He saw secrets, heard whispers of the future, and felt an overwhelming peace he had not known as a child.

And then she was gone.

As usual, some of what he'd seen had vanished already, but a few words and images remained. Love, most of all. Sons, almost as strongly.

"Aren't you finished with that contraption yet?" Eve asked as she swept into the room.

"For the day, yes. But finished?" Lucien shook his head. "I might never be finished." And the idea that he might not be was oddly undisturbing.

It wasn't yet evident that his wife was with child, but soon that truth would be clear to everyone who saw her. He found himself almost as anxious as she was for the coming months.

"We should hurry," she said, unaware of what

had just happened to him. "Daisy and O'Hara will be expecting us."

They were to stop by the newlyweds' house on the way to town and collect them for the Halloween outing. A year ago Lucien would have been disturbed that O'Hara was practically a neighbor, but the man had changed, a little. The O'Haras were a contented couple.

O'Hara had completely blocked his ability to read Daisy, a fact that astounded Lucien. But things had changed in the past couple of weeks. While O'Hara could no longer touch his wife and see her thoughts, he had been surprised to find that when he touched Daisy, he could now connect with the little girl that grew inside her. His own daughter.

Lucien wrapped his arms around Eve. "Since Daisy knows she's having a girl, does that make you curious about our baby?"

"A little," she confessed. "I have considered asking O'Hara, but . . ."

"You don't have to." Lucien kissed his wife.

"What does that mean?"

"I had a visit."

The news did not disturb her. Unnatural visits were common in this house. "A visit from whom?"

"My mother."

Her eyes grew wide. "Oh, Lucien, are you all right?"

He smiled down at his wife. "Fine, really. She's . . . here. Not often, and I may never see her again, but she's here. She's always been with me."

"Of course she has."

"And she told me . . ." He hesitated.

"About the baby?"

"This one and more to come," he said.

"More?" Eve blinked twice. "How many more?"

He grinned. Sons. Six of them, for a total of seven, counting Nathaniel. They would all have his gift, in varying degrees, and they would never suffer for lack of love, or lack of belief in what they could do, or lack of family.

"Evie, love, we're going to need a bigger house."